78-8-2

S. Kraus

Also by Don DeLillo

Running Dog

Don DeLillo

ALFRED A. KNOPF　　New York　　1978

THIS IS A BORZOI BOOK
PUBLISHED BY ALFRED A. KNOPF, INC.

Copyright © 1978 by Don DeLillo
All rights reserved under International and Pan-American
Copyright Conventions. Published in the United States by
Alfred A. Knopf, Inc., New York, and simultaneously in
Canada by Random House of Canada Limited, Toronto.
Distributed by Random House, Inc., New York.

Library of Congress Cataloging in Publication Data

DeLillo, Don. Running dog.

I. Title.
PZ4.D346RU [PS3554.E4425]   813'.5'4   77-26674
ISBN 0-394-50143-8

Manufactured in the United States of America

FIRST EDITION

To Eydie and Phil

Running Dog

You won't find ordinary people here. Not after dark, on these streets, under the ancient warehouse canopies. Of course you know this. This is the point. It's why you're here, obviously. Wind comes gusting off the river, stirring the powdery air of demolition sites. Derelicts build fires in rusty oil drums near the piers. You see them clustered, wrapped in whatever variety of coat or throwaway sweater or combination of these they've been able to acquire. There are trucks parked near the warehouses, some of them occupied, men smoking in the dimness, waiting for the homosexuals to make their way down from the bars above Canal Street. You lengthen your stride, although not to hurry out of the cold. You like that stiffening wind. You turn a corner and move briefly into it, feeling your thighs take shape against the dress's pleasurably taut weave. Broken glass shines like white mica in the vacant lots. The river has a musky tang tonight.

Eastward now, you see four letters spray-painted on the side of a building. Mongrel scrawl. ANGW. But familiar somehow, burning a hole in time. And it comes back now from a distance of more than twenty years. The visit to Salzburg. The cousins, the games, the museum. Four letters engraved on a ceremonial halberd. Your father's explanation: *Alles nach Gottes Willen.*

Weapons have become godless since then. Weapons have lost their religion. And children have grown up to find they have traveled curious distances. You feel it's imminent now, one more corner to turn, someone there, that silent bargaining that has nothing to do with goods or even services; only what you truly are, night-cruising souls agreeing to each other's terms. A dark elation grows with every step you take.

All according to God's will. The God of Body. The God of Lipstick and Silk. The God of Nylon, Scent and Shadow.

The young man drove an unmarked car north on Hudson. His partner dozed in the seat alongside. Turning west toward the river, Del Bravo expected a certain picture to present itself. Stacks of crates and cardboard boxes. A construction scaffold fronting an old building. Trucks and earth-moving equipment. Derelicts around a fire. Experience told him this is what he'd see.

He hadn't expected a woman. Coming this way, striding nicely. She had long hair, darkish blond, and from twenty yards, and closing, he could see how attractive she was. Her black coat was open, revealing a bright red dress.

No kind of professional in her right mind would patrol deserted areas. She was eye-catching all right. If she was in the business at all, she wasn't working streets. An unlisted number. A white high-rise in the East Fifties. To Del Bravo, easing up on the accelerator, she was a discrepancy in the landscape. A welcome sight, sure, but also slightly disquieting —she didn't fit the picture.

After she passed the car, he watched in the rearview mirror as she approached the demolition site, moving in that nice brisk sexy stride. A perennial all-pro, he thought. The radio squawked. He figured he'd swing around the block and catch her again at the end of the same long street. With nothing better to do, he wanted a second look.

"Wake up, Gannett."

"What's doing?"

"Be alert, G.G. There's something I want you to look at."

"Where are we?"

"Just wait'll I make this final maneuver here."

"I think I was dreaming."

"Where the hell is she?" Del Bravo said.

"I was dreaming about rocks. All these big rocks on a beach. They were huge enormous rocks. I was there but I wasn't there."

The street was empty. Del Bravo let the car inch forward. No one in sight. It had taken him very little time to circle the block. At the rate she was walking she should have reached this part of the street right about now.

The fire was untended. There'd been some men standing around the fire in that vacant lot. It was still blazing. No one there. This he considered a near-discrepancy.

The headlights picked up dust, a fairly heavy accumulation. It seemed to be coming from the second-story level of a construction scaffold in midblock. A possible discrepancy. No dust a couple of minutes ago. Dust now. Building should be unoccupied. Crew's gone home.

"You were there but you weren't there."

"That's the way I dream sometimes," Gannett said.

"I want to look in this building here."

"What for, Robby?"

"Hand me the flashlight."

Del Bravo moved through a narrow alley between the gutted building and the one just east of it. Out back he found the windows boarded up, just as they'd been on the street side. He went to the front of the building and took a longer look at the scaffolding. He felt the dust in his eyes and mouth. Gannett watched from the front seat, sniffling a little.

"You're not thinking of climbing, are you, because I'd hate to have to get out of the car to give you a hand-hold."

"We both know the only thing your hand can hold."

"What are you looking for, Robby, so I can show some interest."

"If I reach that strut, I'm up and over."

Del Bravo hoisted himself up a series of interlocking rods and beams until he reached the second-story platform, about eighteen feet above street level. There was an unblocked window here, the one they used to empty the building of its contents. Del Bravo directed the light inside. Piles of floorboards bound together. Large chunks of plaster. Room walls all gone. Plumbing dismantled. He heard Gannett's voice below.

"Floor's liable to give."

The flashlight beam picked her out through clouds of plaster dust just as he was stepping through the window. He took a short-barreled .38 out of the shoulder holster under his lumber jacket and played the beam of light across the floor. He moved slowly forward, immediately wary of protruding nails, more generally concerned by the aura, the presences, a field of unnamed sensation.

She was on her back, vivid in the gray haze, head twisted to one side. There was blood still coming out of her, midbody, beneath the rib cage. All this dust, and the way her head was turned, and the condition of her clothing, indicated there'd been a struggle. A brief one, obviously.

Del Bravo looked for a weapon near the body. Plaster and wood dust filled his nostrils. He smelled perfume as well, and sweat, and noticed that her mascara had run and that the thick layer of face powder was cracked in places. No trace of pulse. The blood came out. He made his way back to the window.

"Call in, G.G."

"What do we have?"

"Body, one, female."

He went over the whole area, stepping over objects, careful not to disturb the positions of things. He put the gun away and squatted by the woman's body. He heard Gannett climbing up the scaffold. Events had been such that the woman's coat had slipped off one shoulder, and her dress, of that shimmering red material, had twisted up toward the left side of her body. Her bra had become loose on the opposite side and he could see it was all padding.

From a position on all fours, he directed the light down under the bra, spotting dark bristles of recently shaved hair. Without touching the body he moved the flashlight slowly over her hands, face, hairline, neck and legs.

Gannett came in the window, panting and cursing. Del Bravo lighted the way for him, watching his partner approach in a hunched manner, although the ceiling was fifteen feet high. Gannett crouched down beside him.

"What do we have?"

"What we have is either a lady with a hormone problem—don't get too close."

"What do you think, Robby, knife?"

"I think definitely knife."

"Doesn't look multiple. I see one entry."

"Or a man with a funny taste in clothes," Del Bravo said.

"If you can get your light under the hair."

"No touch."

"I call it one entry. I'm surprised all this blood."

"Advanced techniques."

"What do you call it, Robby?"

"They don't pay me to count stab wounds."

"I hate these wet ones."

"Seen a lot of wets, have you?"

"Usually with me it's the female that does the stabbing. I don't know how many times I walk in and there's some woman sitting on the sofa, looking a little sleepy, you know, and there's the common-law husband on the kitchen floor with about skeighty-eight stab wounds. And the woman's just about nodding off. Maybe they get tired. All that stabbing makes them tired. You want to put a blanket over them and turn off the radio."

"I think I hear them outside," Del Bravo said.

"I don't know what it is but with me the body's in the kitchen. Always the kitchen."

"Poor people like to be close to the food."

"What do you think, seriously here, one entry?"

"They don't like to stray from the food, even in the middle of a knife fight."

"If it's one entry, they penetrated something vital."

"That's safe. I'd go with that."

"All this blood," Gannett said.

"And it's royal."

"Royal?"

"Don't touch, G.G."

"Right," Gannett said. "A queen."

About half an hour later Del Bravo stood on the sidewalk blowing into his cupped hands. He wore the yellow hard hat that usually sat in the back seat of the car. An ambulance, two unmarked cars and two squad cars were nearby. Fingerprint men and photographers came and went. An emergency service vehicle pulled up. Seconds later a uniformed sergeant spotted Del Bravo and came over.

"Move it, buddy, crime area."

"What?"

"This area's sealed."

With a weary sigh Del Bravo took out his shield and pinned it to his jacket.

"These days, what is it? Everybody's in disguise."

"I know, sergeant."

"Tell me how in the hell people are supposed to know who's the police. All this dressing up. The police don't know each other. Junkies, car boosters, beards, hats. Blind man with a dog, he could turn around and shoot you. It used to be you could go by the clothes. But you can't go by the clothes any-more."

"You go by the sex organs," Del Bravo told him.

Gannett joined them, breathing steam, his arms crossed on his chest.

"We missed the stairway," he said.

"What are you talking about, stairway?"

"Place used to be a restaurant. West side of the building there's an outside service stairway going up to the kitchen. Didn't you go around the west side of the building?"

"I went around the east side of the building," Del Bravo said.

"Anyway that's how they got the victim up there. We're climbing scaffolds. They walked him up the stairs and in the door. There's a door at the top of the stairs, Robby. It wasn't locked."

"I checked the back. I checked the east side, the front and the back."

"Three out of four," the sergeant said.

Arms still crossed, Gannett wedged a hand in each armpit.

"Wouldn't I like to be in Florida right now."

"Go coop some more. Maybe you'll dream about it."

"That's right, the beach."

"He dreams about rocks," Del Bravo told the sergeant.

"Rocks on a beach."

The sergeant waited for more.

"I'm there but I'm not there," Gannett said.

I

1

Lightborne, at sixty-six, took to using a walking stick on his frequent strolls down West Broadway and through the SoHo gallery district. This one spring evening the sole of his right shoe—he wore penny loafers—began flapping soon after he started out. This somewhat undermined the effect he'd sought to create with his walking stick.

He headed back, gingerly, walking on his right heel. Entering a cast-iron building, he rode to the fourth floor in a self-service freight elevator, a drafty contrivance he feared and hated. The vast metal door to his loft bore the legend in red paint:

COSMIC EROTICS

THE LIGHTBORNE GALLERY

He walked through the gallery and stepped past a partition into the area of the loft he used as living quarters. The furniture was dark and heavy, embellished with scroll motifs. An end table leaned a little. The front legs of a desk rested on matchbooks for balance. From a drawer in this desk Lightborne took a small bottle of Elmer's Glue-All and tried to refasten the sole of his right shoe.

About twenty people would be arriving at eight-thirty. They were the core of his clientele and he had some new things to show. Only one fresh face likely to appear. This would be Moll Robbins, a journalist planning a series of articles on sex as big business.

The others were collectors, a couple of people who represented collectors, and the inevitable self-conscious dabblers who were captivated by the novelty of it all. Lightborne didn't mind the latter group. They tended to regard him as an eccentric scholar, a font of erotic lore, and were always inviting him places and giving him things.

Finished with the shoe, he took a pair of grooming scissors and snipped at his sideburns. Then he commenced brushing his hair into a near-ducktail arrangement. Lightborne's hair was silvery gray tinged with a kind of yellowish discoloration, and he liked wearing it long. Finally he put on a string tie and belted corduroy jacket. Not that there was any reason to concern himself with appearance. These get-togethers at the gallery were always informal. The collectors preferred it that way. He served them Wink in paper cups.

Moll Robbins, as it happened, arrived before the others. She wore jeans and a bulky sweater, a tall lean woman who walked in a sort of lazy prowl. Hanging from a strap over her right shoulder was a large leather case.

Lightborne showed her around the gallery, which wasn't the usual clinical space of right angles and clever little ramps. It resembled instead an antique shop in serious decline. There were small tables filled with bronze and porcelain pieces, with stacks of drawings and prints, with books and woodcarvings, vases and cups. There were several pedestals to hold the more interesting pieces, and on the wall were a number of oil paintings as well as enlarged photographs of Hindu temple façades and the lucky phalluses of Pompeii. Along the walls were bins of drawings, more prints, more photographs, and several glass cases full of rings, bracelets, necklaces.

Moll Robbins roved a bit uncertaintly through all of this, fingering the lid of a porcelain teapot (Chinese emperor with concubine, apparently), peering at a coin under glass (Greeks, male, dallying).

"Innocent, somehow, isn't it?"

"It doesn't move," Lightborne said.

"Doesn't move?"

"Movement, action, frames per second. This is the era we're in, for better or worse. It seems a little ineffectual, what's here. It just sits. It's all mass and body weight."

"Pure gravity."

"Sure, a thing isn't fully erotic unless it has the capacity to move. A woman crossing her legs drives men mad. She moves, understand. Motion, activity, change of position. You need this today for eroticism to be total."

"Something to that, I suppose."

When everyone had arrived, Lightborne closed the huge doors and began to circulate. Moll took off her sweater and draped it over the erect member of a plaster vicar, noting that Lightborne was spending most of his time at the side of a well-groomed and neatly dressed man, early thirties, seemingly a business type, the kind of junior tycoon who delights in giving crisp directives to his subordinates.

She spoke with several people, finding them subtly evasive, not exactly reluctant to discuss their interest in erotica but unable to focus their attention on the subject. They seemed rushed somehow, distracted by some private vision, high-type horseplayers, secretly frenzied at the edges.

Lightborne introduced her to the man he'd been talking to. Glen Selvy. Then was led away by several other people.

"What got you interested, Mr. Selvy?"

"What gets anyone interested in sex?"

"We don't all collect," she said.

"Just a pastime. Line, grace, symmetry. Beauty of the human body. So on, so forth."

"Do you spend a lot of money, collecting?"

"Fair amount."

"You must know quite a bit about art."

"I took a course once."

"You took a course once."

"I learned enough to know that Lightborne's better stuff is kept under wraps."

"What can you tell me about Lightborne that he wouldn't want to tell me himself?"

Selvy smiled and walked away. Later, when most of the people had gone, Lightborne talked with Moll in his living quarters. He answered all her questions, explaining that he got started in the business in 1946 when he was down and out in Cairo and managed to come into possession of a ring depicting the Egyptian god of fertility, highly aroused. He sold it to an ex-Nazi for a pretty sum and eventually learned that it ended up on the finger of King Farouk. After that, one contact led to another and he traveled through Central America, Japan, the Mideast and Europe, a worldwide network, buying and selling and bartering.

"What about your friend Selvy? I'm curious. He doesn't look quite the type. What's his collection like?"

"My lips are sealed."

"What do you mean?" she said.

"Some people are here to look. Some to buy. Some to buy for others."

"Fronting."

"Sure."

"Buying on behalf of a person or group that doesn't want his, her or its identity known to the world at large."

"That's grammatically very clumsy but otherwise correct," Lightborne said.

"Do you know who Selvy buys for?"

"Actually I only suspect."

"Someone I may have heard of?"

"Selvy's been on the job three months or so. Fairly good at it. Has a basic knowledge."

"That's all you're saying."

"It's a business full of rumors, Miss Robbins. I get word about things sometimes. So-and-so's turned up a bronze statuette in some sealed-off church cellar on Crete. Hermaphrodite: Graeco-Roman. I hear things all the time. I get word. The air is full of vibrations. Sometimes there's an element of truth. Often it's just a breeze in the night."

Glen Selvy stuck his head around the edge of the partition to say goodnight. Lightborne asked him in for coffee, which was perking on a GE hotplate in a corner of the room. Selvy checked his watch and sat in a huge dusty armchair.

"My man in Guatemala tells me to expect choice items this trip."

"About time," Selvy said.

"Dug up from tombs with his own two hands."

"He's found more tombs, has he?"

"The jungles are dense," Lightborne said mysteriously.

"My principal is certain your pre-Columbian stuff is fake. Do you want to hear what he has to say about the handicraft?"

"Tell him this trip."

"This trip it's different."

"Different," Lightborne said.

He poured three cups of coffee. Moll believed she detected an edge of detachment in Selvy's voice and manner. His reactions were just the tiniest bit mechanical. It was possible he was deeply bored by this.

"In the meantime," Lightborne said, "I can show you a lady with an octopus."

"Another time."

"It's a porcelain centerpiece."

"Seriously, anything stashed back here? If not, I'm off."

"You say seriously. Did I hear you correctly?"

"You heard."

"I was telling the young lady about rumors. The part rumors play in a business like this. Six months ago, for instance, I heard a rumor about an item that could prove to be of interest to any number of people, including your employer perhaps. The odd thing about this rumor is that I first heard it about thirty years ago, originally in Cairo and Alexandria, where my list of acquaintances was colorful and varied, and later the same year, if memory serves, after I went to Paris to live. The item in question was the print of a movie. To be more exact, the camera original."

Lightborne offered sugar, wordlessly.

"I was telling the young lady that movement, the simple capacity to change position, is an important erotic quality. Probably the single biggest difference between old and new styles of erotic art is the motion picture. The movie. The image that moves. This assumes you consider movies art."

"Oh, I do," Moll said.

"In the same league with painting, sculpture, so on."

"Absolutely."

"All right then," Lightborne said. "For several months I kept hearing rumors about this very curious film. People in the business. Collectors, dealers, agents. It's a world of rumormongers. What can you do? But then the noise died. The little hum, it faded away to nothing. I don't think anyone noticed. The rumor was implausible to begin with. Hardly anyone took it seriously. So, silence for thirty years. Not a word on the subject. Then, six months ago, the rumor is revived. I hear it from three people, none of them in contact with the other two. Precisely the same rumor. A film exists. Unedited footage. One copy. The camera original. Shot in Berlin, April, the year 1945."

Lightborne nodded to indicate a measure of absorption in his own commentary. He went to the refrigerator and got a box of Graham crackers. He offered them around. No takers. He sat back down.

"In the bunker," he said.

He took a cracker out of the box and dunked it in his coffee.

"Spell that out," Moll said.

"The bunker under the Reich Chancellery."

"And who appears in this footage?"

"Things get vague here. But apparently it's a sex thing. It's the filmed record of an orgy, I gather, that took place somewhere in that series of underground compartments."

Selvy gazed at the ceiling.

"I don't believe it myself," Lightborne said. "I'm the chief skeptic. It's just the curious nature of the thing. The recent rumor is point for point the same as the original, despite a thirty-year gap between the two. And the few people who believe the thing, at least as a possibility, are able to make some valid historical points. I happen to be a student of the period."

Robbins and Selvy watched the soggy bottom half of the cracker in Lightborne's hand detach itself and fall into the cup. Lightborne used a spoon to gather the brown ooze and eat it.

"In any case I thought it might be useful to trace the story as far as I could, maybe with luck even to its source. Eventually a contact in the business, someone I trust, put me in touch with an individual and we arranged a meeting. He didn't volunteer his name and I didn't ask. Man in his thirties. Slight accent. Nervous, very jumpy. He said he knew where the footage was. Said prints had never been made. Guaranteed it. Said the running time would qualify it as full length, more or less. Then he grew melancholy. I can see his face. A performance, he said, that would surely take its place among the strangest and most haunting ever given. He also said I wouldn't be disappointed in the identities of those taking part. All this and yet he wouldn't give a straight answer when I asked if he'd seen the footage himself or were we dealing in hearsay."

Lightborne stirred his coffee.

"The idea we agreed on was that I would act as agent for the sale. I have the contacts, I know the market, more or less. We further agreed that with sex exploitation reaching the level it has, certainly there'd be no problem finding powerful and wealthy groups who'd be utterly delighted at the chance to bid for distribution rights to something this novel. Think of it. The century's ultimate piece of decadence."

"And it moves," Moll said.

Lightborne sat back and crossed his legs, holding the cup and saucer to his belly.

"So," he said, "a small-time dealer in erotic knickknacks, some good quality, some not so good, and here I am with a chance to act as go-between in some monumental pornography caper. I begin to send out feelers, veiled hints, to this part of the country, that part, to this fellow in Dallas, that fellow in Stockholm. As things begin to happen, as the market heats up, my man suddenly disappears. I have no idea how to reach him. He always insisted he would contact me. So I call people, I make inquiries, I hang around our usual meeting place. Finally I hear from the same man who put us in touch at the outset. X is dead, he tells me. Not only dead—murdered. Not only murdered—done away with under strange, very odd circumstances."

"How odd?" Moll said.

"He was wearing women's clothes."

Selvy looked at Moll Robbins, at the same time motioning for Lightborne to pause.

"What's in that case you've got?"

"Nikon F2," she said.

"It stays inside, okay?"

"I don't know, you've got a fairly nice profile, Mr. Selvy. Might look good somewhere near the tail end of a story, just to break up lines of print."

"It stays or you go."

"And a Sony cassette recorder," she said.

"Take it out, please. I'd like to see it."

"Mr. Lightborne, this is your residence. You invited me to come here. You placed no restrictions."

Selvy picked the leather case off the floor, opened it, took out the tape recorder, turned it over, removed the battery case, opened it, took out the four small batteries and set them on the nearest table.

"Quite a routine," she said. "You must be handy around the house."

"No words, no pictures."

"It wasn't necessary, you know. I'm not about to tape your insipid voice if you don't want it taped."

Lightborne reacted to all this by taking his cup and saucer to the sink and washing them out. Returning, he pushed the box of crackers toward Moll. This time she took one, halving it neatly before taking a bite.

"After this depressing turns of events," Lightborne said, "the whole matter dried up and total silence prevailed. But I wanted to give you a little background, Glen, because just yesterday the smallest whisper reached my ear. If things get interesting again, I think your employer ought to be informed."

"Sure, absolutely."

"As for you, Miss Robbins, you'll have to forgive a garrulous old man."

"It's been interesting, really."

"Who do you work for?" Selvy said.

"*Running Dog*," she said.

He paused briefly.

"One-time organ of discontent."

"We were fairly radical, yes."

"Now safely established in the mainstream."

"I wouldn't say safely."

"Part of the ever-expanding middle."

"We say 'fuck' all the time."

"My point exactly."

"Was that your point exactly? I didn't realize that was your point exactly. I didn't know you had a point exactly."

Selvy got to his feet, saying goodnight to Lightborne and then bowing toward Moll Robbins, clicking his heels together as he did so. She followed as far as the gallery area in order to pluck her sweater from the rigid appendage where she'd left it earlier, returning then to thank Lightborne for his time. He watched her replace the batteries in the tape recorder.

"I was wondering," she said.

"Yes?"

"Is he always in that much of a hurry? Could be a plane he's got to catch. Or commuter train maybe."

"Glen's not the type to hang around and make small talk."

"Of course if I found out who he buys for, and if it's someone interesting and important, and if I use this information in one of the pieces I'm doing, it wouldn't do *you* any good, would it?"

"Wouldn't do me much harm either," Lightborne said. "The collector Glen represents hasn't shown much interest in the stuff I've been coming up with. According to Glen, he may be on the verge of dropping me completely."

They walked out into the gallery and Lightborne went around turning off lights. He looked at Moll from a distance of thirty-five feet or so.

"You mentioned trains and planes."

"Just wondering aloud," she said.

"If you were heading Glen's way, and this is only speculation, you'd probably choose to fly. Although if you didn't like flying, you'd be able to take a train."

"I don't mind short flights. Anything over an hour, I get a little restless."

"I think you'd be all right."

"Trains are fun. I like trains."

"Three and a half hours on a train can be a little tiring."

"You could be right."

"Although Penn Station. If the old structure still stood.

That would make it worthwhile. Just walking in the place. A gorgeous piece of architecture."

"I was also wondering," she said.

"What else?"

"What would I need in the way of clothes?"

"It might be slightly warmer."

"Slightly warmer, you say."

The last light went out and Moll stood in shadow in the open doorway, unable to see Lightborne at all.

"I'm only speculating, understand."

"You're not a meteorologist," she said.

"I only know what God wants me to know."

When she was gone, Lightborne locked the door and went back into the living area, where he took off his jacket, his string tie and his shirt. He went to the wash basin, took his razor out of the cabinet and then removed the top on an aerosol can of Gillette Foamy, noting a bit of rust on the inner rim. He had an appointment first thing in the morning and thought he'd save time by shaving now.

Moll Robbins hailed a cab on Houston Street and twenty-five minutes later was on the phone in her West Seventies apartment, talking to Grace Delaney, her managing editor.

"Do we still have a Washington office?"

"It's called Jerry Burke."

"What's the number?"

She put down the phone and dialed again.

"Jerry Burke?"

"Who's this?"

"I understand you have terrific access to the corridors of power."

"What time is it?"

"This is Moll Robbins in New York, Jerry. We haven't met, I don't think, but maybe you can help me."

"You do movie reviews."

"From time to time, yes, but this is a different sort of thing completely. I'd like you to help me track someone down."

"You were full of shit about the new *King Kong*."

"I don't doubt it, Jerry, but listen I'm looking for a man named Glen Selvy, white, early thirties, six feet one, possibly in government down there. There must be some kind of giant directory of government drones that this man's name is listed in. If you could look into it or ask around or whatever, I'd be forever in your debt, within reason."

"Six foot one?"

"I thought it might be important."

"What do I need his height for?"

"Detective work," she said. "All the particulars."

Glen Selvy drove from the airport to a four-story apartment building in a predominantly black area near the Navy Yard. He'd been living here for several months but the place looked recently occupied. It was severely underfurnished. A number of unpacked cartons were arrayed near the bed. There was a floor lamp with the cord still tied in a neat bundle at its base.

This quality of transience appealed to Selvy. It had the advantage of reducing one's accountability, somehow. If you were always ten minutes from departure, you couldn't be expected to answer to the same moderating precepts other people followed.

He took off his suit coat, revealing a small belt holster that contained a lightweight Colt Cobra, .38 caliber. The Smith & Wesson .41 magnum, with six-inch barrel and custom grips, he kept wedged in a carton near the bed.

Late the next day Moll got a call from Jerry Burke.

"I've been through a number of registers. No results at all.

Then I remembered the Plum Book. *Policy and Supporting Positions.* Many, many government jobs. Descriptions. Names of incumbents."

"Excellent," she said.

"Your man isn't listed there."

"Damn."

"But I came across an appendix in a Senate bulletin and there's something called Congressional Quota Transferrals and it's chock full of names and next to each name there's an alphabetic code that refers you to page something-something. Anyway on this one little list I found a Howard Glen Selvy. According to his code letters he's on the staff of Senator Lloyd Percival."

"Jerry, that's terrific."

"He's a kind of second-level administrative aide."

"Isn't Percival in the news these days?"

"It's been going on for a while, really, but in closed committee sessions. He's investigating something called PAC/ORD. It's ostensibly a coordinating arm of the whole U.S. intelligence apparatus, strictly an above-board clerical and budgetary operation. Whatever Percival's digging for, it hasn't been leaked."

"Secret hearings."

"Every day," he said.

"What do the letters stand for?"

"What letters?"

"PAC/ORD," she said.

"Not many people in Washington could answer a question like that."

"Not many people in the whole world, I bet."

"Personnel Advisory Committee, Office of Records and Disbursements."

"Has to be evil, with a name like that."

"Or why else would Percival be involved?"

"He's a righteous type, is he?"

"Never mind that," Burke said. "What I'd like to know is why you're interested in this guy Selvy."

"It's just he's so cute," she said.

2

Glen Selvy in a three-piece suit walked slowly around the quarter-mile cinder track. There were birds everywhere, wheeling overhead, hopping mechanically in the grass.

Fifty yards away a black limousine turned into the quiet street that skirted the athletic field. Selvy headed over there, watching the back door swing open, his mind suddenly wandering to a nondescript room, a bed with a naked woman straddling a pillow, no one he knew, and then sex, her body and his, relentless crude obliterating sex, bang bang bang bang.

Lomax had a penchant for rented limousines. This was fine with Selvy, whose own car was a cramped Toyota. It was safe to assume the chauffeur didn't come with the car; he'd be someone Lomax knew. Maybe the thinking was that inconspicuousness no longer amounted to much. Or that in a town like Washington a limousine was not readily noticeable. Maybe it was Lomax himself. A personal style. A departure from established forms.

Lomax was pudgy, his hair mod-cut, graying a bit at the temples. He liked to pat and smooth and lightly stroke his hair, although it was never mussed. He was dressed for golf today, Selvy noticed. A set of clubs leaned against the far door.

"I learned something yesterday," Selvy said. "Lightborne knew Christoph Ludecke. Before Ludecke was killed, he and Lightborne had several meetings."

"In what connection?"

"Ludecke claimed to have access to some movie that apparently the whole smut-industry power structure would love to get the rights to. So Lightborne was all set to act as agent for the sale."

"Help from an unexpected quarter," Lomax said.

"Sure, Lightborne. Who figured Lightborne would link up to any of this? It explains the whole thing."

"Does it?"

"The Senator's connection to Christoph Ludecke. Now we know. One way or another he knew Ludecke had this footage. One way or another his phone number, or one of his phone numbers, his least traceable phone number, which we nevertheless traced, ended up in Ludecke's little book. That's the absolute central fact, the core of his involvement. Percival wanted the movie for his collection."

"Does he do movies?"

"This would be the first."

"What's so special about it?" Lomax said.

"It's a genuine Nazi sex revel."

"Wonderful."

"Supposedly shot in the bunker where Hitler spent his last days."

"Grand," Lomax said. "Simply grand."

Off the road a creek meandered east into the distance. In a park a group of young Orientals practiced the stylized movements of *t'ai chi*, a set of exercises that seemed to some degree martial in nature. The tempo was unchanging and fluid, and although there were eight of them involved it was hard to detect an individual dissonance in their routine. Almost in slow motion each man thrust one arm out while moving the other back, this second arm bent at the elbow, both hands extended, fingers together, as though the arms were hinged weapons and the hands not terminal attachments but rather the pointed ends of these weapons. Moves and countermoves. Front leg bending, rear leg stretching. Active, passive. Thrust and drag. A breeze came up, the lighter branches on the trees rising slightly as their leaves tossed in the agitated air. Eight bodies slowly moving in a revolving lotus kick. The creek reappeared at the end of a stretch of elms, swifter here, running in the sun.

"We've got more than enough leverage to use against the Senator."

"I don't make policy," Lomax said.

"We've got the smut collection to use against him. His interest in this movie is just an added twist of the knife."

"I execute policy, I don't make it. I do fact-gathering."

"We know he's got pieces that once belonged to Goering."

"People ask me questions. I frame a reply in terms of giving an answer."

"Among other notables," Selvy said.

"When the time comes, it comes. If he presses these inquiries, we'll tell him what we know and how we'll use it. His constituency will go bananas. Picture the media. Over a million dollars' worth of sexually explicit art."

"No way he can move against us."

"But I don't make policy," Lomax said. "I just gather information."

"Who makes policy? Tell the policy maker. We have whatever we need on Percival. Meanwhile I keep moving paper in his office."

"Double cover," Lomax said.

In the current parlance, Selvy was a reader. He was reading Senator Percival. At the same time he and Percival had a clandestine alliance. No one else in the Senator's office was aware that Selvy had been hired not to help direct the paper flow but to do Percival's art buying.

"But you shouldn't call it smut," Lomax was saying.

"Did I call it smut?"

"You said earlier, his smut collection."

"You've seen the photos, I take it."

"Interesting photos," Lomax said. "You're getting better at it."

"Less rush this time."

"There's nothing shameful about the human body, you

know. Some pleasant surprises in that collection. Some very nice things. I'd say the man has taste. Don't call it smut. You called it smut."

Three Irish setters ran in a field near Reservoir Road, scrambling over each other when one of them changed direction abruptly. A group of schoolgirls played field hockey, wearing elaborate uniforms, their laughter and shrieks seeming to reach the limousine across a particularly clear segment of space, an area empty of distorting matter, so that the listener received a truer human voice, the vivid timbre of animated play.

"We found the woman," Lomax said.

"Where is she?"

"Traveling."

"Whereabouts?"

"The old country."

It was cherry blossom time.

Moll found Washington spiritually oppressive. Government buildings did that to her. Great weight of history or something. Guided tours. Schoolbooks. The last Sunday of summer vacation. I don't feel well, mom.

She wore thong sandals, a loose cotton dress and a hip sash—an outfit she used whenever she felt a deceptive appearance was called for. A date with a man she suspected she might dislike, for instance. She believed herself to be attractive, although not quite this way. Clothes, used in this manner, were a method of safeguarding her true self, pending developments.

Her auburn hair, normally curled and frizzed and shriveled up, had an even more electrified look today. Deep-fried hair. Probably caused by humidity, the condition was extreme enough to be taken as a style.

Along a corridor in the Senate wing she moved in her

somewhat wary manner behind a group of reporters who were trying to keep up with Lloyd Percival. The Senator, still wearing orange makeup from an earlier TV appearance, answered only certain questions, and those curtly, talking out of the side of his mouth. He was sixty, a large man, beginning to go fleshy, with something of a burdened look about him, small tired eyes blinking above those folds of loose skin.

He wheeled right, strode past an enormous mahogany clock topped by a bellicose eagle, made another right toward a flight of stairs, and as though by hidden signal the reporters stopped pursuing and dispersed, leaving Moll to follow alone, right into an elevator reserved for senators and staff, out into another corridor, around a corner, keeping about seven feet behind him, just so he'd know she was there.

"Out with it."

"Moll Robbins."

"Print or broadcast."

"*Running Dog* magazine."

"*Running Dog*," he said.

"Yes."

"You people still in business?"

"Barely."

"Capitalist lackeys and running dogs."

"Someone remembers," she said.

He pushed open a large door, looked inside, looked back at Moll, cocked his head, paused and shrugged, saying: "What the hell, come on in."

It was an enormous ornate men's room. No one else in sight. Spotless tile, gleaming fixtures. Faint aroma of balsam fir and lime. Percival stooped over a wash basin.

"I have to get this makeup off."

"I saw it," she said.

"What, the show?"

She waited for him to raise up a bit so he could hear above the gushing water.

"That man seemed confused."

"Who, the moderator?"

She waited for his head to emerge again.

"Yes."

"He's always confused. The fella's all image. He can't talk about something like PAC/ORD. He's a bunch of little electronic dots, that's all he is. The fella's so folksy he ought to do his news show in a living room set, wearing slippers and smoking a pipe, in front of a crackling fire."

Moll took a towel from a shelf and put it in his outstretched hand.

"They ought to hire a kindly old lady to bring him disaster bulletins on a tray with his raisin cookies and hot chocolate."

"See, we thought at *Running Dog* we'd do something different."

"How different, I'd like to know."

As they spoke Moll had a distant sense of Memorable Event Taking Place, and could hear herself describing it to friends—"*So we're in this U.S. Senate men's room and he's got his head down inside a Florentine marble wash basin and I'm checking out the urinals to see if they have state emblems on them, like Delaware pisses here, and this one's Kansas*"—

A toilet flushed down at the end of a long row of stalls. The stall door opened and an elderly black man came out, fastening his trousers. Moll watched him approach.

"How are you today, Senator?"

"About as well as can be expected, Tyrell, under the circumstances."

"I know the feeling," Tyrell said.

He took a brush out of his white jacket and moved it through the air behind Percival's shoulders and midback, eyeing Moll for the first time, at least openly. It was a look, combined with a haughty shrug, that said, *I don't know what you're doing here but this is the wrong place to be doing it.*

In the corridor the Senator walked at a more reasonable pace.

"We'd like to take a relaxed approach," she said.

"My so-called human side."

"It's fairly common knowledge you spend much of your free time at your Georgetown house. That might be the place to talk."

"I have aides who screen people like you. Why weren't you screened?"

"Will you do it, Senator?"

"*Running Dog*—Jesus, I don't know."

"Our problems are strictly financial. We don't get many complaints about content or format."

"You run nudes?"

"Occasionally."

"Male and female?"

"Female."

"Pubic hair?"

"Airbrush."

They seemed to be coming to a door that led to the street.

"Nice to know the old values aren't dead," he said.

They stood blinking in the sunlight.

"I don't want to talk about the closed-door hearings."

"Truthfully, I'm not the least interested. I want to discuss your other activities, Senator. Your reading habits, your family, your thoughts on contemporary life. Your hobbies, your pastimes, your diversions."

She took a cab to the airport, and about a minute before the plane taxied out to the tarmac to be cleared for takeoff, Glen Selvy walked up the aisle toward her seat, spotting her and nodding. About fifteen minutes into the flight he returned, told her there was an empty row of seats toward the rear of the plane and asked her to join him.

She gave him her limpest category of response, a visual autopsy, but eventually followed.

"Travel to Washington often?"

"Film gala at the Kennedy Center. I do some reviewing. In New York to see Lightborne?"

"I may get around to seeing Lightborne, yes."

"Nice old turkey," she said.

She dozed the last ten minutes of the flight. When the plane touched down she was startled, coming awake abruptly, her hand reaching out to grasp Selvy's on the arm rest. He looked at her without expression, making her feel he'd been observing her precisely that way all the while she was asleep, and she found she liked that.

They shared a cab and sat in stalled traffic for a long time, finally reaching midtown just as daylight was fading. Moll suggested they find a jazz club she used to go to years earlier, somewhere in the stunned landscape of East Third Street. It turned out to be long gone but they found a dive around the corner and went in for a drink.

Selvy took off his tie and jacket and rolled up his shirt-sleeves. He began drinking shots of Jim Beam. First he sipped a fraction of an ounce off the top, downing the rest athletically in one swallow. The grimace and flush of pleasure hard-earned. Moll started out with scotch and water. Feeling guilty about the water, she switched to rocks.

They talked a while about various things they'd drunk in different places they'd visited around the world. A man sitting nearby, with a bandage around his head, said he was too drunk to go home by himself. This meant they would have to take him home. It was the code of Frankie's Tropical Bar, he said. The man was Dominican. He said he didn't care whether they took him to his home or their home, as long as they took him home. He said he knew who killed Trujillo.

"I believe in codes," Selvy said.

They went out to find a cab. The man with the bandage around his head walked right into a fat woman. She hit him in the mouth. He looked around for something, a weapon. He saw a bicycle and picked it up. In the dark he couldn't tell the bicycle was chained to a fence. He started toward the woman, intending to ram her with the bicycle or to throw it at her. He was jerked back toward the fence and fell on top of the bike, catching his hand in the spokes.

Moll took Selvy by the arm and led him along a line of cars waiting for the light to change. At the end of the line they found a taxi and got in. They headed uptown and then west. Selvy dropped her in front of her building and then went on—somewhere.

Early the next morning he turned up at her door. He strode in, a noncommittal look on his face, and scanned the premises.

"Welcome to Falconhurst," she said.

Brown walls. Espresso machine. Silverplated telephone. Acrylic stepladder. Black banquette. Spherical TV. White plastic saxophone.

"The walls are brown."

"I considered mulatto."

"Chocolate-brown."

"But finally decided what the hell."

"The previous tenant was gay, wasn't he?"

"They're his walls," she said.

"You ought to put some plants on the stepladder."

"I kill plants."

"That type, are you?"

"They die in my embrace."

She was wearing a floor-length rugby sleepshirt. On her feet were tennis sneakers, laces undone. The shirt accentuated her height in ways she thought interesting. She watched Selvy open the refrigerator and take out a bottle of Coke, which he drained in two quick gulps. He hadn't shaved and looked a little menacing. He stood with his back to the refrigerator, arms folded, watching her.

It occurred to Moll he didn't look much like the man she'd first seen at Cosmic Erotics, the junior exec with the crisp manner. The night of drinking had given him a strange pale aura, a quality of relentlessness. It was almost a form of competence, this ability to suggest a dark force in one's own makeup. She'd sensed it while they were drinking at Frankie's Tropical Bar but the aftereffect was even more telling, this spareness about him, a hard-edged overriding disposition, the kind of single-mindedness she didn't confront in the course of an average day.

Howard Glen Selvy. Second-level administrative aide. Assistant to the assistant.

The small bedroom looked out on a vacant lot that might have been a Zen garden of rubbish. As she knelt at the edge of the bed, Selvy, behind her, put his hands under the long garment she wore and moved them along her calves, lifting the shirt as he did so. Moll bent back to raise her knees and he slipped the garment up over them and his hands moved to her thighs and hips as the phone rang, and to her belly then, and breasts, his forearms tight against her ribs, lifting her a little. She crossed her arms to pull the shirt over her head, the phone ringing, and then sat in the middle of the bed to watch him undress, which he did with a curious efficiency, as though it were a drill that might one day save his life.

There was an element of resolve and fixed purpose to their lovemaking. He was lean and agile. She found herself scratching his shoulders, working against his body with uncharacteristic intensity. He began to sweat lightly, to take deeper breaths, and his stubble scraped her face and neck. She took her left hand away from his lower back and stretched the arm way back and began tapping on the brass post at the head of the bed, hitting it with her knuckles in time to the rhythm of Selvy's breathing, and then her own, as the sounds they made began to blend.

They were tied up in a ball. They were compact and working hard. Who is this son of a bitch, she thought.

She sat naked in the dining area, her legs extended along the length of an antique church bench, or at least a section of one. Selvy stood leaning against a bookcase, wearing long johns and drinking another Coke. She hadn't noticed the long johns when he was undressing; obviously he'd removed them in one motion with the trousers that concealed them. She thought he looked great like that, leaning as he was, head tilted to drink, in that archaic underwear, an English lancer on the eve of Balaclava. She took another bite of yogurt, glancing at the telephone as it began ringing once more.

"Is that the office?"

"Yes," she said.

"What do you want to do?"

"Play tennis."

"Great."

"Except it's impossible without waiting for hours or joining a private club or suddenly coming into great wealth and building your own rooftop court."

"Ridiculous."

"You know where we can play?"

"Last night in the cab after I dropped you off we went by some courts in this remote little area in Central Park, a hundred feet off the road but in a place where you can't stop the car. We'll walk. It's easy from here. No problem."

"You're crazy."

"Do you have an extra racket?"

"Nobody plays tennis in Central Park just by walking out the door and making a left turn."

"Come on, get dressed."

She spooned a final bite of yogurt out of the carton she held between her thighs and then went into the bedroom to get some clothes on, hearing Selvy dial a number on the phone. When she was dressed she found him waiting by the bedroom door. He went inside to dress and she called her boss, Grace Delaney, at the office.

"I couldn't answer when you called."

"Obviously."

"Percival's willing, I *think*. I also think he'll talk to me at his place in Georgetown, where the collection's almost got to be."

"You don't really believe he'll let you anywhere near it."

"I believe he will, Grace."

"Put your dreams away," she sang, "for another day."

"Well, he *will*, I talked to him, we sort of struck up a tiny little rapport."

"Why are you whispering?"

"We went to the men's room together."

"Spare me the details."

"See you later maybe."

"Who's there that you're whispering?"

"I'm taking care of a sick friend."

"What's he got, the clap?"

"Always a joy to talk to you, Grace."

Rackets in hand they walked through the park in a northeasterly direction. Selvy pointed out a clearing in some trees beyond a children's play area. They could make out two courts, both empty.

"Ever get bombed on sake?"

"Sure," he said.

"Once, on one of those high-speed trains to Kyoto, I think it was, I nearly did myself in."

"Dutch gin's good for doing yourself in."

"Where?"

"I was in Zandvoort for the Grand Prix."

"Grand Prix of volleyball, I suppose."

"What do you mean?"

"Look," she said.

"Those aren't tennis courts, are they?"

"Those are volleyball courts," she said.

They decided to play anyway. Because the nets were so high, they hit underhand shots exclusively and did a lot of dipping and knee flexing, using strange body English. A small girl watched from the top of a sliding pond nearby. Eventually a certain lunatic rhythm began to assert itself. The players got the feel of things. They appeared to enjoy playing within these limitations and started keeping score more diligently.

Moll chased an errant serve down a small hill and when she came back up to courtside found that Selvy was about forty yards away, heading across the lawn, racket in hand, toward a black limousine that was parked on the grass. The back door opened and he got in. She watched the car bump down off the curb back onto the roadway and then swing left and pick up speed, passing behind a knoll and out of sight.

The small girl standing atop the sliding pond also watched, from a somewhat better perspective. Moll looked at her and shrugged. The girl pointed, her index finger tracing the direction of the car. Finally her arm dropped to her side and she came sliding down the shiny ramp and walked off toward a group of parents and other children.

Moll stood for a while, scanning the area, two tennis balls in one hand, the racket in the other. One of the children shrieked, in play, and when Moll turned in the direction of the sound she saw Selvy walking toward her along a paved lane between two rows of benches. He was still fifty yards away when she said, softly: "You forgot your racket."

She was back on the church bench, wearing Selvy's long johns this time. He came out of the bathroom, still a little wet, with a towel around his waist, grinning at the sight of her in his underwear.

"I just used that towel."

"Doesn't matter," he said.

"Get a clean towel."

"I'm fine. I'm happy. Leave me alone."

He sat at the table, facing her, his thumbnail nicking the label on the bottle of Wild Turkey she'd set out.

"We may be the start of a new kind of human potential group," she said. "Wear each other's clothing."

"It's probably been done."

"Get in touch with each other's feelings by exchanging clothes. I see it becoming big. Huge rallies in ballparks and concert halls. When people join the movement they have to fill in forms telling what size clothes they wear. We need a name for it."

He leaned across the table and poured an inch of bourbon into the glass she held in her lap. Then he filled his own glass and got some cold cuts out of the refrigerator and sat back down.

"Apparel Personality Exchange," she said.

"Some mustard on this?"

"APE."

"You're in the wrong business," he said. "You ought to be promoting, merchandising."

"My father was an advertising immortal."

"It shows."

"You mean the apartment. Really, I'm not all that consumer-oriented or brand-conscious. It's just a phase I went through about a year ago. I bought a lot of shiny stuff and maybe I regret it. But my father, getting back to that, he did the midget campaign for Maytag. It made him an immortal."

"I guess I missed it."

"Wash a midget in your Maytag."

"I did miss it."

"We used to argue all the time. It was awful. I thought he was the absolute lowest form of toad in the whole sick society. I was living with Penner then. And I'd see my father

year and we'd have these all-out screaming fights
he consumer society and revolution and all the rest of
it. I remember seeing *Zabriskie Point* about then and that
scene at the end when the house blows up and all those
brightly colored products go exploding through the air in
slow motion. God, that made my whole year. That was the
high point of whatever year that was. And I tried to get old
Ted Robbins to go see it, just out of spite, out of petty mal-
ice, all those packages of detergent and powdered soup and Q-
tips and eye liner and that whole big house, boom."

"Who's Penner?"

"Remember Gary Penner? The demolitions expert who
traveled all over the country blowing up things. Dial-a-
Bomb."

"Yes," Selvy said.

"Feared coast to coast. FBI wanted him badly. He was J.
Edgar's secret obsession. I lived with Penner for seven months.
Running Dog was in its prime then. We used to run statements from Penner about once a month hinting at what bank
or whatever target in what city was due to get it next. I
actually wrote the statements. Oh, it was a weird time. Weird
times were upon us. Penner was *the* strangest son of a bitch. I
mean he was wrapped up in explosives beyond human com-
prehension. He was also the meanest bastard you'd ever want
to come across."

"But you like mean bastards."

"Fortunately I like mean bastards."

"He got it how?"

"Some woman shot him, finally. Motel in Arizona. About a
year after we split up. *Running Dog* did an obit with a black
border."

Feeling a sneeze coming on, Selvy got up, moved away
from the food on the table, whipped the towel off his waist
and got it up to his nose just in time. Then he tossed the towel
in the direction of the open bathroom door. They looked at

each other. She downed all but a few drops of bourbon. Then she put her thumb under the elastic band of the long johns, pulled it away from her belly and poured the last of the liquor down into the opening. She watched Selvy react interestingly and involuntarily. She got up, put the glass on the table and walked toward the bedroom, touching him lightly as she passed.

When Moll woke up later it was early evening. A soft rain was falling. It seemed to hang out there rather than actually descend. She felt a chill and reached down to the floor for the sheets and bedspread. She started to place them carefully over Selvy's body, in order not to wake him, when she realized he was watching her. She bit his shoulder and licked at his nipples. He moved, resettling himself, eyes closed now, as she kissed his lids and brows and moved the tips of her fingers across his chest.

"I know whose limousine that was," she said.

He faced the ceiling, eyes closed.

"Senator Percival, wasn't it?"

With her finger she traced a hank of hair around his left ear.

"I know you work for him, Glen. He's an avid collector of explicit art. You scout for him and do his buying."

Her hand on his chest rose and fell with the beat of his even breathing.

"He can't do it himself, obviously. You do it for him, following his instructions, presumably, and using administrative cover. Look, we may or may not end up using Percival in the series I'm doing but if you can help me get at the collection, great, fantastic. If not, I understand. I may be able to manage it myself."

She watched his eyes come open.

"I even know your first name," she said.

Before she knew what was happening, he was kneeling between her legs and hefting her up toward him, his hands at her hips, making her arch, and then was in her, cleanly, and driving, using his hands to force her body tighter onto his. Her head back on the pillow, pelvis way off the bed and knees up, she watched him grimace and stroke and then had to close her eyes, abandoning the visible world to enter this region of borderline void, his nails burning into her hips.

When she woke this second time it was the middle of the night. She half dreamed various things, a run-on series of images, and slept, and woke again. She kept picturing Selvy in a military setting, a barracks usually. He's standing around in white cotton boxer shorts, a dog tag around his neck. Maybe she was mixing Monty Clift into it, in *From Here to Eternity*. She pictured Selvy doing a hundred pushups in his white shorts. She pictured him sitting on a cot, spit-shining his boots. She pictured him running laps, his rifle at high port, sweat beginning to dampen his combat fatigues.

Without turning his way or reaching an arm across the bed, she knew he was no longer there.

3

People who don't make the trip every day have a tendency to grow silent as the train passes through Harlem. It isn't shock or gloom so much as sheer fascination that brings on the hush. The pleasure of ruins. The eye's delight in finding instructive vistas. It's so interesting to look at, so numbly colorful, especially from this distance, and while moving through.

Selvy got off at the Bronxville station and took a cab along Palmer Road. They turned left across an overpass and into a quiet street in the less expensive section. Klara Ludecke lived in a small attractive house on this street.

His instructions weren't specific. She'd been traveling in Europe. Why and precisely where. He didn't care to get involved in side issues, such as her husband's murder, being concerned only with the dead man's connection to the Senator and the leverage it provided.

Her face was a near circle, though pretty. She was somewhat broad of figure, maybe thirty years old, and spoke in an accent that was pleasant to hear even in its odder journeys through certain words. She led him to a dark parlor and then sat waiting in a straightbacked chair, hands folded on her knees.

"You've been away, Mrs. Ludecke."

"To Aachen, in West Germany."

"Your husband was born there."

"Yes, in 1944, I believe."

"Why this particular time to travel? Your husband had just been murdered. You spoke once to the police and then disappeared."

"My husband has relatives there, still. I wished to see them. You must understand I needed to be close to people who loved him. I was not capable to deal with things."

"You've come back—why?"

She made a sweeping gesture to indicate the house, possessions, legalities, disengagements.

"You're not staying."

"It would be impossible."

"Are you going back to Germany?"

"I don't know. Perhaps that's what I'll finally do. At least my husband's family is there. His own father died seven months ago but there are brothers and sisters who have been very kind to me, and Christoph's mother as well."

"Your husband was a systems engineer—correct?"

"You're not one of the policemen I talked to after it happened."

"No," he said.

"Who are you?"

Clipped to his belt holster was a device called a field-strength meter. He took it out, raised the small antenna attached to it, and then tuned the meter to sweep the frequency band. Checking the needle he probed the north side of the room. From the bookcase he took a 1961 World Almanac. Embedded in the narrow space between the spine and the binding was a small audio device. Selvy disengaged the single transistor in the oscillator circuit. He looked at Klara Ludecke. She didn't know whether to be surprised or angry.

He took out his wallet and showed her a set of credentials linking him to something called U.S. Strike Force, Internal Projects.

"Special investigative unit."

"What is special about me?"

"Your husband didn't die under what I'd call normal circumstances, Mrs. Ludecke."

"When is murder normal?"

"Beyond the fact that he was murdered, there were unusual details."

"Abnormal, perhaps you would prefer to say."

"Words."

"Abnormal," she insisted.

"Yes, why not?"

"Anyone would agree. A grotesque death. And it's interesting that you haven't spoken a word about the people who killed him. Circumstances so abnormal that this small detail is completely overlooked."

"No, wrong."

"Perhaps this aspect of the crime isn't part of your special investigation. You're not interested? It's too routine for specialists. You're bored with that question?"

"I'd like to discuss the matter of acquaintances."

"Would you really?"

"Your husband's work took him to Washington on occasion."

"This is correct. Washington and the surrounding area."

"Washington in particular."

"I wouldn't say that, no."

"According to the original police inquiry—"

"The police," she said. "The police know nothing. Sex crime, that's all they know. It's the people in the special investigation who know what's important and what isn't. They know where to look. How deep, how shallow. The police. They photograph the body. They make chalk marks on the floor. They check their files on deviates and the killers of deviates. That satisfies them. They have such experience in these areas. Who am I to complain?"

Klara Ludecke raised her eyes to an angle level with his.

"How special can this investigation be if you haven't even asked about Radial Matrix?" she said.

Selvy picked up a plastic disk from the coffee table in front of him, a scenic paperweight, three-dimensional vista of rolling hills, and studied it a moment. He watched the woman rise from the chair and walk through the dark parlor and along the equally dark hallway, where she opened the front door and held it, not taking her eyes off the opposite wall as he walked past her into the sun.

Later that same day he rode an escalator down to the Capitol subway with Lloyd Percival.

"You're due at Lightborne's when?"

"Tomorrow night," Selvy said. "Auction."

"What, more Guatemalan stuff?"

"Apparently."

"We see nothing but stiff pricks lately. What I wouldn't give for a single mushy prick. Might be a whole new approach. Jesus Christmas, what happened to the esthetic element? Tell Lightborne. The subtlety, the complexity, the simple charm. All he seems to show us are junkyard pieces."

"He knows, Senator."

"Just heard from some friends in Amsterdam. Someone's come up with a plaster-and-polystyrene copy of a Bernini I've always admired."

"*Saint Teresa in Ecstasy.*"

"Right, some young Dutch sculptor."

"Lightborne's got a vicar he did."

"What kind of vicar?"

"A vicar with a stiff prick, Senator."

"Why did I ask?"

"Anyway."

"Anyway what this Dutch fella's done is to lift the folds of Saint Teresa's habit way up around her thighs and to place her knees well apart without changing the original position of the feet. Hell, it was already there. All he's done is highlight it. Her ecstasy always was sexual."

They were the last two people to step onto the small electric conveyance and it started immediately.

"Bernini might not agree."

"Don't quibble, Glen."

"Not to mention Saint Teresa."

"Are you a prude?"

"Possibly."

"Interesting fella. You're an interesting fella."

"What about the angel?"

"He's changed the configuration of the arrowhead but only slightly."

"To make it more phallic."

"Marginally so," Percival said.

"The sacred and profane."

"Special form of eroticism, isn't it? Always been attracted to it myself. It pleases the Lord that only a few of us have the wherewithal to pursue such attractions."

They got off the subway and took an elevator to the third floor of the Dirksen Building.

"Magazine wants to make me look human."

"Which?"

"*Running Dog.*"

"Stay away," Selvy said. "It's not my department of course."

"Why?"

"They'll burn you."

"How do you know?"

"They're after controversy. They're dying and need a fix. Even if they do the piece they promise, you'll be hemmed in by autopsy reports, photos of entry and exit wounds, who killed Brown, who killed Smith, who killed Jones. They deal in fantasy."

They walked down a corridor toward the Senator's office.

"It's not your department of course."

"Absolutely not," Selvy said.

"Your duties are strictly administrative."

"Their editor's unstable. Grace Delaney. A lush. Used to spend all her time raising bail for well-hung Panthers."

Lightborne leaned forward to grimace, inches from the mirror, checking his teeth for traces of the grilled cheese sandwich he'd had for dinner. He turned on the cold water, wet his index finger and then ran it several times across his clenched teeth.

He cleared a space in the gallery and set out folding chairs and a bench, deciding finally not to bother hauling the armchair out here. He went around turning on lights. In his jacket pocket he found a slightly bent Tareyton King and he blew on it several times to remove microscopic lint and then began searching for a match, the cigarette held between thumb and middle finger, an idiosyncrasy he'd copied from a titled Englishman he'd once done business with. With no matches to be had, he finally turned on the hotplate and was waiting for it to warm when the first of the bidders arrived.

Eventually eleven people sat in the gallery as Lightborne made final adjustments. Glen Selvy carried a chair out of the living area and sat against a wall, slightly apart from the others. Lightborne showed a carved wood fertility figure.

Noted its characteristics and advised as to period, precise handiwork involved, where found and how. A well-tanned man named Wetzel was the sole bidder.

A copper statuette with a lesbian theme also went without competitive bidding. Wetzel captured a bronze satyr—once owned by Fulgencio Batista, Lightborne said—after an encouraging flurry of bids against three other people.

Lightborne pushed a trunk on rollers into the auction area. He undid the belts, used an enormous key to open the trunk and then, with the help of a couple of men sitting up front, removed a three-foot-high volcanic stone phallus that pointed upward from a base of a pair of testicles larger than bowling balls.

The piece was variously chipped, pockmarked and discolored. It had character. Lightborne invited the bidders to take a closer look, and most did. Then he delivered a brief interpretation of the piece and opened the bidding.

Wetzel said, "That thing is about as pre-Columbian as an Oldenburg clothespin."

"Who said pre-Columbian? I said it was dug out of a tomb in the jungle. Who specified a date?"

"Your man chiseled the damn thing in his backyard."

"He knows tombs no one else knows," Lightborne said. "They're in the densest areas. You can't get in there except on foot, hacking."

"Hacking," Wetzel said.

"Professor Shatsky was supposed to be here to authenticate. He's late, evidently."

"Shatsky."

"The Jewish Museum."

"What the hell does the Jewish Museum know about Guatemalan pricks? This particular prick isn't even circumcised."

Lightborne made a gesture of pacification.

"Go easy on the Anglo-Saxonisms," he said.

An hour later the whole thing was over. A full-fledged disaster. Lightborne poured some Canadian whisky into a shot glass and sipped it. He got out a box of marshmallow cookies and ate three of them whole, washing them down with small amounts of rye.

Bottles of Shasta and Wink sat on tables in the gallery. Someone's cigar still smoldered in an ashtray. Lightborne took the bent Tareyton out of his pocket and used the acrid cigar to light it. He locked the door, turned off the lights and slipped behind the partition.

A sixty-watt bulb hung over the wash basin, swaying a little in the breeze from an open window. Lightborne poured some more rye and sat by the phone. He dialed the operator and asked her to get a Dallas number, person to person, collect.

After some delay the call was accepted by Richie Armbrister, known as the boy wonder of smut, a twenty-two-year-old master of distribution and marketing who lived and worked in a barricaded warehouse in downtown Dallas.

Armbrister controlled a maze of one hundred and fifty corporations which numbered among their activities and holdings a chain of bookstores, strip joints and peep movies coast to coast; massage parlors and nude-encounter studios, southwest U.S. and western Canada; outlets for leather goods and mechanical devices west of the Mississippi; sex boutiques, topless bars, topless billiard parlors across the Sunbelt; a New Orleans car rental firm with topless chauffeurs. He took few vacations and had no hobbies.

"Lightborne, how are you? Always a pleasure to speak to a knowledgeable person, what with all these second-raters who work for me."

"I understand the business is getting tight, Richie. I mean legally speaking, as far as successful prosecutions."

"They'll never find me. I have too much paper floating around. I'm very well hidden, believe me. Holding companies in four states. Dummy corporations. I don't exist as a person. I'm not in writing anywhere. I'm sitting behind all that paper."

"Legal fronts, wonderful."

"So speak," Armbrister said, his high-pitched voice seemingly on the verge of cracking.

"Remember the business we talked about some months ago."

"Sure."

"It's hot again," Lightborne said. "I got a phone call that sounds encouraging."

"You're encouraged."

"It could be nothing."

"I'm still interested. Full-length movies. First-run. The field's been denied me so far. Some bad luck. A series of small incidents. Organized crime, you know. The families. They're involved in full-length."

"It could be nothing, Richie."

"But the trail is hot again."

"It's warm. I'd say warm, realistically."

"What do you need, Lightborne?"

"To show some money."

"All my money's tied up in cash."

Lightborne realized he was being called upon to laugh and with an effort he managed to do this.

"Hey, I bought a plane," Richie said. "I'm going to Europe to do some business. We gutted the whole passenger section and redid it. It's big, it seats thirty-one, a DC-nine. Maybe I'll stop in New York on the way back. We'll get serious about this thing."

"I know Europe well," Lightborne said with no particular conviction.

"First we go to England to look at the theater setup. Then Hamburg or Stockholm, I forget which, for the shops, to see if we can push our rubber line. Then maybe Amsterdam for bondage items, to check out their expertise."

Lightborne was suddenly exhausted and wished only to stretch out on his cot and go to sleep. He stared into the dimness, nodding to the rhythms of the voice on the other end. There was a remark, a brief expectant silence, and then Richie's manic laughter came swimming across the continent.

"Ha ha," Lightborne said at the first opening.

The next day he walked into a railroad diner near Chinatown. He was a couple of minutes late and breathing heavily as he hurried the length of the room and sat next to Selvy at the counter.

"We discussed footage, you recall."

"Yes," Selvy said.

"Would he be interested?"

"Oh, he'd be interested."

"Tell him it could be on."

"I'll tell him."

"Tell him to forget about past failures."

"It's on. I'll tell him."

"Never mind the stuff from the jungle, tell him."

"This is different," Selvy said.

"Of course it's still sight unseen. It's still a question of plausibility."

"You were the chief skeptic, last time we talked about it."

Lightborne ordered soup and absently ran the edge of a matchbook under his fingernails.

"Common knowledge there was a steady flow of women in and out of the SS guard rooms in the bunker," he said. "All told there were hundreds of people in the bunker. It was an elaborate operation, running the country from down there, what was left of the country."

"All those people, things could happen, you're saying."

"On the other hand when we talk of the old boy himself, this is when I become highly skeptical once more."

"Hitler."

"He was too feeble to take part in anything like that. He

was partially paralyzed, he was under sedation much of the time. In his last days he wasn't well at all. Eva Braun. Eva Braun certainly wasn't a candidate for a mass sexual exercise. Not the type. Of course she liked movies. She once worked for a photographer. But that's of little matter."

"Very little," Selvy said.

"On the other hand there were the early days with Geli Raubal. His niece. Story goes he forced her to model for dirty pictures. Close-ups and such."

"Who drew the pictures?"

"He did," Lightborne said.

"Hitler."

"So you have this pornographic interest. You have the fact that movies were screened for him all the time in Berlin and Obersalzburg, sometimes two a day. Those Nazis had a thing for movies. They put everything on film. Executions, even, at his personal request. Film was essential to the Nazi era. Myth, dreams, memory. He liked lewd movies too, according to some. Even Hollywood stuff, girls with legs."

"You're building a case. You're tilting."

"It could be nothing."

"You're a student of the period."

"Did I say that?"

"I believe I recall, yes, you said that."

"You see, he's endlessly fascinating. The whole Nazi era. People can't get enough. If it's Nazis, it's automatically erotic. The violence, the rituals, the leather, the jackboots. The whole thing for uniforms and paraphernalia. He whipped his niece, did you know that?"

"Hitler."

"He used a bull whip, story goes."

Lightborne broke a saltine cracker and dropped the pieces into his tomato soup.

"Not that I don't remain skeptical," he said. "I remain highly skeptical."

"About the existence of the film itself or just the people taking part, their rank and such?"

"About both of those plus one other thing, which is the commercial prospects such a document would have. I call it a document to dignify it. Is there really any demand for such a thing? Is this what people want out of pornography? Maybe it's too historical. Maybe it *is* a document. I'm asking myself. What do people want? Is there a strong fantasy element involved? Will this kind of material help people upgrade their orgasms?"

Selvy couldn't help laughing.

"I like your walking stick," he said.

"Someone noticed. You're the first. Up until now, nobody saw it. I paid money. This is African wood, right here. The handle is a monkey if you notice."

"Nice stick, very."

Lightborne called for the check, noting that his companion had only a cup of coffee before him on the counter.

"Don't bother," Selvy said. "He pays."

"And you think there's a chance he'd be interested."

"Oh, he'd be interested all right. I know it for a fact."

The routine. Cab, terminal, plane, terminal, car. He moved through it apart from other people, sitting in aisle seats, standing at the edge of waiting lines, unobtrusively watchful, last on, first off. He found a place for his car on Potomac Avenue and headed into the building, skirting two small boys playing on the stairs outside his apartment.

"Hey, you the landlord?"

"No."

"Where you belong?"

"Hey, white."

"What you be doing here?"

"Hey, white."

"Where you belong then?"

He took a shower and waited for time to pass. He didn't mind the waiting. Somewhere to be at 1500. No one he knew, or might talk to in the intervening period, would ever suspect the nature of his business. It was carried on beneath the level of ordinary life. This is why it made no difference where he lived. It was all the same, mere coloration for the true life, for the empty meditations, the routine, the tradecraft, the fine edge to be maintained in preparation for—he didn't know what. In preparation for what?

He lived in the off-hours. He created his own operational environment, having little outside direction, no sense of policy. Periodically he reported to a house near the Government Printing Office, where he was given a technical interview, or polygraph, or lie detector test.

He was a reader. He read his man. There was nothing cynical in his view of the world. He didn't feel tainted by the dirt of his profession. It was a calculated existence, this. He preferred life narrowed down to unfinished rooms.

That afternoon at three Selvy stood outside a restaurant on M Street, Palacio de Mexico, as the limousine approached and the back door slowly swung open. There was a fully grown St. Bernard on the front seat next to the driver and three St. Bernard puppies mauling each other across the length of the rear seat. Lomax had squeezed himself into one of the jump seats and he motioned Selvy toward the adjoining one.

"I took them running," Lomax said.

"They haven't stopped."

"They needed the exercise. Dogs this big. It's crazy, having them in the city. Maybe I'll buy land somewhere."

"Fairfax County."

Lomax took one of the puppies in his lap and began stroking its neck. The car moved past the Executive Office Building.

"I saw Klara Ludecke," Selvy said.

"And?"

"She wants to know why she's a widow."

"Only natural."

"That's what I thought. Only natural she'd get around to asking."

"Is she in contact with Percival?"

"I doubt it."

"Any clue as to what she was doing back home?"

"Relatives, she says."

"I hear different," Lomax said.

The car headed west now, turning sharply on its approach to the Key Bridge. A long silence ensued.

"Why would she mention Radial Matrix?" Selvy said.

Lomax tossed the puppy back onto the seat.

"She mentioned it, did she?"

"She mentioned Radial Matrix."

Lomax took a box of throat lozenges out of his pocket and put one in his mouth. The car headed south on 29, the Lee Highway. Lomax pushed his way onto the rear seat and began playing with all three puppies, letting them scramble over his head and neck. Up front the fully grown dog sat looking straight ahead.

"The lady's natural curiosity raises a question," Selvy said. "It's not in my jurisdiction but, still, I've wondered lately."

"Mo here's gonna be stronger than a goddamn moose."

"Who killed Ludecke?"

"I'm looking at Percival," Lomax said.

Selvy thought this was stupid to the point of imbecility. He watched Lomax try to extricate himself from the roistering dogs.

"The Senator's just a high-toned smut collector. His thrills are vicarious, strictly. Murder is too powerful an idea for someone like that, even on a contract basis."

"Stay on Percival."

"That line of investigation has nothing left to yield. He wanted the Berlin film. He knew Ludecke had it. It doesn't go beyond that."

"I'm looking at Percival," Lomax said. "And don't call it smut. You keep calling it smut."

Selvy glanced out the window at a frame house with a plastic pool on the lawn and about half a cord of firewood stacked under the front porch.

"There's an outside chance some magazine may do a piece on the Senator's collection."

"Christ," Lomax said.

"There goes our advantage."

"Ain't it the truth."

"So?"

"I'll get back to you."

"In the meantime," Selvy said.

"In the meantime, go to New York."

The limousine pulled into a gas station and then swung across the road and headed back toward Washington.

"I just got back from there," Selvy said.

Both men knew this wasn't a complaint. It was an indirect form of acquiescence, a statement of Selvy's willingness to blend with the pattern, to travel an event to its final unraveling.

All the way back Lomax remained slumped in his jump seat, talking to the dogs.

4

The office was cluttered and bright, a sizable room with a fireplace that didn't work. Grace Delaney sat behind a teak desk, swiveling gradually toward the window behind her. Moll presented her argument, with gestures, trying not to be distracted by police cars wailing down Second Avenue. Men with guns. That was the aspect of things no one would be able to change. She sensed she was losing Delaney to the view.

"That's it, Grace. Finis. Das Ende. I can be in Georgetown before the dew is on the rose, or whatever."

Running Dog's offices were divided among three sites. A duplex in an East Side brownstone. A suite in an office building way across town. And someone's house in Sunnyside, Queens.

This of course was the brownstone, top floor, rear, looking south, view of ailanthus trees and small gardens. Grace Delaney was a carefully tailored woman, slim and angular, whose face and hands often appeared to be flaking. She faced the window now, her back to Moll, who sat on the liquor cabinet, waiting for Grace to think of something to say.

"All right. Personal level. It's not the kind of thing that turns me on."

"What do you want, a nude torso in his freezer?"

"It's not political. It has no ramifications."

"You're wrong, Grace."

"Could be. Prove it to me."

"He's got a man on staff who runs around the country buying this bric-a-brac. That's travel dollars plus the guy's salary."

"This sun feels so good."

"Obviously taxpayers' money."

"You're boring me, Moll."

"Sex is boring?"

"I guess I miss conspiracy."

"Like how?"

"A sense of evil design."

"Well, Percival's investigating this PAC/ORD operation. That's where the evil design lies, presumably."

"That's it, see, I miss an element of irony."

She swung around in her chair to face Moll.

"Our investigation into Percival's affairs should yield precisely what the Senator's investigation into PAC/ORD will eventually yield. I miss the symmetry of this."

"Grace, we're not weaving Persian rugs."

Delaney took a silver flask out of her desk and had two quick snorts, her head jerking mechanically.

"Conspiracy's our theme. Shit, you know that. Connections, links, secret associations. The whole point behind the series you're doing is that it's a complex and very large business involving not only smut merchants, not only the families, not only the police and the courts, but also highly respectable business elements, mostly real estate interests, in a conscious agreement to break the law. Or haven't you heard."

"I heard."

"If you examine the matter, Percival's got nothing to do with any of this. He's an art collector with a taste for the erotic. I see it, if at all, as a fun thing."

"What can I say?"

"I don't see it as major."

"You're telling me not to pursue it."

"I miss ramifications."

"One last talk with the man."

"He won't let you anywhere near his collection."

"I have possible access without him."

"How?"

"Mysterious source."

"Close to the Senator?"

"Close enough."

"I have my doubts."

"Let me work on it."

"Knucklehead," Delaney said.

Her voice was husky and a little intimate and sometimes made insults sound like endearments. Often she purred obscenities. In her carefully tailored way, surrounded as she was by photos and layouts, by crushed paper cups, overflowing ashtrays, cellophane mobiles, by books and scattered magazines, she managed to suggest the rigor that dwells at the heart of successful concealment. Moll watched her pour lotion on her wrists and over the backs of her hands and then slowly, dreamily even, begin rubbing it in. They knew about this even in Sunnyside. It was the way she dismissed people.

It was late afternoon when Moll hailed a cab that took her past the Little Carnegie, where a special Chaplin program was playing. She found Selvy waiting in her apartment and decided not to ask how he'd gained entry. Bad taste, such questions. An insult to the ambivalence of their relations.

Her sweater crackled as she pulled it over her head. Static cling. Current in the tips of her fingers. When he touched her, she jumped. They crashed together onto the bed. The mild shocks ceased as their bodies came to resemble a single intricate surface. She began tossing her head, free and clear of garments, straddling him, noting the blends and scents rising.

Their eyes locked. A reconnoitering gaze. She sensed his control, his will, a nearly palpable thing, like a card player's unswerving determination, the furious rightness of his victory.

She ran a finger along his mouth. He lifted her then, driving with his hips, pounding, so high she tumbled forward, a hand on either side of his head for balance. They remained that way, reaching the end slowly, without further bursts and furies. On hands and knees she swayed above him, licking her lips to moisten them against the dry air.

Propped on an elbow he watched her walk out of the room. When she came back she brought a can of beer, which they shared.

"You have a third baseman's walk."

"I walk crouched," she said.

"Like you've been spending a whole career too close to home plate, expecting the hitter to bunt but always suspicious, ready to dart one way or the other."

"Suspicious of what?"

"He might swing away."

"So that's my walk. A third baseman. What about my body?"

"Good hands," he said. "Taut breasts. A second baseman's."

"I just remembered something."

"Won't get in your way when you pivot to make the double play."

"We're going to the movies. I just realized. There's a Chaplin program at the Little Carnegie and we've got four and a half minutes to get down there."

The dictator in uniform.

Each of his lapels bears the double-cross insignia. His hat is large, a visored cap, also with insignia. He wears knee-high boots.

The world's most famous mustache.

The dictator addresses the multitudes. He speaks in strangulated tirades. A linguistic subfamily of German. The microphones recoil.

The story includes a little barber and a pretty girl.

An infant wets on the dictator's hand. Storm troopers march and sing.

The dictator sits on his desk, holding a large globe in his left hand. A classic philosophical pose. His eyes have a far-away look. He senses the vast romance of acquisition and conquest.

The celebrated scene.

To a Lohengrin soundtrack, the dictator does an eerie ballet, bouncing the globe, a balloon, this way and that, tumbling happily on his back.

The dictator weeps, briefly.

The little barber, meanwhile, studies his image as it appears on the surface of a bald man's head.

The dictator welcomes a rival tyrant to his country. The man arrives in a two-dimensional train. The leaders salute each other for many frames.

The prerogatives of dictatorship are easier to establish, they learn, when there is only one dictator.

There is a ball in the palace. The dictator and his rival eat strawberries and mustard. A treaty is signed. The two men team up.

The dictator goes duck-hunting and falls out of his boat. Mistaken identity.

The barber, or neo-tramp, who is the dictator's look-alike, assumes command, more or less, and addresses the multitudes.

A burlesque, an impersonation.

In a restaurant nearby, Moll said, "The really funny thing is that I remember the movie as silent, and it's not of course. I even forgot the speech at the end. Incredible. But I guess the visual memory is what dominates. I'll tell you what I never, ever forget when it comes to movies."

"What?"

"Who I saw a particular movie with."

"Who you saw a particular movie with."

"I never forget who was with me at a given movie, no matter how many years go by. So you're engraved, Selvy, on the moviegoing part of my brain. You and Charlie Chaplin forever linked. Charlie said he would never have made *The Great Dictator* later on in the war or after the war, knowing by that time what the Nazis were capable of. It's a little naïve, in other words. He also said something strange about the dictator being a comedian. But Charlie's so related in my mind to silent film that I completely forgot this was a talkie. Ten, twelve years ago it must have been. Probably more. Fifteen maybe."

"Shut up and eat."

"I do run on at times."

"Just a bit," he said.

Over dessert she said, "Let's go drinking downtown."

"Serious drinking."

"Our original hangout. Some serious drinking. A couple of roustabouts out on the town."

"What's it called, I forget."

"Frankie's Tropical Bar."

"Can we find it?"

"Ask any cabbie. It's famous."

"The guy with the bandage on his head."

"Who tried to throw a bicycle at that fat lady."

"It all comes back," he said.

"Local color. Good talk. Festive music. Disease."

At two in the morning they were still there. Two men and an elderly woman sat at the other end of the bar. On a step leading down to the toilets another man sat sprawled, mumbling something about his landlord working for the FBI. The FBI had placed cameras and bugging devices not only in his apartment but everywhere he went. They preceded him, anticipating every stop he made, day or night.

"Ever get swacked on absinthe?"

"Missed out on that," Moll said.

"Serious derangement of the senses."

"I went through a disgusting mulled wine phase several years ago. It started in Zermatt and I allowed it to continue much too long and in far too many places."

"Doesn't beat a Caribou," Selvy said.

"Yes, very nice. But not to be mentioned in the same breath as a Bellini, which goes down especially well if you happen to be lounging on your terrace in Portofino, overlooking the bay."

"Nothing beats a Caribou."

"This is boring," she said. "Stupid way to converse."

"You're in Quebec City. Picture it. Twenty-two below zero Celsius. People running around everywhere. It's Carnaval. Somebody hands you a glass that's pure alcohol plus red wine. You take a drink. Three days later your body comes hurtling through a snow-blower."

"Dull. Stupid and dull."

Huge stains, as of disruptions in the plumbing, covered part of one wall. The place smelled. There were inclines in the floor, some unexpected grades and elevations. An unfinished mural—palm trees—covered a section of the wall behind the bar.

"Where are you from?" Moll said.

"Originally?"

"Originally, lately, whatever. Or are you the kind of person who sees himself as a man without a history—no past, no relatives, no ties, no binds. You're the kind of person who sees himself as a man without a history."

"But you like that kind of person."

"I like that kind of person, true."

"Because they tend to be mean bastards," he said.

"And I like mean bastards."

"They tend to be very, very mean."

"And I'm attracted to that, yes."

The bartender was a Latin with a terrible complexion. His shirt cuffs were folded over twice. He seemed to tiptoe back and forth, a stocky man, his head wagging. The lighting in the room was dim.

"Arak," she said. "I got wiped out on arak—where?"

"Cyprus."

"Cyprus, that's right. Although I don't think I've been to Cyprus. No, I've never been to Cyprus. So that's not right. You're clearly mistaken, Selvy."

"It wasn't Cyprus and it wasn't arak. It was ouzo and it was Crete."

"Well, now, I admit to having been on Crete."

"And it was ouzo, not arak. You've never touched a drop of arak in your life."

"I don't think I like ouzo. So why would I want to get wiped out on it?"

"You thought it was arak," he said. "But it wasn't. And it wasn't Crete either. It was Malta."

"It was malteds. It was chocolate malteds."

"Right. That's correct. You're making sense for a change."

"Do I get to see the collection?"

"Not a chance," he said affably.

"Is it in Georgetown?"

"Forget it."

"He'll see me. I know he'll *see* me. Whether or not he'll grant me a real live interview is a whole 'nuther question. But I couldn't care less about the whole thing unless I know the collection's in his Georgetown house. I just want to get near it, understand. I want to know I'm close. So is it in Georgetown? I want to know I've got half a chance."

Selvy was drinking Polish vodka. He drained his glass and pushed it several inches toward the inner rim of the bar. The man sitting on the step near the toilets hadn't stopped talking about the FBI. He was able to see the cameras and listening devices. They were installed everywhere he went. If he went to another bar around the corner, they would be there. If he took a bus uptown, he'd see the little bugging devices, the little cameras under the seats and along the metal edges of the windows. People kept telling him he had the DTs. But the DTs were when you saw rats and birds and insects. It was little cameras he saw. Tiny transmitters. And they were everywhere.

The bartender filled Selvy's glass. The old woman at the other end of the bar started an argument with one of the two men who were with her. It was her son, evidently. The bartender stared at Moll.

"Headhunter Zombie," she said. "It's coming back to me.

This hotel bar someplace—the Dutch Leewards? Where are the Dutch Leewards? You mix in papaya, peach nectar, some dark rum, some more dark rum, some light rum, some lime juice, some shaved ice and I think some honey. Add a dash of bitters."

The first three-round burst took out the bartender and sent glass flying everywhere. Moll felt herself thrown to the floor. There was a second burst, a three-part roar, little explosions everywhere, things flying, and she was aware of Selvy's hand leaving his hip with a gun in it. This had happened earlier, two seconds perhaps, and was just registering, and there was blood also registering, coming down on her from the top of the bar. She flattened herself against the angular surface where the bar and the floor joined, digging in, her whole body, glass registering, crashing everywhere, and the old woman's voice.

Selvy took a head-on position, prone, to avoid presenting too wide a target. He noted muzzle flash. Gun bedded in his hand, he moved his fingertip to the trigger and applied pressure, straight back and unhurriedly, letting out his breath but not completely, just to a point, holding it now as the gun fired, only then exhaling fully.

He watched for motion out on the sidewalk. Single gunman, he was almost certain, auto-firing in short bursts. For a brief moment he lost a sense of where the man was, then realized he was standing in the doorway, trying to sort out the chaos inside. AR-18. Severe muzzle climb. Son of a bitch is wearing ear muffs and shooting glasses. Thinks he's on a firing range.

Answering the burst, Selvy fired twice. The whole place was breaking apart with noise, bullets, flying glass. The man who'd been sitting on the step crawled moaning toward the door, trailing blood, one arm limp. The gunman was out of the doorway, moving, hit possibly. Selvy had the distinct impression he'd been hit.

He got to his feet and stepped over the crawling man. He heard a car move off. The old woman lunged at him and he gave her an elbow that drove her to the floor. There was still a roar in his head but the street was quiet and he didn't bother checking for blood. It was academic really, whether he'd hit the man. No concern of his. A technicality.

He returned the .38 to the break-front holster on his belt. Moll came out on the sidewalk. Her expression was comical. She seemed more amazed by the fact that he'd been carrying a gun than by the rest of it, the man spraying the place with automatic fire, the dead and wounded.

"I saw him," she said. "I looked up at the end. What was he wearing? He looked so strange. He stood there trying to see into the room. He was wearing something on his ears and face."

"Tinted glasses. Shooting glasses, for ricocheting bullet fragments. And ear protectors, for noise."

"Who was he? There are people dead in there. What the hell happened?"

"I don't think he was familiar with the weapon. He was letting the muzzle climb when he fired. That weapon's designed to prevent that."

"But who the hell was he? What happened?"

"He had his right elbow at the wrong angle. He had it pointed way down. Your elbow should be straight out, parallel to the ground, firing that particular weapon."

"Jesus, will you stop?" she said. "Will you tell me what happened?"

Her sweater and shirt were covered with the bartender's blood. She stood there trembling. He gave her a crooked little smile and shook his head, genuinely regretful that he wasn't able to bring some light to the situation.

A couple of kids came out of a doorway to approach Selvy near the shattered front of Frankie's Tropical Bar.

"We see the whole thing."

"How much you give us to testify?"

"We make a deal, man."

"It was Patty Hearst with a machine gun."

"No, man, it was Stevie Wonder. You see his headset? He was shooting to the music."

II Radial Matrix

1

She parked at the very limit of a dead-end street overlooking Rock Creek. It was a warm evening, kids chasing each other in a playground just yards away. The house was red brick, fairly large, attached (how strange, she thought) to a common brown frame house that seemed totally out of place here. How strange and interesting. She approached the brick house, noting that the door-knocker was a bronze eagle.

Lloyd Percival made flattering remarks. He remembered what she'd been wearing on their previous encounter in the corridors of the Senate wing. And commented on the reduced frizz-content of her hair. They sat around a cherrywood cocktail table in a large room filled mostly with period furniture and decorated in spruce green Colonial wallpaper. The first hour was boring, at least for Moll.

"And Mrs. Percival?"

"Spends most of her time back home. Doesn't like Washington. Never has. We've grown apart, I'm afraid. Divorce in progress."

"What does she do?"

"She curls up with the Warren Report. She's been reading the Warren Report for eight or nine years. Nine years, I make it. The full set. Twenty-six volumes. She wears a bed jacket."

"You have two married daughters."

It went on like this. Percival had a second drink. He sat stoop-shouldered in a wing sofa, his deep friendly voice droning on. Even with his beady eyes and his small and somewhat flat-top head, Moll found his presence genial and even serene. He was the kind of man people feel at ease with. Large, shaggy and quietly ironic. She curled up in her chair, enveloped by the room's cozy mood.

"I still don't understand why I didn't have you screened. We screen people like you."

"My fried hair. Disarmed you."

"I know what you really want to talk about."

"Do you?" she said.

"You don't want to talk about my family, or my views on world affairs."

"Don't I?"

"Let me do something to that drink."

"No, it's fine."

"You want to talk about the hearings."

"Actually, no, you're wrong."

"You want to talk about PAC/ORD."

"You're so wrong, Senator."

"Not that I blame you," he said. "They've got mechanisms. Undercover channeling operations. They've got offshoots. It's damn shocking. At this late date, you'd think I'd be impervious to what those people dream up. Not so."

"Senator, the truth is I wouldn't think of asking you to divulge what goes on in closed-door hearings."

"What about this boss of yours?"

"Yes?"

"Grace Delaney," he said. "I hear unflattering reports. She's had dealings with radical groups, among other things."

"A woman with a past. Isn't that what makes us interesting? For men, it's lack of a recorded past that proves so fascinating. Women, no. It's the shadows behind us that do the trick."

"Your own, for instance, I would dearly love to hear about."

"I used to live with Gary Penner. Dial-a-Bomb?"

"I do recall, yes. The name's familiar."

"It should be, Senator. He blew up half your goddamn state about ten years ago."

They shared a laugh over that. Unfolding slowly, Percival's long body rose from the sofa. He shuffled to the liquor cabinet, bringing a bottle of Jack Daniel's back to the cocktail table with him.

"You understand nothing I tell you is to be attributed. It is not only unattributed. It is undocumented, unfounded and unreal. I deny everything in advance. Whoever leaked this stuff to you, whichever committee counsel, is not only breaking the law; he's totally misrepresenting the facts."

"What you're saying, really, Senator, is that you decided at some point that *Running Dog* is precisely the publication this kind of story cries out for. No one else would touch it since you've no intention of providing the slightest clue to its authenticity."

"None of it ever happened. I repeat. It's all lies. I find it utterly inconceivable that such things could find their way into the pages, so on, so on, so on."

He told her that PAC/ORD—the Personnel Advisory Committee, Office of Records and Disbursements—had been set up, on the surface, as the principal unit of budgetary operations for the whole U.S. intelligence community. Dealing strictly in unclassified areas, the agency had been established in response to criticism of soaring intelligence expenditures.

Covert operations were beyond its scope. Hiring, firing, paying, promoting, budgeting. This was PAC/ORD territory, on the surface, and it did not extend beyond the legal, administrative and clerical areas. Thousands of people in a number of agencies. PAC/ORD was not unlike the personnel department of a large corporation.

On the surface.

Beyond that, however, the Senator's investigating committee had learned that PAC/ORD had a secret arm, the kind of
cover setup known as a proprietary. This was Radial Matrix, a
legally incorporated firm with headquarters in Fairfax
County, Virginia. Radial Matrix—the term itself was mean-
ingless—was a systems planning outfit. They advised on, and
installed, manufacturing and shipping systems. Their clients
included firms across the U.S. and in a number of other coun-
tries. In the last three years they'd become a huge success,
with several spin-off operations and activities. The only overt
connection between PAC/ORD and Radial Matrix was a
contract the latter had to install a new computerized wage
system on behalf of the former.

The only overt connection.

Radial Matrix was in fact a centralized funding mechanism for covert operations directed against foreign governments, against elements within foreign governments, and
against political parties trying to gain power contrary to the
interests of U.S. corporations abroad. It was responsible for
channeling and laundering funds for unlisted station personnel, indigenous agents, terrorist operations, defector re-
cruitment, political contributions, penetration of foreign
communications networks and postal agencies.

So on, so on, so on.

"If you study the history of reform," Percival said, "you'll
see there's always a counteraction built in. A low-lying surly
passion. Always people ready to invent new secrets, new
bureaucracies of terror."

"Don't get carried away on my behalf."

"It's only fair to point out that these PAC/ORD activities are fairly small-scale, as far as I can tell, compared to the
CIA extravaganzas that brought on the thirst for reform in
the first place, and of course they're being run by some of the
same people. My point is that these activities satisfy the historical counterfunction. They fill those small dark places. And

they're illegal. Run counter to the spirit and letter of every law, every intelligence directive, that pertains to such matters."

One of the marvels of all this, the Senator continued, was that Radial Matrix, strictly as a business enterprise, was enjoying such enormous success. Surely this was an unexpected development to the folks at PAC/ORD, who couldn't have expected their modest creation to become such a world-beater.

Moll told the Senator she didn't think any of this was very startling, considering past developments and revelations. Percival had an answer for that.

One final level of operations.

Radial Matrix was currently run by a man named Earl Mudger. Handpicked by PAC/ORD, he was former commander of a fighter-bomber squadron (Korea) and long-term contract employee (Saigon desk, Air America) of the CIA. He'd had civilian experience, briefly, in the late fifties, with a firm specializing in production flow systems and automation.

Mudger turned out to be the right man for the job—too much so, it seemed. He fell in love with profits. The profit motive became more interesting to him at this stage of his career than pay records or secret bank accounts or whatever fancy paperwork is necessary to maintain agents in the field and deliver money into the hands of favored political leaders in this or that country.

The Senator poured himself another drink and put his feet up on the cocktail table. First traces of slurred speech.

"What's happened is that PAC/ORD has lost control of its own operation. Radial Matrix has become a breakaway unit of the U.S. intelligence apparatus. Nobody knows what to do about it. Mudger's completely autonomous. They're afraid to move against him. Public scrutiny of the funding mechanism is unacceptable. And it could happen if they try to remove him. Anything could happen. Including disclosures of how Radial Matrix has managed to be so successful."

"I'd like to hear."

"Mudger hasn't forgotten his field training. He uses the same methods in business he used in espionage activities. In actual combat. That's why the firm's a whopping success. The man's made his own set of rules and won't allow anyone else to use them. He's got all kinds of links, organized crime and so on. And he's just sitting out there in the countryside running up profits. Recent scheme is diversification. Systems planning has apparently begun to seem dull. He wants to diversify."

There was a silence as they pondered this.

"What you have in Mudger," the Senator said, "is the combination of business drives and lusts and impulses with police techniques, with ultrasophisticated skills of detection, surveillance, extortion, terror and the rest of it."

"It's like what Chaplin said in connection with *Monsieur Verdoux*. The logical extension of business is murder."

Percival shuddered, a bit theatrically, to indicate his feelings on the subject. He leaned forward to freshen her drink. She waved him off, smiling politely. He got some ice cubes from the bucket on the liquor cabinet and carried them back in his left hand, watching them slide into his glass one by one. Streetlights were on outside. No further sound of children playing. Moll watched him drink quietly. He finished one, started another.

"I like tall women," the Senator said.

"So he wants to diversify."

"Let me ask you something."

"Sure."

"Did you ever smoke grass?"

"Did I ever smoke grass? Yes, Senator, in my time."

"I guess you must have."

"Being a woman with a past," she said.

"What I wanted to know. Do you have any with you?"

"Sorry."

"It's something, candidly, I would have liked to have done. Some years ago with my youngest daughter, when she was about twenty or so, I thought we should do this because I knew she smoked, I knew she smoked."

"You thought it would bring you two closer together."

"I really wanted to," he said.

"Where, in the Capitol rotunda?"

He finished his drink and poured another.

"I like tall women."

"I'd be interested in hearing more about this Earl Mudger person. If you want this thing to see print, you ought to tell me everything you know. He wants to diversify, you say."

"I wonder this."

"Yes?"

"What can I call you?" he said. "Candidly."

"Moll will do."

"Moll, can you keep a secret?"

"Sure, try me."

"I was in contact with a man. Never mind details, like name and such. We met at a party. First there was a party. New York gallery opening followed by a party. You know the agenda. The talk: politics, sex, movies and dog shit. You know the kind of thing. Then a second party that branched off from this. A small, small gathering of like-minded people. Very small. We had interests in common."

"Like what?"

"That's not part of the secret. That's a different secret."

"Please go on," she said.

"This man I met. The second party. I found out later he was a systems engineer. Did contract work for Radial Matrix. Strictly on the up-and-up. Not connected with their covert function. But this was learned later. At the party he had something to sell. Something I was interested in buying. We were like-minded people there. Conversation flowed mostly in one direction. And I learned about this man's proposal to sell. So we talked and made arrangements to talk again. In my position, being the position I hold, this was done discreetly, taking enormous precautions. But I did give him a certain phone number where he could reach me. This was done because he refused to be contacted himself. There was total insistence on this. What I also later learned was that in his work for Radial Matrix, strictly on the up-and-up, he and Earl Mudger struck up an acquaintanceship. See, Mudger was interested in making the same buy I was. Diversification. His plan to diversify. So then before we could even talk again the man I talked to is found stone cold dead in some condemned building in New York. But this is just between us. Deep background. Because I trust you."

"I understand."

"So now, I'd be willing to bet, there are two investigations going on. I'm investigating them. And I'd be willing to bet they're investigating me. Blackmail in mind. Purposes of blackmail. So we must tread lightly. Everything we do is subject to extreme cautionary procedures."

She watched his head fall forward. Two minutes later he snapped awake.

"I'm curious about the house, Senator."

"Do you have any grass or not?"

"I love looking at other people's houses."

"I want to smoke grass with a tall woman."

"Show me around, why don't you?"

"If I show you around, we have to go to the bedroom. You have to be shown the bedroom just as much as other rooms. All rooms count the same in a house when it's being shown."

"Show me the bedroom, Senator."

"Call me Lloyd," he said.

He struggled to his feet and held out his right hand. She took it and allowed him to lead her up a short staircase. At the top of the stairs he fell down. He got up, with her help, and then headed into the bedroom, where he fell again. She watched him crawl toward the king-size canopy bed.

"Where's your housekeeper? Don't senators have housekeepers? Some little old granny to button the trap door in your pajamas."

"Gave her the night off."

"Part of your seduction scheme, was it? Jesus, Lloyd, too bad. All that trouble for nothing."

"It's all lies. I repeat. We never had this talk."

She helped him up on the bed and waited until his breathing grew steady and he passed beyond the outer edges of sleep. Then she went down the hall and turned left, interested in finding the easternmost end of the house, the surface that abutted the brown frame structure next door.

The walls here were lined with antique sconces and turn-of-the-century handbills and steamship prints. She examined three small rooms. In the last of these were two banister-back chairs, a spinning wheel and a Queen Anne writing table. Moll noted the position of the fireplace. East wall. The screen was not in place before the open recess. It was leaning against one of the chairs.

Cleanest fireplace she'd ever seen. She moved closer, bending to inspect. It wasn't a working fireplace. No flue. Nothing but solid brick above. She leaned further into the recess. The back section was hardwood. Probing in the dimness, she touched a small latch. When she lifted it and applied pressure, the section swung open. A priest's hole. She moved through hunched way over, not actually crawling. Immediate sense of confinement. Near-total darkness.

This constricting space ended after she'd moved forward fifteen feet. Standing full length she felt along the walls on either side. Her hand found a dimmer-switch and she eased it out and turned it about ninety degrees.

She found she was standing on a grillwork balcony overlooking an enormous room of Mediterranean design. She walked down a closed staircase lined with stained glass panels, abstract. The floor below was parquet with a centered rectangle of peacock tiles. There were large tropical plants.

On the walls were perhaps fifty-five paintings. Pieces of

sculpture stood among the plants. There were small displays of pottery, jewelry and china. A stone fountain depicted a woman on her knees before an aroused warrior. Mounted in a tempered glass segment of one wall was a bronze medallion scene of Greek courtesans. There was a large bronze on the tiled rectangle: two men, a woman.

Moll moved first along the walls, looking at the paintings and drawings. Very nice, most of them, all labeled. Icart. Hokusai. Picasso. Balthus. Dali. The Kangra school. Botero with his neckless immensities. Egon Schiele with his unloved nudes. Hans Bellmer. Tom Wesselmann. Clara Tice.

She crossed the floor several times, studying the sculptures, the pottery, the section of hand-carved choir stall—naked woman with gargoyles. She realized there were no doors or windows. He'd had the whole house sealed from the inside, all openings bricked and plastered over. Portable humidifiers for the plants. Elaborate lighting system. The only way in or out was through the fireplace in the "real" house.

Her camera case was in the car. She debated getting it. Now that she'd found the collection she didn't know what to do about it. Maybe Grace Delaney was right. It lacked ramifications. It wasn't political. It was strictly private, isolated from the schemes and intricacies. She was inclined to let the Senator win his point. Radial Matrix was the story here.

On another level she was curiously indifferent to the objects around her. This was despite their high quality, the dramatic space, the secrecy of the whole setup, the handsome trappings, the subject matter itself. The strongest thing she felt was a sense of the work's innate limitations. She recalled what Lightborne had said about old and new forms. The modern sensibility had been instructed by a different kind of code. Movement. The image had to move.

From his window Selvy could see a colorless strip of the Anacostia River. He hadn't shaved in two and a half days, the first time this had happened since his counterinsurgency stint at Marathon Mines in southwest Texas, a training base for paramilitary elements of various intelligence units and for the secret police of friendly foreign governments.

Shaving was an emblem of rigor, the severity of the double life. Shaving. Proper maintenance of old combat gear. Seats on the aisle in planes and trains. Sex with married women only. These were personal quirks mostly, aspects of his psychic guide to survival.

He'd broken the sex rule and now he had nearly three days' growth. But the routine still applied. The routine in one sense was his physical movement between New York and Washington, and the set pieces of procedure, the subroutines, that were part of this travel. In a larger context the routine was a mind set, all those mechanically performed operations of the intellect that accompanied this line of work. You made connection-A but allowed connection-B to elude you. You felt free to question phase-1 of a given operation but deadened yourself to the implications of phase-2. You used expressions that contained interchangeable words.

The routine was how your mind had come to work; which areas you avoided; the person you'd become.

He'd known from the beginning that Christoph Ludecke was a systems engineer. When the break developed—Senator linked to transvestite—the dead man's occupation was among the first things looked into.

He'd also known that systems planning was the cover Radial Matrix used in its role as funding mechanism for covert operations. Obviously. Radial Matrix—an abstraction personified by Lomax, his sole contact—was the entity he worked for.

The connection was unexpected. It didn't fit the known world as recently constructed. It was a peculiar element in a series of events otherwise joined in explainable ways.

This was where the routine was important. He stuck to the

routine. The routine enabled him mentally to bury this queer bit of intelligence, Ludecke and Radial Matrix, a conjunction of interests that could only lead to areas he wasn't privileged, or competent, to enter. He wasn't a detective, after all. He didn't build models of theoretical events surrounding a criminal act. Nor did he concern himself with policy.

Ludecke was linked to the Senator. It wasn't within Selvy's purview to meditate on additional links, even when they might pertain to his own ultimate sustenance. Especially then. This was why the routine existed.

In his right hand, as he stood looking out the window at nothing in particular, was the .41 magnum, loaded with expandable bullets. Selvy's regard for the implements of an operational mode became a virtual passion where handguns were involved. He went regularly to the range to work on sight alignment and trigger control. He dry-fired, he used live rounds. He practiced grip and finger positions. He worked on various steadying exercises.

This, too, was the routine.

He kept the chambers clean. He took precautions against fouled bores and corrosion. He owned any number of lubricants, brushes, swabs, preservers, conditioners, degreasers and removers.

To Selvy, guns and their parts amounted to an inventory of personal worth. He controlled the weapon, his reflexes and judgment. Maintaining the parts and knowing the gun's special characteristics were ways of demonstrating involvement in his own well-being.

These pieces, laid out at his fingertips, resembled nothing more than routine hardware. Still, there was order in this grouping; distinct precision. He could see how each surface was designed to adapt to at least one other surface. The interrelationships accumulated and spread. Things fit.

Where the routine prevented Selvy from seeking human

links, it prompted him to study the interactions within mechanisms.

At the range he worked on stance, breath control, eye focus. The idea was to build almost a second self. Someone smarter and more detached. Do this perfectly and you've developed a new standard for times of danger and stress. He stood at a forty-five-degree angle to the proposed line of fire. He tried to avoid locking his elbow. He fired, focusing his master eye, the right eye in his case, on the gun's front sight.

The handgun is intimate. A functional accessory. You wear it. It fits you or doesn't, and vice versa.

He found it reassuring to handle the parts, to know their names and understand their functions. Attention to detail is a form of vigilance. There were no shadings in his willingness to use the stopping power at his disposal. This was very clear, this resolve. It affirmed his bond to the weapon itself.

Evening. The room was dark. He didn't move from the window to turn on a light.

Sex with an unmarried woman. Two and a half days without a shave. Minor lapses. He saw the humor in his idiosyncrasies. The routine still applied. That's what mattered most. The routine applied to the extent where he didn't actively speculate on who that might have been who was standing in the doorway of that run-down bar directing automatic fire across the room, or what the reasoning behind it was, or who was supposed to get hit.

In a storeroom on H Street, Moll Robbins went through *Running Dog's* files, such as they were, on Earl Mudger.

From bases in Japan he led strikes by F-84Es against selected enemy targets in Korea. These strikes were operational tests of refueling procedures as much as combat missions. He also coached the football team, 116th Fighter-Bomber Wing.

Still in Korea he resigned his commission and spent a year in special paramilitary programs run by Air Force Intelligence, an open-ended term of duty.

He left to return to civilian life as Vice-President, Distribution, Process Management Systems, a firm with headquarters in Oklahoma City.

Three years later he appeared as chief training officer at Marathon Mines, an abandoned silver mining site in rough country north of the Rio Grande, where antiguerrilla specialists taught survival techniques and conducted war games.

In Laos he was a contract officer attached to Air America during operations secretly directed by the CIA.

In Vietnam, still on a contract basis, he recruited and directed CT teams against the Vietcong. Later he helped set up a network of provincial interrogation centers, where Vietcong suspects were tortured. Then he ran a cover operation in Saigon, hiring mercenaries for special operations.

It was while Mudger was on loan to Special Forces for unknown duties that he became something of a legend in Vietnam. Apparently he established a feudal barony complete with loyal ARVN soldiers (loyal to him, not the government) as well as pimps, black marketeers, shoeshine boys, war refugees, bar girls, deserters, pickpockets and others. It was suspected to be a drug operation with a thriving sideline in black-market piasters. As head, Mudger dispensed land, money, food and other favors.

He also set up a private zoo in the jungle outside a village called Tha Binh. He managed to stock it with tigers, wolves, elephants, peacocks, snakes, leopards, apes, zebras, monkeys, hyenas and hippos.

Virtually all this information Moll found in a single clipping, most of it color background for an AP dispatch that detailed Mudger's exploits during the fall of Saigon. Waving a Browning automatic he commandeered a C-123 transport, rigged for defoliation, and crammed most of his people

aboard, along with seventeen of his animals, on the day before the city fell.

Lomax put his feet up on the jump seat. He opened his
briefcase and took out a red folder.

THE DORISH REPORT

A confidential reporting service

He turned to the first page and began reading.

Sir:
 An investigation has been conducted pursuant to your
request and authorization concerning Grace B. Delaney,
Managing Editor, Running Dog magazine, a property of
RD Publications, which person resides at 116 East 61st
Street, New York, N.Y. 10021, in order to ascertain Grace B.
Delaney's background, reputation and responsibility. The
results of our investigation are set forth below under head-
ings designed to facilitate your perusal and analysis.

The headings were: Identification, Background, Personal
Relations, Credit, Litigation and Finances. Lomax scanned
Personal Relations before any of the others but eventually
found Finances to be more to the point. Tax matters in par-
ticular.
 At the bottom of the last page was a statement in italics:

This report is made available to you at your express re-
quest, as you have employed us for that purpose. It is a
privileged and confidential communication, and the infor-
mation contained herein is not to be disclosed to others,
verbally or otherwise.

It concluded: The Dorish Report, Investigative Confidentiality for the Special Needs of the Seventies.

Trying to hail a cab on H Street, Moll watched the black limousine gradually come to a stop in front of her. The driver was square-jawed, dark suit and cap. The man sitting in the rear, opening the door toward her, was wearing sports clothes and moccasins. He smiled pleasantly.

"Come on, I'll take you."

"Where?"

Shrug.

"To the Senator," she said. "That it?"

Smile.

"The Senator wants to apologize, does he?"

Smile.

"I'll have to take a raincheck," she said. "Tell him next time."

"No rainchecks. We don't give rainchecks."

"Tell him thanks anyway."

"It's urgent," the man said.

His face didn't quite indicate that. The smile was still there but only technically, no longer bearing traces of pleasantness. But it wasn't urgency that had replaced it. Just impatience, she thought. Still, the strangeness of it kept her from walking away. She was feeling a little disassociated. Limousine, driver, Senate aide. If Percival wanted to talk to her, it would be foolish, considering the revelations of the night before, to put him off.

She got into the car, sorting a number of thoughts at once. She noticed they were heading west on K Street. The man in sports clothes lit a cigarette.

"He's at his Georgetown place, is he?"

The man patted his sideburns, one at a time.

"Taking some time off, is he, from his onerous duties on the Hill?"

They passed Washington Circle and were on a freeway skirting the channel. They turned onto a bridge approach and Moll twisted in her seat and looked out the back window, realizing that was Georgetown they'd just left behind.

She began reading road signs aloud, not knowing quite why. At a certain bend in the road, sunlight filled the interior of the car and when she glanced down at the material covering the back seat she saw it was covered with dog hair.

Soon they were passing Falls Church and heading into intermittent countryside, fields of black Angus grazing. The car slowed occasionally for extended stretches of motels, plant nurseries, supermarkets, auto and truck dealerships. Streams and brooks were called runs here. Roadside shops advertised Civil War relics.

2

Lightborne wore a hat with a little feather stuck in the band. It was a gift from one of his customers, who thought it would go well with his Norfolk jacket. He wore the hat just this one time, an after-dinner stroll through the gallery district. It made him feel like a veteran sportswriter covering the Army-Navy game on a clear and brisk November day. Or like a man out for a Sunday drive in his Buick Roadmaster in the year 1957.

The phone was ringing when he got back to the gallery. It was Richie Armbrister, the twenty-two-year-old smut merchant, calling from a special hookup aboard his customized DC-9, which had just landed at JFK.

"I'm back from Europe, Lightborne. We came down in the dark. I hate nighttime landings."

That squeaky voice sent little tremors rippling through Lightborne's nerve apparatus.

"Hear that music? That's my disco. People are dancing. They danced right through the landing. Listen, I want to ask.

Is it still warm? Full-length, I mean. The business you mentioned. How hot's the trail?"

"I'd say very warm, Richie, without fear of overstating."

"Good, listen, we'll talk. I'm coming over there. It's a layover, for maintenance. I definitely want to explore this thing. The more I talk to people, the more I hear about profit potentials with first-run. I made new connections in the European capitals. Features. They're feature-crazy. Exhibitors are hollering for more product. So I think I want to get my toe in the water, Lightborne. Eventually distribute worldwide maybe."

These last remarks Richie delivered in a subdued and earnest manner. An encouraging development. Lightborne was heartened.

"Betty's Azalea Ranch," Moll said.

The man read a newspaper.

"Topside Pool Supplies."

About a hundred yards beyond the Centreville Free Will Baptist Church, the limousine turned into an unmarked dirt road. Half a mile in, they passed a one-story L-shaped building, both wings very long, no landscaping out front. Farther on, maybe two miles, the car stopped in a grove of scarlet oaks near a large stone house. Two Shetland ponies stood in a split-rail cedar corral. There was a pond to the side of the house and some stables beyond that.

They got out of the car. Moll watched a small helicopter setting down in a field nearby. Two men hopped out, both wearing skin-tight jeans, denim jackets, sunglasses and Stetsons. They walked toward the back of the stone house as the helicopter slowly rose, slanting now toward the deep woods in the distance. The men were Orientals, she was quite sure, looking boyish in those narrow pants and small-scale western hats.

Earl Mudger stood in the doorway. Moll was aware her escort had paused, leaving her to approach the house alone.

Mudger wore a blacksmith's apron and heavy-duty gloves. He was a thickset man with curly hair trimmed close, with ash-blond eyebrows and a strong jaw, slightly jutting—the picture of a man who wouldn't yield easily to aging. His eyes were a fine silky blue. He had a bent nose, broadly columned neck and something of a surfer's numinous gleam—his eyes and hair and brows shining just a bit, as though bleached by the elements.

She followed him to a wicker table set under an oak tree. He took off his gloves and apron and tossed them onto one of the extra chairs. An old woman, an Oriental, brought out lemonade and some cookies. Moll could tell Mudger fancied himself a charmer. Tough but winsome. She set her face to Executive Chill.

"Let's us talk some."

"Fine," she said.

"Fact number one, everything Percival told you last night was exaggerated by a factor of seven."

"What did he tell me last night?"

"I can replay it for you any time. Fact number two, it doesn't matter anymore because I'm no longer involved with PAC/ORD, or Radial Matrix, or Lloyd Percival. Born free, that's me. No more attachments. I'm shaking loose. Time to retire."

"A life of meditation," she said.

"Fact number three, you've got the alliances all mixed up, assuming you believe what the Senator's been telling you. Did you ever wonder how Percival's select committee gets their input? Lomax is Percival's man. Lomax is the source of every-thing the committee knows."

"Who is Lomax?"

"Man in the limousine."

"I've mistaken him twice for the Senator's man. Once in New York, I *think*. Now here."

"You weren't mistaken," Mudger said. "Loyalties are so interwoven, the thing's a game. The Senator and PAC/ORD aren't nearly the antagonists the public believes them to be. They talk all the time. They make deals, they buy people, they sell favors. I doubt if Lomax knows whether he works for PAC/ORD or Lloyd Percival, ultimately. You have to understand, agencies allow this to go on all the time. People know what's happening. But they allow it. That's the nature of the times. You go to bed with your enemies."

"I assume you feed Lomax false information."

"Tell you what," he said. "Sometimes this is so much fun, I'd do it for nothing."

"Who is Glen Selvy?"

"No idea."

"Howard Glen Selvy?"

"Not a leaf stirs."

"Bullshit," she said.

"I like your smile."

"I'm not smiling."

"I thought that was a smile. I mistook that for a smile. Have some lemonade, why don't you?"

"These are Vietnamese, these people you've got here?"

"We have some Vietnamese here, definitely."

"That you got out just in time."

"I've had hairier moments. So have they. Compared to the life most of these people have had, getting out of Saigon was on the level of an escapade."

"Ho Chi Minh City," she said.

"Yeah, Ho Chi Minh City. A lark with firecrackers."

Moll nibbled on a cookie and drank some lemonade. She couldn't shake the feeling she'd crossed an invisible frontier into another way of life. The rules were different here. Sitting in the shade. White wicker and lemonade. Ponies motionless in their small corral.

"Back that way along the road," she said. "Radial Matrix?"

"Right."

"Thriving, by all accounts."

"Systems. It's one of the areas we still excel in."

" 'We' meaning Americans."

"Nothing but."

"In Vietnam you were involved in drug trafficking, no?"

"We did some of that. We were a link. As I say, I've un-linked myself. Too much software, hardware, so on. Technology. The whole thing's geared to electronics. There's a neat correlation between the complexity of the hardware and the lack of genuine attachments. Devices make everyone pliant. There's a general sponginess, a lack of conviction."

"You had your own zoo in Vietnam."

"Checking up on me."

"A little," she said.

"My pride and joy, that zoo. We got to the point where we were making exchanges with real zoos halfway around the world. We had an animal dealer from Michigan come all the way out to see our operation. I had more gibbons than I could use. I was laying off gibbons the way bookmakers lay off excess bets. I had this rare type lynx, Eurasian, almost extinct, this one variety, and we bred it successfully in captivity. I tell you what, that made my war."

"Victory after all."

"We won far's I'm concerned. Revise the texts."

"What sort of retirement plans—forgive the skeptical look."

"Domestic bliss," he said. "My wife's off having a baby, matter of fact."

"Nice."

"I'm fifty-two years old."

"Interesting."

"Wife number three."

"Not bad."

"She's a gook," Mudger said.

Apron and gloves. Helicopter landing in a field. She recalled what Percival had said before his sour mash whisky slowed him to a crawl. One set of rules. Mudger's. Nobody else gets to use them. Vietnamese in cowboy hats.

"Not that I don't have something to fall back on," he said. "Aside from domestic bliss."

"I've got a shop in the basement. Sometimes I go down there and work half the night. Do a little planing, a little sanding. Lock things in vises. It's good for the soul. Punch holes in metal, do a little buffing. So anyway I got to fooling around with a small machine of my own devising that tests the hardness and content of steel. Machines that size do hardness alone, normally. I can tell you high carbon, low carbon, how much nickel or manganese. Is this boring?"

"Sort of."

"The machine has a thing called a diamond tip penetrator. I trademarked it as the Mudger tip."

"A little better," she said.

"I'm building a large shop about twenty miles south of here. If things work out, I'll be filling contracts for Radial Matrix."

She watched him light up a little at the irony of that.

"This is what's called negotiating a termination," he said.

He laughed, eyes not leaving her face. She judged him the kind of man deeply pleased by the appreciation of others. He would be a studier of faces, eager to gauge people's reactions to things he said. Robust men were always like this.

"It's real work," he said. "Doesn't involve secret transmitters, hot mikes, all the rest. Like for instance"—she watched his face shade with amusement—"I can let you hear dialogue and other noises pertaining to last night's amorous activities."

"Involving whom?"

"You and the Senator, of course."

"Never happened. Sorry to disappoint."

"It doesn't necessarily have to happen," Mudger said. "All we need's your voice and his, which we have. The rest is purely technical."

"You make it happen."

"Sure."

"In this case has it already happened or is it pending?"

"I don't know. Lomax would know."

"Being the Senator's man, Lomax might push the wrong button. Scramble the voices beyond recognition. Or erase the tapes."

"It's a little more complicated than that."

"You've got me thinking I've done something wrong."

Mudger seemed to grow serious. He sat sideways in his chair, left arm extended, resting on the table, his right arm hanging over the back of the chair.

"When technology reaches a certain level, people begin to feel like criminals," he said. "Someone is after you, the computers maybe, the machine-police. You can't escape investigation. The facts about you and your whole existence have been collected or are being collected. Banks, insurance companies, credit organizations, tax examiners, passport offices, reporting services, police agencies, intelligence gatherers. It's a little like what I was saying before. Devices make us pliant. If *they* issue a print-out saying we're guilty, then we're guilty. But it goes even deeper, doesn't it? It's the presence alone, the very fact, the superabundance of technology, that makes us feel we're committing crimes. Just the fact that these things exist at this widespread level. The processing machines, the scanners, the sorters. That's enough to make us feel like criminals. What enormous weight. What complex programs. And there's no one to explain it to us."

That night Mudger stood behind the bar in his living room, mixing himself a drink. He put his glass down on the red folder, the Dorish Report. Lomax sat near the French doors, looking at a magazine. The doors were open, revealing a small Buddhist shrine in the garden beyond the patio.

"Been meaning to ask."

"What's that, Earl?"

"Why was the subject carrying a gun?"

"I don't know."

"He's over there in Percival's office, reading, isn't he? Or hanging around some art gallery. I'd like for you to tell me why he's carrying a gun."

"Earl, he shouldn't have been."

"Is he some kind of cowboy? What is he, a junior G-man? Because I thought we trained people better than that."

"It was contrary to procedure."

Mudger was sitting at the bar, his back to Lomax.

"This business with guns. He's, what, some kind of sportsman? Shoots fucking bear with a handgun?"

"He was on the Lower East Side. Maybe he thought it was dangerous."

"He was right, it turned out."

They both laughed.

"Who'd you press into service?" Lomax said.

"I called Talerico. He's in Canada these days. We've done things for each other before. Always worked out. Tal said he'd see what he could do."

"That's what he did?"

"He got some guy from Buffalo. His old jurisdiction. Supposed to be a weapons expert. Famous for midnight raids on National Guard armories."

"Who?"

"Augie the Mouse."

They both laughed.

"So Augie goes in there wailing," Mudger said. "He's got his fancy little two-pound Kevlar vest. He's got yellow glasses and ear protectors. He's wearing everything but platform shoes. And he's wailing, he's got this AR-18 and he's strafing the place, he's busting it up."

"What happens, he gets hit."

"He gets hit but doesn't know it. When he gets home he takes off his armor and sees this little hole in it. So he starts feeling his chest, his belly. He tells his driver maybe it got deflected into his lungs. He starts coughing and spitting, looking for blood. Finally his driver shakes out the vest and this small lead mushroom hits the floor. Which isn't the worst of it. Ignorance of technique. The worst of it is that he's supposed to isolate the subject before going to work. The subject's supposed to be a-lone. Not a sin-gle wit-ness in sight."

"You got the Saint Valentine's Day massacre."

"Jerk-off. I told Talerico. Where'd you find this jerk-off?"

"Augie the Mouse."

Mudger laughed, hitting the bar with the palm of his hand.

"Tell you what, it was my fault. Ought to have used different people."

"Such as?"

"Tieu to dac cong."

"That's not your average man in the street they'll be dealing with," Lomax said. "I have to tell you I felt a little surge of pride or satisfaction or what-have-you when I got word he walked out of the bar without a mark on him. Plus putting a bullet in the Mouse. I felt gratified, Earl, truth be known. Certain amount of my own time and effort invested there. This is the best penetration I've run, frankly. I don't think your adjusters will find this is just another day's work."

Mudger shrugged. The phone at his elbow rang. He picked it up, listened a while, said something, listened some more. Lomax went out on the patio. It was a warm night. He stood in the garden watching Mudger put down the phone and say something over his shoulder at the same time. Lomax walked back into the room, belatedly realizing what it was Mudger had said.

"Congratulations, Earl."

"Where's your glass? We'll have another drink."

"How's Tran Le doing?"

"She's fine. She's great. Never better."

"I couldn't touch another drop, honestly."

"An eight-pounder," Mudger said over his shoulder.

"What is it, a fish?"

"Where's your glass?"

"Maybe just a wee snort, to mark the occasion."

"Where's your fucking glass?" Mudger said.

Lightborne stepped off the train and walked through a tunnel under the tracks. On the other side he entered the depot. Klara Ludecke was sitting on a bench near the newsstand. In her lap, for purposes of identification, was a copy of *Running Dog* magazine. Lightborne's spur-of-the-moment idea.

He nodded and she followed him back out. Early evening. They walked toward the underground passageway he'd just come out of. The sole on Lightborne's right shoe started flapping.

"I'm authorized," he said, "to hand over the agreed sum in cash once the film is in my hands."

"I'll be happy to see it go."

"Can I assume it was your husband who gave you my name?"

"My husband gave me three things. He gave me your name. He gave me an address in Aachen. And he gave me the key to a storage vault located at that address."

In the passageway Lightborne lowered his voice, wary of the effects of echo.

"Have you seen the footage?"

"He wanted me to have nothing to do with it."

"Did he tell you anything about it at all?"

"He only told me Berlin, under the Reich Chancellery, during the Russian shelling."

On the opposite platform the flapping sole began to annoy Lightborne, and he suggested they sit for a while on one of the plastic benches.

"And so the film has been in a vault in Germany all these years."

"Air-conditioned storage vault," she said. "To preserve it properly."

"I myself first heard of the item some thirty years ago."

"When my husband was killed I knew that was the reason. He refused to sell at their price. At first they agreed on a price and when the screening was to be. Then Christoph demanded half payment in advance. This was turned down and he no longer wanted to talk with them. They put pressure in so many ways. He still refused. We see what happened."

"Whose price?" Lightborne said. "Who put pressure?"

"I don't think you want to know."

"Do you know?"

The train from New York went roaring by, knocking them back a little in their seats, rippling the pages of the magazine she held once more in her lap.

"I know the name of a company in Virginia. I insisted to tell the police there is something to find there. They treated me as though I were a child. Sex crime. Obviously it could be nothing else. They were almost too embarrassed to discuss it with me. Only sex, it could be. The things sex killers do. One knife wound in the body, I reminded them. Where is the mutilation, the mess? So exact, this sex killer? No, no, they tell me. He picked up the wrong fellow. It happens all the time."

Another train approached, heading south. They went down the steps near the taxi shack, fleeing the vibration and noise, and ended up strolling in little circles in the parking lot.

"After Christoph was buried, I went to Germany. It was done half in rage. I wanted the film, to possess it myself. I thought to own it would make my husband real again. As though it would give me power. As though the murderers would be taunted. Having it in my hands would make everything real. He died for something. Here it is. This round container with straps. Now I understand. Of course," she said, "I've calmed down since then. Now I only think to sell it. I want to be paid for my husband's death."

"Yes, and it's much, much better to conduct this kind of transaction in an atmosphere of mutual composure."

She laughed wryly.

"All I want now is to see the last of it. They've put their listening devices in my house, they've broken in when I was not at home, they've made phone calls at all hours. I'm sick of this business. Deeply ashamed and disgusted. I know I'll be cheated out of the movie's true value. Still, I want to be rid of it as soon as possible."

"There's no question of cheating," Lightborne said. "My client doesn't operate that way. Once you hand over the film, you'll be given a transferral fee. Then my client's technical people will check to see just what we have. Is it a camera original, the master, as I've been hearing? Can we make a workprint for editing? Can we correct whatever defects? There's a dozen questions like this, most beyond my own scope. If there's no soundtrack, can we add one? What about final printing?"

"I only know Berlin, the Reich Chancellery, when the Russians shelled the city."

"Then of course the ultimate question. The content itself. What is actually on film. Once this is looked into, you and I can discuss further monetary installments."

"I know I'll be cheated. It doesn't matter. As long as you take it away."

They crossed the street and walked slowly past a row of shops. Lightborne went into a paint store, just closing for the day, and asked if he might borrow a rubber band. He looped it twice over his right shoe to keep the sole from flapping. Then he and Klara Ludecke went back through the tunnel to the depot and sat on the bench near the newsstand.

"There is a single container," she said. "It's quite large, metallic. I think steel. I don't know how many reels are inside. Meet me on Fifty-seventh Street between Sixth and Seventh avenues. Two weeks from today, noon, south side of the street. I'll place the object in your hands."

"Where, exactly, on the south side of the street?"

"Walk up and down. I'll find you."

"I'd like to ask," Lightborne said. "If you know anything about the history behind all this, I'd be interested in hearing."

"You're interested in the Nazis?"

"In the period, the era. The great collapse. People in overcoats listening to Bruckner. Hitler handing out vials of poison."

"This is theatrical, the swastika banners, the floodlights."

"The wedding banquet," he said. "The execution of Fegelein in the garden. The burial of the wolfhound and her pups."

"You respond to the operatic quality, the great flames."

"Yes, the Russian guns in the distance, the strange celebration in the bunker when they mistakenly thought Hitler was about to kill himself."

"The last meal was spaghetti," she said.

The New York train pulled in, the 7:13. Lightborne decided he was sufficiently interested in the circumstances surrounding the movie to wait for the next train, assuming she could tell him something.

"Christoph's father was an officer with a tank unit that defended against the Russian advance on the Oder."

"Marshall Rokossovsky, maybe."

"I was fond of him. Heinz Ludecke. A shy, humorous man. In the war he had a cousin—I don't know his name. He was a stenographer attached to the Führerbunker in Berlin. The main task of this cousin was to record conversations between Hitler and Goebbels."

"Yes, they liked to reminisce," Lightborne said.

"In the confusion at the end, Heinz was taken prisoner by the Russians but managed to escape with false papers. Eventually he ended up in a British camp for refugees and foreign workers. Here he came across his cousin, who carried Belgian papers and a parcel which he obviously regarded with the greatest concern. It seems Hitler's valet had been ordered to burn all of the Führer's possessions and effects. This parcel alone had been smuggled out of the bunker by Heinz's cousin and he insisted that Heinz take possession of it on the theory that he was less vulnerable to interrogation and arrest."

"They didn't burn his portrait of Frederick the Great," Lightborne said. "He gave specific orders the portrait was to be spared."

"You hardly need me, Mr. Lightborne."

"I'm sorry, go on."

"It might be best if you produced your own movie."

"Please continue, Mrs. Ludecke."

"Heinz managed to resume a more or less normal life. His cousin vanished completely, never to be seen again, as in a fairy tale. Of course all this I learned from my husband. Whether or not Heinz ever viewed the film, even Christoph never found out. When Heinz died, not so long ago, Christoph went to Germany and took possession of the movie, something he could not do while his father was alive because Heinz would not relinquish it."

"Why didn't he destroy it, I wonder."

"He was devoted to Hitler, and remained so all his life. If he saw what was on the film and if it is the filth some people believe it to be, I'm quite sure he would have destroyed it. Most likely he never saw the movie. I don't know. Perhaps there's another answer. The film itself may provide the answer. Or it may do nothing of the kind. In any case it was after my husband acquired the film that he started the fresh rumors of its existence."

"To heat up the market."

"To create a fever, yes. Not the happiest of strategies, was it?"

"A sad business," Lightborne said with feeling.

"You know the circumstances?"

"Merely in outline."

"He was wearing my clothes when he was killed."

"To avoid detection. Those people were putting pressure."

"It was something he did from time to time."

"A preference."

"He would go into the city."

"I see."

"He said it was only the clothes. He didn't have relations with men, he said."

"Was he telling the truth?"

"I don't know," she said. "They knew him in that district. Truck drivers near the packing plants. They called him the Red Queen, for the dresses he wore, always red, my dresses. I knew. I permitted it."

Lightborne sensed he was supposed to be touched by this. People with their enlightened attitudes. The best he could do was nod his head slowly, suggesting thoughtful consideration. Good time to change the subject.

"I'm forced to wonder, Mrs. Ludecke. Why a two-week wait before you hand over the container? Frankly I'd hoped to have it in my hands today or tomorrow."

"I'm considering another offer."

Lightborne grinned, a nervous reflex.

"Lovely," he said. "All this talk about being so eager to get rid of it. That's wonderful."

"I had to allow the other party some time. The other party asked for time. It was common courtesy."

"Common courtesy, that's wonderful. I'm always charmed by alliteration. The child in me."

She seemed amused by her own bold tactics. Caught in the midst of all these vortical energies, she'd found, at least for the moment, an approximation of calm, or perhaps it was objectivity, a view of herself uninfluenced by tragic emotion.

"It was funny about Heinz's cousin," she said. "Heinz said that people in the British camp asked his cousin over and over and over again: 'What was Hitler really like?'"

3

Selvy sat on the roof of his building, eating a peach. There was a warm breeze from the west, where the sun hung on a tremulous rim, all ruddle and blood. When the metal door began swinging open, twenty yards away, he moved the peach to his left hand. It was Lomax, in his polyester knit trousers and white belt and shoes, trailed by three kids who lived in the building.

"How do I get rid of them?"

They followed him to the ledge where Selvy sat.

"What you supposed to be doing here?" one kid said.

"This ours, white."

The smallest kid rubbed his sneaker against the side of Lomax's shoe, scuffing it slightly.

"They followed me up four flights," Lomax said.

"The limo's been stripped by now," Selvy told him. "Your driver's long gone."

"I came in a cab."

"What is it, unofficial visit?"

"How long have you lived here? Have you lived here all this time? Why don't you live where everybody else lives?"

All this time the kids had been crowding around Lomax, baiting him, ridiculing his clothes. Selvy noticed he was sweating, really irritated. The small one scuffed his other shoe. Selvy watched him clench his fists. He was very tense. He didn't know what to do.

"It getting dark, white."

"You're being where you don't live, man, and it getting dark."

"Pizz on you, white."

The small one scuffed his shoe again. One of the others ran his hand along the top of the ledge, coming away with ash and tar. He moved in now, feinting with the other hand, then reaching out to smudge Lomax's tartan slacks, a move half aggressive, half defensive, the kid drawing away quickly, his action comically stylized, head bobbing. Lomax pulled a Walther automatic out of the waistband holster under his jacket. He was shouting, waving the gun in their faces. They backed off slowly, eyes white in the dimness. The small one chewed gum. They didn't know whether to be impressed or scared. They seemed to believe Lomax. He was riled enough to start shooting. As they got close to the door they relaxed a little. A trace of swagger crept back into their style. They went through the door strutting a little, shaking their asses.

Lomax was still shouting, calling them names. Selvy watched him holster the gun, his hand trembling a bit. He quieted down finally and took out a handkerchief and spat into it a few times. Then he put his right foot up on the ledge and began cleaning the scuff marks off his shoe. Selvy finished eating and tossed the peach pit over his shoulder into the air shaft.

On the 8:13 heading back to Grand Central, Lightborne considered two aspects of the situation. First, whoever held the footage had to contend with an element of danger. Second, Christoph Ludecke tried to sell the thing outright—half payment up front—without allowing the buyers an advance screening. Aside from being naïve, this attempt indicated that the movie wasn't quite the commodity it was rumored to be. Ludecke wanted to get what he could and disappear. It also indicated there were huge sums involved.

A little later that evening Lightborne's phone rang. The man at the other end didn't identify himself by name.

"You're acquainted with Glen Selvy."

"Yes," Lightborne said.

"He's been acting as my representative."

"You collect."

"That's right," the man said. "And Glen told me recently you might have an unusual item to offer."

"Certain commitments have been made."

"But the matter hasn't actually been settled."

"Depends on interpretation," Lightborne said.

"I gather the widow is proving difficult. She and I have talked. My problem is that I'm not in a position to verify the item's value. I need someone to handle details. Of course if you're already acting on behalf of another collector, we've got nothing to discuss."

"It might be I could work something out," Lightborne said. "How do I reach you?"

"You don't."

"Why not let Selvy handle it?"

"I don't know where he is. He hasn't shown his face for days. Doesn't answer his phone."

"Well, then."

"She wants to hear from me."

"There's the matter of my own fee," Lightborne said. "I'm happy to mediate, to bring people together, to work out touchy details. But this is turning into an operation where the utmost delicacy is required. The risks involved are considerably more than I'm normally willing to expose myself to."

"You want adequate recompense."

As they bandied vague phrases, Lightborne realized why the voice at the other end sounded so neutral, so free of cadence, ornament or regional flavor. The man had been trying all along to disguise it. Lightborne was tempted to point out that he'd always had a pretty fair idea as to the identity of Selvy's principal. It was a small world, smut, and even those who spent time in the more affluent haunts were sooner or later known to all the rest, the marginal drudges, eking out their mean existence.

"History is so comforting," he told the man. "Isn't this why people collect? To own a fragment of the tangible past. Life is fleeting, and we seek consolation in durable things."

This was Lightborne's speech to new collectors. Whether or not it applied to such an object as a ribbon of film was a question that didn't engage his interest right now.

"Pretty sunset," Lomax said.

"Isn't it, yes."

"Why don't you live where everybody else lives?"

"Get to the point."

Lomax offered him a cigarette.

"You're being referred to as the subject."

"An adjustment's in progress then."

"They want to adjust, definitely."

"Frankie's Tropical Bar."

"Right," Lomax said. "Someone from out of town. Some jerk-off. You parked one in his vest, case you didn't know."

"The weapon was firing *him*."

"Right, that's right, a regular jerk-off."

"Why is it felt, Lomax, that I rank as a subject?"

"Call me by my first name."

"I don't know your first name."

"Arthur."

"What's behind the adjustment?" Selvy said.

"You first of all made an arrangement with Ludecke's widow. You and she are trying to market the Berlin film together."

"Joke."

"Her house was miked. You deactivated the damn thing. It was felt in some quarters this was highly incriminating."

"It never occurred to me, frankly, it was one of our devices. No reason I know of for us to be listening. If we're listening, Arthur, why don't I know about it? Find a bug, you ought to squash it."

"It wasn't appreciated, tampering with audio surveillance. The feeling in this outfit concerning devices of any kind is close to religious. You ought to know that."

"What else?" Selvy said.

"Secondly, your involvement with *Running Dog* was taken into account."

"Elaborate."

"That woman you've been seeing. What's to elaborate?"

"You know, it's interesting, the first thought I had that night was that she was the subject. Her article on Percival. Then I thought, Christ this is insane. No way. I'm half hallucinating this thing. They wouldn't come down that hard. Insane, totally."

"You were the subject," Lomax said. "Of course it wasn't supposed to happen that way. You were supposed to be alone. And you were supposed to be unarmed. But you were holding. Why were you holding? There's no justification for that."

"I mean shit, Arthur, you nearly shot three kids just now. Do you need a gun, your job?"

"It's the business, I guess."

"The business."

"Or maybe we're just gun-totin' folks."

Selvy waited for Lomax to stop chuckling.

"We go to bed."

"You go to bed," Lomax said. "Thanks for your candor."

"But that doesn't involve me with the magazine."

"Our information's different. Our information's that you were pointing Robbins in the right direction. I think recent events prove this to be the case. But that's all behind us. I came on my own, by cab, to let you know they want to adjust, period."

"What recent events?"

"She found the collection, Robbins."

"Not with my help," Selvy said. "Not with any help from me."

"That annex sensor you rigged in the fireplace. The readout indicates that wasn't Percival going through on the night in question. Much lighter person. She was there that night. I can play you the tapes."

"What's my motive?"

"Motive, obvious, sex, clearly."

"Sex, clearly."

"It's been known to happen," Lomax said. "The lady wants to make a name. She's tapping away on her Olivetti. The exposé of the half century. When she hits a dead spot, you fill it in for her. Hump, hump, tap, tap. When she needs a tactical lead, you provide it."

"You said information. Your information's different. But this is speculation, it's gaming."

"Hard information behind it. Granted, they didn't wait for all the input. They tried to adjust a hell of a lot sooner than they should have. But you *were* Robbins' source, weren't you? So in retrospect it was justified. Technically you can fault them for being premature. It was handled badly. We've been doing that. There's been some slippage. I'm frankly concerned."

Selvy was tired of this. It brought things to the surface, or close to it—things he didn't care to know about. Textures, entanglements, riddles, words. It compromised the routine.

"What I came for, ultimately," Lomax said in the midst of a deep breath. "There's a new operation in progress. This time you're looking at something different is my understanding."

"What am I looking at?"

"An assassination team of former ARVN rangers."

"How many?" Selvy said.

"Two in number."

"Carrying what?"

"I'm not sure."

"Been nice chatting," Selvy said.

"They're part of a kind of special project. A pet project. Pulled out of Vietnam at the very end and then brought over here."

"I'm glad to hear they're gainfully employed, the little fuckers."

Lomax stood with hands in pockets, the edges of his sport

coat drawn back. There was an alligator stitched on the breast pocket of his knit shirt. A plane banked over the river after takeoff from National. Lomax checked the tar on his pants.

"Want you to know," he said. "I'd like to undo it completely. Whole process."

"Don't."

"I'm thinking of getting out myself. Stand clear for a while. Get a perspective."

"Sure, your dogs, the puppies."

"Buy a place in the country."

"They need room to run," Selvy said.

By midnight he was on Interstate 95 north of Philadelphia. In the back seat of his Toyota were some clothes and a couple of cartons packed with various possessions. He smoked and listened to the radio. Fixed limits and solid dark. After a while he turned off the radio and rolled down his window. The highway was almost empty but a roar filled the interior of the car, an air blast so integral to travel on major routes that he couldn't break it down to component sounds. So much his own car. So much the sparse additional traffic. So much the power of night.

Moll Robbins sat looking into the keys of her typewriter. On the wall to her left was a neon display, bluish white, a smoking gun. At her elbow, which rested on the table before her, was a glass of iced tea and half a cruller. The limp white page in the typewriter was blank.

When she got up and looked through the peephole to find it was Selvy who'd just knocked, she discovered she didn't fully welcome the visit. Something in her resisted his appearance just now. Bad timing, that was all, probably.

"What time is it?"

"I don't know," he said.

"I'm awake, oddly enough."

"I like your robe. It's not your kind of thing, though, is it?"

"The gunfighter. Sit down, I'll get you something. It's not a robe, it's a tea gown. I'm drinking tea."

"I'm drinking whisky," he said.

"What else? The gunfighter's special. NYPD's been looking for you, hill and dale, ever since you rode into the sunset. I get calls regularly. Precinct, homicide, missing persons."

"They know my name?"

"Nope."

"What'd you tell them?"

"You were a pickup. I picked you up. You were too cute to resist."

"Plausible," he said.

"Sure, good girl, except you're not Clark Gable and I'm not Jean Arthur. Any of it begin to make sense to you?"

"Afraid not."

"The police have some leads, apparently."

"Cops don't know shit. Forget cops."

She poured him a drink. He looked drawn and spare and a little dangerous, reminding Moll of the first time he'd turned up at her door. She left the bottle and sat across the room, studying him.

"Something new in here."

"What?" she said.

"Neon."

"Guess I couldn't resist. More flash. Transience and flash. Story of my life. I realize looking around this place that I don't have any furniture in the strict sense. I stack clothes in those modular boxes in the bedroom. I work at a folding table. I have a wall unit. It's just as well, isn't it? If you don't live in a house on your own piece of property, there's no point owning real things. If you're floating in the air, ten-twenty-thirty stories up, might as well live with play objects, shiny balls and ornaments."

"It's a gun. I didn't see at first from this angle. A six-shooter."

"I saw it the day after. Couldn't resist. Also the story of my life. Not being able to resist."

"Resist what?"

"Whatever I don't see clearly."

He gestured toward the typewriter.

"If I'm interrupting, say so."

"I wasn't getting anywhere."

"Where do you want to get?"

She leaned well forward, peering at him, her hands hanging down over her knees, almost as though she was getting ready to slip off the end of the ottoman, an impromptu comic bit.

"Who are you, Selvy?"

He sat back in his chair, an intentional countermotion, a withdrawal, and smiled in deep fatigue, self-deprecatingly. He appeared to be disassociating himself from whatever significance the question by its nature ascribed to him.

"Who is Earl Mudger?" she said.

"Don't know."

"Who is Lomax?"

"Lomax. Don't know."

"Of course I have my own versions of the answers to all these questions."

"I can't corroborate."

She reached over to the table for her iced tea. It was the middle of the night. She was remotely tired, knowing it wasn't the kind of weariness that leads to immediate sleep. The reverse probably. Getting to sleep would be labor, prolonged exertion. The ice in her glass had melted, making the tea flavorless.

"What is it like, secrecy? The secret life. I know it's sexual. I want to know this. Is it homosexual?"

"You're way ahead of me," he said.

"Isn't that why the English are so good at espionage? Or why they seem so good at it, which comes to the same thing. Isn't it almost rooted in national character?"

"I didn't know the English controlled world rights."

"To what?"

"Being queer," he said.

"No, I'm saying the link is there. That's all. Tendency finds an outlet. I'm saying espionage is a language, an art, with sexual sources and coordinates. Although I don't mean to say it so Freudianly."

"I'm open to theorizing," he said. "What else do you have?"

"I have links inside links. This is the age of conspiracy."

"People have wondered."

"This is the age of connections, links, secret relationships."

"What would you think of this?"

"What?"

"If I told you this," he said.

"Tell me."

"*Running Dog* is a propaganda mechanism."

"Who for? You're kidding."

"I don't know who for."

"That's bullshit, Selvy."

"You're right, I'm kidding."

"I don't like that smile."

"Just a little joke."

"Granted, it's a crappy magazine. Granted, we play to people's belief in just what I've been talking about. World-wide conspiracies. Fantastic assassination schemes. But we are not anybody's mechanism."

"I'm not even smiling, look."

"I mean granted, we do things in the schlockiest way imaginable. You'd better be kidding."

"A kidder," he said. "I like to kid."

"Whose mechanism?"

"Can't you take a joke?" he said. "Don't you know when someone's joking?"

"Because it makes me think of how we named the goddamn magazine. Except we meant it ironically, of course. Using the Hanoi line then current. The familiar taunt."

"What taunt?"

"Imperialist lackeys and running dogs."

"All comes back."

"Perfect name for a radical publication, considering the temper of the times. The name had impact then. It fairly sparkled with irony."

Moll this time slipped down the side of the ottoman to sit crosslegged on the floor.

"We almost named it *H. C. Porny.* H. C. Porny was a cartoon character we'd planned on using. He was supposed to represent the government. More precisely the government plus big business. Short, fat, leering old man. We'd hoped, see, to replace Uncle Sam as a national symbol."

"H.C. meaning Hard Core."

"Our cartoonist OD'd, unfortunately. OD meaning overdose. And that was the early end of H. C. Porny. Where were you then, Selvy?"

"Fasting."

"I'll bet you were. Praying and fasting. People had flag decals. Everybody had something. People had bumper stickers. AMERICA—LOVE IT OR LEAVE IT. So this friend, it's clear as day, this well-meaning friend gave me a sticker of my very own, which I thought was so devilishly clever I immediately proceeded to affix it to the bumper of my little Swedish car. VIETNAM—LOVE IT OR LEAVE IT. And don't two guys come staggering out of a bar on Eighty-sixth Street while I'm stopped for a light? And don't they see my sign and start pounding on my car until the whole thing gets out of hand and there's a mob of people and I end up with a broken ankle and my car half wrecked?"

"Passions quicken in wartime. We see this time and again."

"Sure, sex was in the parks and streets. What lovely urgent folly. But what were you doing, pal? We're waiting to hear."

"I was preparing for the desert."

"You were oiling your goddamn .38."

"That was my desert period."

"You were leaping through burning hoops for a better America."

She watched him close his eyes and go to sleep. It took only seconds. Pure of heart, she thought. She found some brandy in the cabinet and sat a while drinking, watching him sleep. The digital clock in the wall unit had stopped days earlier at 4:01. 4:01 sounded about right. She finished the brandy and got up off the floor, creaking a bit. Selvy's head was tilted left. She put her hand to his face: sleep and warmth. Then the other hand, framing him. He opened his eyes finally. She waited for him to adjust to his surroundings.

"What would you do differently, knowing what you know now?"

"What do I know now?" he said.

There was an interval of dusky sex. Both half asleep, alternately active and listless, they lay diagonally across the bed, breathing deeply and evenly, muttering at times. It must have been a dream, she thought later, seeing him naked in the dawn, a dream in first light, crouched rigidly by the window, body leaning slightly forward, arms enfolding his knees, head lowered, a dream in gray space, motionless, absolutely still, she thought later, as though he'd learned from some master of the wilderness how to suspend even the rhythms of his breathing.

4

The maroon and gold pimpmobile, double-parked outside a nude-encounter studio, drew a crowd of admirers, largely because its rear window was custom-fashioned to resemble a lightning bolt.

It's Times Square Saturday night. Everybody's in costume. Cowboys, bikers, drag queens, punk rockers, decoy cops, Moonies, gypsies, Salvation Army regulars, Process evangelists in dark capes, skinhead Krishna chanters in saffron robes and tennis sneakers. Glitter and trash everywhere. Hot pants, blond wigs, slouch hats, silver boots. Late-season heat blasts. Waves of humid air pour over the crowds. Horns blowing, engines revving, music wailing from loudspeakers in record stores. There is swamp fever in the air. Everybody's soaked through with sweat, eyes glassy and distant. Priests, doormen, movie ushers, French sailors, West Point cadets, waitresses in dirndls, Shriners wearing fezzes.

The two men seemed composed, totally untroubled by the heat. Selvy had first noticed them an hour ago and about a mile away, near the Coliseum. Now they were standing on a corner watching the quasi-Hindus dance and chant. They were both small, both in western boots; one wore dark glasses. They thought the chanters were funny. They stood laughing at them, pointing occasionally.

Selvy crossed the street. A kid with a walkie-talkie moved with him nearly stride for stride as he headed north on Broadway. Magic massage. Topless pinball. Scandinavian skin games. The kid was gangly, maybe sixteen, with the supercharged look of a once bright child who'd failed to develop. The walkie-talkie had an antenna that measured roughly ten feet, tall enough to scrape the bottom of theater marquees, and so the boy kept toward the edge of the sidewalk, often balancing on the curbstone itself. At Forty-fifth Street, he put the set to his mouth.

"Code blue," he said. "Prepare to activate all units. People in the street, take your positions. Camera one, code blue. This is a take. Give me a reflector over here. This set is closed. Camera's rolling, you people. Everybody's live. We are shooting live. This is a live action scene. Prepare sound stage to record. All right, you cab drivers, let's hear it. Watch those cables, everybody. Closing the set to all but essential personnel. Nude scene, nude scene. Get it moving, everybody, please. Am leaving the district. Repeat. Am leaving the district."

Overloaded with static, random brain noise, he stepped off the curbstone and went striding diagonally across the street, trailed now by four smaller kids. Selvy found an Irish bar on Eighth Avenue. He knocked back a couple of Jim Beams and waited for something to happen.

The blank of tool steel was cherry-red. Earl Mudger held it to the anvil with a pair of tongs, rough-forging the shape he wanted with a double-faced hammer.

He took off his gloves and put on a pair of goggles. He held the steel blank to a grinder belt, further shaping and sizing, removing excess metal.

Leaving the goggles hanging from a hook, he went into the next room, where there was a band saw, a drill press, a lathe, a grindstone and a small heat-treated furnace. He heated the steel blank for twenty minutes, then immersed it in quenching oil.

Back in the smaller of the two basement rooms he set the blank on the metal base of the testing machine he'd designed himself. It was fitted with wheels, gauges, handles, weights, a fulcrum arm and a precisely sized diamond tip, and it measured the hardness of steel. First time the blank tested out high, as he'd anticipated. Too brittle at that level. He reheated it for an hour. After it cooled he tested again. About right this time. It wouldn't break or chip easily. It would hold its cutting edge.

He took off his apron and lit up a cigarette. Then he lay

supine on a long workbench, watching the smoke drift toward
the ceiling. Upstairs the baby was crying.

The man next to Selvy drank beer. He wore a touring cap
well down on his forehead, almost touching his nose. His bills
and change were set before him in a small puddle of beer.

"You a TV type?"

"No," Selvy said.

"The old Madison Square Garden used to be right across
the street there. We used to get TV types coming in here all
the time. Knick fans, Rangers. I mention it because I'm promoting something sensational. Madison Avenue should give it
a look."

He waited for Selvy to ask what he was promoting. Selvy
kept an eye on the mirror. They were in the bar. He saw them
take a booth near the men's room. One of them had a mustache, very sparse. The other, with sunglasses, had a tapering
face. Both wore light windbreakers.

"What I'm doing is a contest to the death. Man versus
polar bear. Combat supreme. Polar bear is vicious. Polar bear
can decimate a herd of reindeer in like a matter of minutes.
I'm lining up this guy Shunko Hakoda. A sumo wrestler. He
goes three-fifty, easy. His agent's hedging right now but I
think we got the numbers. Meanwhile I'm negotiating with
the president of Malawi to hold the fight there. I'm envision-
ing a large cage in the middle of a soccer stadium. You're
asking yourself where we'll find a polar bear in Malawi."

Selvy eased off the bar stool and walked out. He headed
back toward Times Square, taking the same route. Naked
karate. Pagan baths. A battle-scarred Cadillac moved slowly
down Broadway, a man's foot hanging out one window. It
weaved on past, bumpers caked with mud, streaks of dirt
across all four doors. Selvy watched it plow into the back of
the maroon and gold pimpmobile. Tinkling glass. Little puffs
of dust. The onlookers were overjoyed. They glanced at each

other wide-eyed as if to confirm the dimensions of the event.

In seconds the owner-pimp emerged, wispy beard, a trifle hassidic in his mink hat and understated black velvet suit. He moved in little scat steps, half a dancer, aggrieved and restive in this sidewalk crush, already eyeing the Cad, which sat throbbing in a patch of broken glass and chunks of rusty dirt dislodged from the fenders.

Selvy was pinned by a dozen spectators. He reached out for an awning support in order to avoid being swept in a given direction against his will. Over the heads of some teenage girls he saw the two men at the edge of the crowd, earnestly discussing something. He couldn't tell whether they'd spotted him. Also hard to tell what they might be carrying under those loose-fitting windbreakers.

The doors of the Cadillac slowly opened and bodies of various sizes and types became visible. The car was full of Hispanics (official police designation), maybe ten or eleven, at least three of them children. The crowd turned its attention back to the pimp.

Selvy used the awning support to stand fast while most of those around him took about four involuntary steps into the street. Traffic was halted at the scene of the accident. Whole masses of onlookers were rocked one way or another by sudden imbalances elsewhere in the crowd. A police siren sounded at a steady volume with the car unable to make progress in the stalled traffic.

Selvy forced people aside and made it to the nearest open doorway. He climbed a long flight of stairs. The walls on both sides were full of graffiti. At the top he turned and looked back. Then he walked down the corridor. He passed several rooms with small curtained booths, a few people milling about. He passed another room with a man standing in the doorway.

"Photograph live nudes," the man said sleepily.

Selvy turned right into another corridor. He stopped by a window. Down on the street a mounted policeman was moving through the crowd. He passed another open door. Gadgets, novelties, devices, creams, ointments, marital aids. Wholesale only. At the end of the corridor was a black metal door with two words painted on it in vivid red: NUDE STORYTELLING.

Selvy looked behind him. Then he opened the door and stepped inside. The outer office consisted of a desk, a telephone and a couple of chairs. A chubby black man in a porkpie hat sat at the desk, smoking a cigar. He had a racing form spread in front of him.

"Be a short wait," he said.

"Who's doing the storytelling?"

"Not me, guarantee."

"How much per story?"

"Cost you upwards of thirty-fi' dollars for a half-hour story, depending."

"How much minimum?"

"I let you get away with fifteen down. What I'm saying, the basic story is fifteen. Activities can run you a little more."

"All right," Selvy said.

"You a cop, Jim?"

"Just want to hear a nude story."

"Because if this is a sweep of the area, you ought to be sweeping anywheres but here. What I'm saying, it's all seen to."

"How long do I wait?"

"Pick out a chair, Jim. There's a story in progress."

Mudger trued up the cutting edge with a coarse hone. He found this mysteriously pleasing. There was a lightbulb directly overhead so that he could determine the best sharpening angle by noting the shadow cast by the blade on the stone, and its gradual disappearance. Sight, sound, touch. He maintained a steady pressure as he moved the blade-edge into the stone.

The shape of tools. Proportions and heft. The satisfactions of cutting along pencil lines, of measuring to the sheer edge of something and coming out right, of allowing for slight variations and coming out right, of mixing fluids and seeing the colors blend, a surface texture materializing out of brush striations.

Cleaning up grit wheels. This made him happy. He liked the touch of rough surfaces. He liked the sounds things made when excess finish was removed. Sandpapering, grinding, buffing. He liked the names of things.

It was midnight. He went into the washroom. Standing over the commode he tried to spit into the stream of urine as it emerged. On the third try he connected, watching the blob of spit go skipping into the bowl.

He set to work on the handle. It would be burl maple. The names of things. Subtly gripping odors. Glues and resins. The names. Honing oil. Template. Brazing rod. The names of things in these two rooms constituted a near-secret knowledge. He felt obscure satisfaction, something akin to a freemason's pride, merely saying these names aloud for Tran Le or her grandmother or the two men, Van and Cao. Carborundum. Emery wheel. Tenon and drawbore. You couldn't use tools and materials well, he believed, unless you knew their proper names.

Cleaning up grit wheels. Hand-stitching a leather sheath. Doing your own heat-treating.

Sharpness: dry-shaving a square inch of your forearm with a freshly honed blade.

By heat-treating the steel blank himself, he knew he was sacrificing some of the exactness a commercial firm would provide. But he preferred it this way. *His* instrument start to finish.

He fitted a brass guard to the steel. Then he took two slabs of burl maple and roughed out a fit. He sanded, applied epoxy and set rivets. Ought to hold forever.

When the unit was dry he leveled out the finger grooves

and used the belts and sanders to get the handle down to a tighter, firmer fit.

He buffed the wood and brass to a fine sheen. Then he alternately polished and sharpened the blade, finally using various buffing wheels to get the edge and finish he wanted.

Sharpness: the sight of blood edging out of a cut in your thumb.

He climbed the back stairs to the kitchen and opened a can of beer, taking it with him up one more flight to the bedroom. He moved quietly past the cradle and looked at Tran Le curled in bed. Her face was touched pearl gray by a night light nearby. She was the most beautiful woman he'd ever seen, a Saigon bar girl at fourteen, leaning against a parked jeep eating an Almond Joy when he first set eyes on her eight years ago. He took off his shirt. When he sat on the edge of the bed, she turned toward him.

"Sleep," he said.

"Where Van is, Earl?"

"Out of town. With Cao."

"Business."

"They be back maybe tomorrow, next day. You sleep."

"Sleep," she said.

"Maybe Van come back with gift for his sister. This because Van know she such a good little wife. Earl tell Van. She is de sweetest little wife in de whole wide world."

Mudger's rudimentary speech often degenerated into stock Negro dialect, catching him unaware. All those recruits he'd trained and pained. The less power you have, the more dominance you maintain in secondary areas. Speech rhythms, foot speed, hair texture. He finished his beer sitting on the edge of the bed. He needed only a couple of hours sleep. Then he'd watch the sun come up.

The woman was young with a healthy reddish face, oval in shape, and large brown eyes. Her hair, center-parted, billowed evenly to either side. She wore an ordinary shift and sandals.

Selvy watched her walk to the outer office. The room was medium sized with a few vinyl chairs, a coffee table and a lamp constructed out of a football helmet. In a corner was a folding bed, doubled up, on casters.

"Stony, is this all?"

"What you see."

"They said two minimum."

"Man's been waiting."

"I'm kind of beat, frankly."

"Tell him a story, Nadine. Man's entitled."

"Being I'm new, I won't make waves. But ordinarily there'd be a tussle over this. Two's the minimum, Stony, and you know it."

"Do him a quickie, hon, and we'll all go home."

She sat across from Selvy. Her knees had a tender sheen. He liked shiny knees. He also liked her voice, a modified drawl. It took her a second or two to gear up to the introductory routine.

"Goes like this: you're allowed to pick one story out of the following three. More, you pay extra. Each story runs ten minutes, depending. Longer of course for activities. Okay. 'Flaming Panties.' 'The Valley of the Jolly Green Giant, Ho Ho Ho.' And the 'Story of Naomi and Lateef.' The second one's mostly gay, just so we get our preferences right."

"Wouldn't I want a man to tell it?"

"Look, who knows?"

"You're new here."

"My second full week and I'm ready to bow out. Quit while they still love you. How much did you give Stony?"

"Fifteen down."

"Just checking," she said. "You have to do that with horseplayers. Okay, pick one."

"I'll try 'Naomi and Lateef.' "

"You're only the second person to pick that. Most everybody picks 'Flaming Panties.' It's really sick, too. The mind that comes up with stuff like that."

"They're not your stories."

"I don't make them up. I just recite them."

"I thought they were your stories."

"If I made up 'Flaming Panties,' I don't know, I think I'd run a sword through my body. It is *the* sickest."

Selvy heard the man in the outer office talking to someone. He seemed agitated, although the words weren't clearly audible through the closed door.

"If you get stimulated by the story, pay attention, you can give me an extra ten if you want, or an extra twenty, depending. We leave it up to customer preference. What's wrong?"

"Nothing," he said.

"That's just Stony making life hard for the kid who brings his sandwich."

Selvy nodded.

"The 'Story of Naomi and Lateef,'" she said, standing momentarily to unzip the shift down the back, then stepping out of it and sitting down again. She looked at him impatiently.

"What?" he said.

"If you keep your clothes on, it means you're a cop."

"I see. I didn't realize."

"Nude storytelling, it says on the door."

"Everybody, that means."

"You're catching on," she said.

"There are some people I'm trying to avoid, more or less."

"We all get naked. If you don't, you're a cop. That's what they told me. I'm also supposed to say we recommend the twenty-dollar activity, which is the one we need the bed for. That goes in at the part we came to before."

"I've got a better idea."

"Of course if you're ashamed. We get all sorts. Maybe we can work out a compromise. I don't think a person ought to be forced to get undressed in front of a stranger. It's just every-body's so casual about their bodies."

"There are some people I'm trying to avoid. What say you and I go out and get something to eat. Come on, put on your dress, we'll go. Is there a back way?"

"Whoa, big fella."

"I'll take the twenty-dollar activity. Just not here, okay? We'll grab a bite, come on."

"Come, go; eat, sleep; dress, undress."

"Nadine. Is that your name?"

"Yes."

"How old are you?"

"Never mind."

"You'll never reach twenty if you hang around here much longer. I'm your last chance."

"At least you're smiling. You'd better be smiling."

"Come on, we'll go to Little Rock."

"What a thing to say."

"Get your clothes on."

"My sister lives in Little Rock," she said.

Dressed, she led the way through a series of storerooms. They emerged in a larger room occupied by a woman wearing black boots, a long black military shirt and an iron cross hanging from her neck. The shirt included a red armband with a black swastika set inside a circular field of white. The woman sat smoking, her feet propped on the top rung of a small ladder.

"Passing through."

"You're the new one."

"Nadine Rademacher. Hi. How's business."

"Sucks," the woman said.

"Enjoy your break."

"Who's Johnny Lonesome?"

"Just a hanger-on," Nadine said. "Can't get rid of the kid."

In the corridor they passed the same man Selvy had seen earlier, standing in a different doorway this time.

"Photograph live nudes."

"Angelo, why don't you go home?" Nadine said.

"Busload of Japanese coming down from the Hilton."

At the top of the stairway Selvy asked Nadine to wait a moment. He followed the same route he'd taken after entering. Turning the corner into an empty hallway he palmed his .38 and held it flat against his thigh. Went past the window, the room full of novelties. Opened the black metal door. No one there. Stony's racing form on the desk. He walked through into the studio. Empty. He holstered the gun and went out to find Nadine.

The street was even more crowded than it had been. Apparently there'd been action. Squad cars, an ambulance, a TV crew. People made faces for the camera. Selvy scanned the crowd, then led Nadine along the front of the building and down a cross street to the nearest restaurant. It was a dark cellar, a steak place, and the waiter wore spats. Only two other tables were occupied. An extramarital affair at one. Judge Crater at the other.

"My drama teacher talked me off L.A.," Nadine said. "He kept saying New York. New York actors. Character actors. People with faces."

"He seemed to think faces were important, did he?"

"He kept saying faces. People with faces. He said I wouldn't learn anything in a place where there's just one basic face."

The waiter glided by.

"Kitchen's closing if you want to order."

The old man nearby, with long white stringy hair, sipped his complimentary cordial.

"So you're an actress," Selvy said.

"Aspiring."

"That place you work at."

"It was all a storage area. Is that what you mean? Why is it set up so everything's so hard to get to? They kept materials there. Books, rubber and leather, film equipment, editing equipment, everything. Then somebody in the organization decided to open it up to street trade, even though it's hidden away on the second and third floor. It's the accountants, Stony said. A tax matter. You're not a cop. We established that. Am I right?"

"Right."

"Talerico," she said, fixing him with a meaningful look.

"Familiar."

"There's two of them. Paul. That's the one who's here. One of the New York families, as you can well imagine. Pornography, trucking, vending machines. Don't you love it? That's the legitimate end. The other one. That's Vincent. He's upstate or somewhere. They're cousins, I think."

"I know the names," Selvy said.

"Vincent's in charge of acquiring, Stony said. Acquisitions. He specializes in first-run movies. When they can't get rights by bargaining, they send Vincent. He gets the film. He just takes it. Then they make their own prints. Then they distribute."

She hunched way down in her chair, conspiratorially, her face just inches above the table top.

"They call him Vinny the Eye. Don't you love it? It's so dumb, I love it. I've only seen Paul. He was in the other day. Everybody went around saying, *'Paul's here, Paul, he's in the building.'* I was disappointed in Paul. I was not impressed. It was disillusioning for a country girl like myself. I think Vinny's the Hollywood one. The dresser. The fancy gangster type. It's really dumb. I wish he'd come around so I could see him."

When the food came she didn't waste time, obviously hungry. Watching her eat relaxed him. It occurred to Selvy he hadn't been hungry in years. He'd experienced weakness and discomfort from lack of food. But he hadn't desired it really, except to ease the discomfort. He tried to recall the last time he'd felt a real desire for food.

"Are you seriously going to Little Rock?" she said.

"Thereabouts, sure, why not."

"Ever since I've been working in that place I keep thinking the whole world smells of Lysol."

"You owe me a story, you know."

" 'Naomi and Lateef.' "

"I might change my mind," he said.

"All I know, I'm not doing 'Flaming Panties.' That story's so sick I've been changing it little by little. A little every day. I don't care who complains. It's a story that relies on combinations. Incest is just the beginning. It *starts* with incest. Then near the end it just becomes reciting words. Some words I just won't say. It piles on the phrases. It becomes red meat."

"Your customers."

"They laugh, mostly. Some get embarrassed. You'd be surprised."

"Sitting there naked, laughing."

"Sheepish nudes, I told Stony."

"So some words you just won't say."

She finished chewing the last bite of baked potato.

"Who are you trying to avoid anyway?"

Selvy looked toward the old man, who sat rigidly staring into space.

"*Tieu to dac cong.*"

He gave her a delayed smile, self-consciously weary, and signaled for the check.

Outside a police towaway crew was about ready to haul the battered Cadillac. Tourists were interested in the pimpmobile. A man, two women and two children posed for pictures, using the car as background. When they were finished, two other women and three children moved into position along the front door and fender. A conventioneer wearing an enormous name tag crouched in the gutter, inserting a flash cube in his Instamatic.

Earl Mudger stood on the patio, facing east, barechested despite the chill, a mug of coffee in his hand. He liked being the first one up, coming down in the dark to start the coffee perking. He would roll his shoulders as he moved around the house, would swing his arms occasionally, feeling the stiffness ease away. Ever since he could remember, in whatever house or barracks he'd lived, with whatever people, family or military, he'd always been the first one up.

With pale light intensifying, aspects of sunrise visible through the trees, he went back into the kitchen. On the counter lay a manila folder and a spool of magnetic tape. He poured more coffee into his mug and sat on a stool, opening the folder and scanning the topmost page, a document headed: *Department of the Treasury, District Director, Internal Revenue Service.* Beneath this was a white label with a long series of numbers arrayed across the top, followed by Grace Delaney's name and home address.

Mudger began turning pages, glancing at audit forms, photocopied documents, photocopied checks and bank statements, agent evaluations, notices of "unfavorable action." He closed the folder and regarded the tape spool. It contained confidential information on the accounts of roughly five hundred taxpayers and had been acquired by Lomax from the same source, an IRS supervisor who had access to restricted files. Among the data was further information relating to Grace Delaney's account.

Mudger finished his coffee and went downstairs. He rechecked the fit and worked some more on the handle section. Then he put on his magnifying glasses and studied the blade.

The knife was a modified bowie. It had a broad sweeping single-edged blade with a clipped point. Overall length was about eleven and a half inches. The blade measured seven and a quarter.

There was a display panel, a hinged triptych, fastened to the wall above a work table. Mudger's knives were exhibited here, some he'd made himself, others turned out by custom knifemakers.

. . .

They had sex in the front seat of Selvy's car, which was parked in the barren dells near the West Side Highway. It was an act they knew would take place as they walked through the dark streets to the car. It helped dispel certain disquieting energies. Times Square Saturday night.

"My hotel's right near that restaurant. Why are we doing it here?"

"I'm a little crazy tonight."

"Try reaching that ashtray and push it closed."

Stale cigarette butts. Smell of various plastics that made up the interior of the car. They straightened up finally. She sat on the driver's side, back resting against the door, her feet up on the seat. Selvy looked straight ahead. A silence, followed by:

"Naomi is this buxom Israeli girl who we find bathing one day in a stream that runs through her kibbutz. She has giant white breasts, etcetera etcetera, nipples, etcetera. So then along comes Lateef, who's an Arab army deserter. Well, to tighten the script, they meet and fall in love and just screw and screw and screw, doing it where they won't be discovered. Forbidden love with a capital F. I'm skipping the details, understand. There's a lot about Lateef's Arab pecker, which you probably don't mind if I glide over. Anyway one day we find them having a picnic on the Golan Heights. It's very star-crossed and tender."

"Wait a second."

He was looking in the rearview mirror. Nadine turned her head, intending to lean back out the open window and check what it was he'd seen.

"Don't do that."

Nobody said anything for the next four or five minutes. Selvy kept his eye on the mirror. He seemed engaged in deep and melancholy thought.

"It's getting daylight," she said.

He got out of the car, walked around to her side and stood leaning against the door, smoking.

"We ought to get my clothes. One thing, I won't mind leaving that hotel. More Lysol. Night clerk's insane. Pigeons in the elevator. One more week here, I'd be ready to fall on my sword."

He was interested in knowing precisely what instruments, devices, tools they might be carrying. It would put things in perspective, having that information. It would clarify the relationship, subject to adjusters.

"Glen with one *n*," she said. "If you're bent on avoiding someone, how come you're standing in plain sight outside the selfsame car that you're getting ready to drive away in?"

He reacted as though coming out of a trance, a state of detachment from his present surroundings. Yet there was an element of alertness in his features, his whole body, as though at the center of that dazed state he'd found a level clearer than any thus far accessible to him.

He was facing east, watching the tops of buildings take on color in the hazy light.

1) A gut-hook skinning knife.

2) A fillet knife with a rosewood handle.

3) An Arkansas toothpick with a buffalo-horn handle.

4) A bowie weighing fifty-one ounces, with a ten-inch blade, scalloped butt cap and brass collar.

5) A throwing knife, minus handle.

6) A hunter with a cholla cactus handle.

7) A hunter with a dropped-point blade and a stag handle.

8) A boot knife with an ivory handle.

9) A stiletto.

10) A palm dagger.

11) An English-style bowie in a strictly decorative buckskin sheath.

12) A survival model with a hollow steel handle to accommodate codeine pills and water-purifying tablets.

13) A combat knife with a mahogany handle.

14) A combat knife with a brass guard and a five-inch blade.

15) A combat knife, walnut handle, set in a leather sheath.

16) A combat knife with a double-edged point and a seven-inch blade.

17) A combat knife with a double-edged point and an eight-inch blade.

5

The coffee table was new, inset with a plexiglass terrarium full of dwarf trees and shrubs. Grace Delaney talked into the phone, girlishly twirling the cord with her free hand. Eventually she went into her swivel routine, ending up facing the window. She hadn't yet poured skin cream on her hands, so Moll stayed put, studying the bonsai, marveling at the other woman's ability to produce convincingly intimate laughter.

Grace turned toward her, placing the phone in its cradle. "We were saying."

"You miss a sense of solid footing."

"Moll, a single unnamed source."

"We go with that all the time. That's why Percival handed me the story. We're totally irresponsible. He knows it gets picked up elsewhere once we run it."

"We ain't running it, swee' pea. It's essentially a blind item, the way you've written the thing. It's couched in the most excruciatingly vague terms."

"I use names," Moll said. "I name Mudger. I name Radial Matrix."

"It's convoluted and tricky and elusive beyond anyone's ability to salvage. It's a ten-thousand-word blind item. Clunk. It goes down like pig iron."

"What do you want changed?"

"I told you, it's unsalvageable. We can't build this elaborate dream structure using a single unnamed source who's already told you he denies everything in advance. The Senator's intent on moving you off his collection. That's about the only basis this story seems to have."

"He doesn't know I'm *on* to his collection."

"Knucklehead, of course he knows."

"Grace, goddamn."

"Want some coffee?"

"No."

Delaney opened a desk drawer and gestured questioningly.

"Okay," Moll said. "What is it?"

"Vodka."

"Okay."

She took the silver flask and drank.

"He knows, Moll. Of course he knows. He's got resources. He's got people all over the place. He's a fucking senator, isn't he?"

"I don't like these plants."

"Don't be stupid. They're beautiful."

"Too carefully sculptured. They don't look real."

"Go do your sex piece," Delaney said. "That was the original idea, wasn't it?"

"It's what led me precisely to the thing I ended up doing."

"Time's awastin', Moll."

"We've gone with riskier things."

Delaney reached for the hand lotion. Her secretary came in, a middle-aged woman named Bess Harris. Moll gave her the flask as she went by, and she put it on the desk. Grace picked it up and drank.

"Want to hear my theory?" she said. "This is my world view. What the whole thing's about, ultimately. Lloyd Percival and Earl Mudger and you and me and Bess and all of us. The bottom line."

"Go ahead," Moll said.

"All men are criminals. All women are Mafia wives."

"Stupid. Very stupid."

"I was married to the same man for eleven years. I did his bidding. Not fully realizing. His *silent* bidding. Somehow, mysteriously, unspokenly. It's built into the air between us. It's carried on radio waves from galaxy to galaxy."

Bess Harris drank from the flask.

"Not for a minute," Moll said. "I don't believe word one."

"I'm a Mafia wife."

"Grace, shut up."

Delaney took the flask from her secretary and drank.

"The ultimate genius of men. Do you care to know what it is? Men *want*. Women just hang around. Women think they're steaming along on a tremendous career, toot toot. Nothing. Nowhere, I'm telling you. Men *want*. Bam, crash, pow. The impact, good Christ. Men want so badly. It makes us feel a little spacey, a little dizzy. What are *we* next to this great want, this universal bloodsucking need of theirs? Bess, get the hell out of here. What are you doing here?"

"It doesn't reach me," Moll said.

"I have been backed into so many bloody corners, it's reached the point where I just react automatically. I am so tired. I am so up against it. Bam. I am so old. You wouldn't believe."

"You're not reaching me."

"They're crazy. That's their secondary genius. They're totally, rampagingly insane. Examine it. Really think. They're nuts."

"Who are you talking to?" Moll said.

"And we're their wives. We live with them."

"Because you're not talking to me."

"Examine it. Your own life. Dig really deep. It's there. One way or another, it's their game you play. Just so you know that. Just so you don't believe otherwise. Because forget it, you're not your daddy's little girl anymore."

"I know, Grace. The radio waves. The galaxies."

"Think it out. Dig down."

"Give me the flask, Grace."

"I am so old and tired."

"You won't go with the piece," Moll said. "Tell me so I can get out of here."

"I was against your idea about Percival's collection for the reasons I pointed out to you. Whatever they were. Lack of design, of political implications. This is a different issue, granted, this piece here, because there *is* design, there *are* implications, there *is* a web of sorts, a series of interconnections. But I can't and won't run it."

"Because you're old and tired," Moll said.

"Because it's too shaky. Too iffy. Not enough footing. I do miss that. A sense of solid footing."

"Thank you."

"Are we still friends?" Grace said.

Moll took a cab to the magazine's West Side office, where her own cubicle was located. She went to work reediting a piece written by a professor of Eastern European studies. He asserted that Russian parapsychologists, at the prodding of the KGB, were close to perfecting a system of assassination by mental telepathy. Moll, actually, didn't doubt it. She started playing with titles as the phone rang.

"Your old lemonade-drinking buddy."

"Who?"

"Earl Mudger."

"What do you want?"

"I'm heading your way."

"That so?"

"To do a little business. And I wonder if maybe you and I can get together and finish our talk."

"Weren't we finished?"

"Tell you what, I didn't think we'd hardly begun."

"Call me," she said.

"I'm thinking next Tuesday's probably when I'll be there. That sound about right?"

"Call me."

What you couldn't get from the printed page, the news clipping or court transcript, was the force of someone's immediate presence, the effect it had, someone's voice, mannerisms, the physical element, the eyes and body. Grace Delaney, for instance. Her eyes, her inflections, the way she'd moved in her chair as she was speaking. These told Moll there was a hidden reason why she didn't want to run the piece on Radial Matrix. Glen Selvy in long johns, his crooked mouth and frozen gray eyes. Mudger's blue eyes. Earl Mudger's voice talking about Lomax and Senator Percival, the fact that the former is the latter's chief source of select information, in a blacksmith's apron, his high shoulders, the twist in the bridge of his nose. Mudger's voice on the subject of his zoo in Vietnam. Mudger's eyes glancing at the old lady setting lemonade on their table, white wicker, the Shetland ponies grazing. Eyes, bodies, voices. The personal force. It's never the voice that tells the lies. Beware of personality. Dynamic temperament, beware.

These musings took place alongside Moll's search for a catchy title. KGB linked with ESP was too much alphabet. Telepathic hit-men. The idea was to work it into a larger framework without telling the whole story in the title. Or were you *supposed* to tell the whole story in the title?

Briefly she saw the man with ear protectors and tinted glasses standing in the door of Frankie's Tropical Bar, the weapon jumping in his hands as he fired.

Selvy had trouble concentrating. The miles were slowly unrolling at the back of his brain, leading him toward a vanishing point, deep sleep, the end of conscious scrutiny. He stood by the window of the small cabin. The place was called Motel in the Woods. The girl was in bed, asleep. It suited him to think of her as the girl. The girl is decent company. The girl does not complicate matters.

They would be here in a couple of minutes.

It was interesting that he'd done it again. Sex with an unmarried woman. Well, he'd been a little crazy that night. Sex with an unmarried woman in the front seat of a car parked on a city street and all the time he was being pursued by a pair of highly motivated combat veterans. Foreigners. Indifferent to local sex customs.

In a way his whole life in the clandestine service was a narrative of flight from women. To restrict his involvements to married women was to maintain an edge of maneuverability. He was able to define the style of a given affair, the limits of his own attachment. It suited him. Life narrowed down to intense segments. The equal pleasures of arrival and departure. They felt the same way no doubt, some of the women in question. Their comings and goings were regulated by external factors. It added force and depth and degree to sex. Selvy used these outer pressures to keep his role within certain well-defined limits.

He tried to concentrate.

The girl did not compromise the routine to any great extent. The girl was decent company. Would not unsettle things. Would not open up avenues of neurotic involvement. She was breathing quietly now, dreaming, he hoped, of some pastoral scene.

When he heard the microbus come up the bumpy motel road, he slipped out the door and walked through the darkness to the last cabin on the path to the woods. This cabin he knew to be unoccupied. His car was parked in front of it.

He stood at the edge of the woods, ten feet from the car. He watched the VW bus pull up at the adjoining cabin, also vacant. They got out, looking weary. They left the front doors open. One of them headed this way, checking his car, Selvy's. The other went back to the bus, probably to turn off the headlights.

Selvy walked out of the woods, showing the .41 magnum. The first ranger reacted but Selvy had the gun to his face, still walking, coming on, and the ranger back-pedaled, his arms at

RUNNING DOG / 136

his sides now, flush, apparently to indicate nonresistance. He backed into the side of the car, went down and then tried to scramble to his feet. Selvy, keeping an eye on the second ranger, put the gun right to this one's mouth, muzzle first, cracking teeth and driving the man back to his haunches against the front tire.

To keep him there, Selvy hit him across the left cheekbone with the gun butt. The other ranger was climbing into the back of the microbus. Selvy took an old pair of handcuffs out of his back pocket. He turned this one on his stomach and bent one leg way up behind him, limber little devil, cuffing the ankle to the opposite wrist. The second ranger closed the rear door.

Selvy searched this one, finding only a small knife with a slender tapering blade. He dropped it in the window of his car. Then he went to the VW and opened the rear door just a crack, inserting the mag in the opening, showing about four inches of barrel. No reaction. Not a sound. He opened the door slightly wider.

The ranger was squatting in the dark, holding a knife in his right hand, an inch above floor level. He was motionless. He was still as a wood carving. He waited there, facing Selvy, head-on.

The latter nodded and closed the door. He went into the vacant cabin and stood by the window. The ranger came out of the microbus and dragged and lifted his buddy into the front seat. Then he got in next to him and backed slowly down the motel road and out toward the highway.

Lomax sat at a corner table watching Earl Mudger make his way across the dining room of the Executive Towers Motor Inn, off Arlington Boulevard.

"It's about time we heard some news from the field. It's overdue. What are you drinking, Earl?"

"News. There's news."

"I just have to outright say it. I think it's a mistake. Selvy may have been leaning some. But I don't think he had an arrangement with the Ludecke woman."

"Who's Selvy?"

"The subject," Lomax said. "I think he may have been edging toward something. But I don't think he was there. I think he may have been helping the Robbins woman put some moves on the Senator. Personal reasons. He wanted off that assignment."

"He squashed my bug."

"Earl, he may not have known."

"He was trained to know. He knew. Of course he knew."

Lomax groomed his sideburns with the tips of his fingers. The waiter brought drinks and menus. He said something they didn't catch. People sitting nearby were turning to look at the bar. Mudger and Lomax glanced that way. Two men and a chimpanzee were seating themselves at the bar. They didn't react to the attention they were getting, and in moments people went back to their food and drink. The chimp wore a leisure suit with flared trousers.

"The FCB matter," Mudger said.

"She's still playing. She has to play. IRS has been breathing heavy ever since her days as a Panther bagwoman. They're looking at fraud."

"Can we get them to ease off, if and when?"

"No," Lomax said. "It was all I could do to get the file and tape."

"Does it matter?"

"I don't think so. She has to believe we have influence there, and she's aware they want to prosecute. We're buying time, that's all. Considering our lack of resources these days, it's all we can really hope to do."

"Been meaning to ask. How is it you're using these Dorish Reports? Granted, we're a corporate entity. But don't we have our own intelligence? If we don't, why don't we? I hate to think we have to use the same investigative service General Motors uses, or Chase Manhattan."

"It's ironic, Earl, but Selvy was in the process of putting together a report on FCB. We phased into adjustment before he was finished. With Selvy out, Earl, we really have no one fully capable."

"How did that happen, in fifty words or less?"

"How that happened, Earl, is when you broke away from PAC/ORD that was the end of our supply of trained investigators. We're not at all strong in the investigative area, Earl, these days. We're strong in the paramilitary area. We've got counterterrorists we can call on, for whatever it's worth, more or less around the clock."

"You think I failed to anticipate."

"In a matter like the FCB matter, we don't need but a single capable investigator. We don't really have one, sad to say. Thus the Dorish Report. Thus getting down on all fours to beg favors from an old friend at IRS."

"Tell you what let's do."

"You want me to shut up," Lomax said. "You think I'm being a little preachy. Okay, good beef here. Let's order."

Lomax chided himself for being slow to realize that Mudger was in a foul mood. He couldn't help being disappointed. He'd expected a word of commendation for his resourcefulness in gathering intelligence on the FCB matter. Now he'd have to wait for the right moment to bring it up again, or forget it completely.

FCB was the way they referred to Grace Delaney. It meant Flat-Chested Bitch.

Mudger kept looking over at the chimp. The restaurant manager was talking to the two men who flanked the animal. It seemed to Lomax from this distance that he was content to let them stay as long as nothing unseemly happened.

"I'm making moves," Mudger said. "That's how you keep going. You renew yourself. Systems planning is fundamentally lacking in one important respect."

"You've said. People."

"People, correct."

"Earl, it's peaked."

"I've been studying pornography for a long time now. Hell of an interesting field. Dynamics involved. The psychology. Interesting element. Strange arrays of people. Pacts and alliances and accommodations. That intrigues me. Systems is all formulation. Essentially sterile concepts. I miss human interest. The war was full of human interest."

"The thing has peaked, Earl."

"Multimillions. Close to a billion, including the soft stuff."

"You've had success employing unique methods. You go into smut in a big way, you'll find these methods aren't so unique."

"Don't I thrive on challenges?"

Lomax patted the top of his head.

"Isn't it all business? When you come right down to it? Isn't the whole thing just a slam-bang corporate adventure? Arthur? Isn't it?"

Lomax didn't like these moods.

"The profit on hard-core movies is awe-inspiring. You can make an X for fifty thousand and get a return in the millions. You don't even have to make. Alternatives exist. I've got people. I'm already tied in. All I need is product."

Mudger turned once more to glance at the bar.

"The chimp is ape family," he said after a while.

"I didn't know."

"Did you know that?"

"No," Lomax said.

"Most intelligent member, although some would dispute that."

"I'm a dog man."

"Some would say gorilla."

"Dessert, Earl?"

"Did you ever watch animals? Steadily watch? Because

there's things you can learn from watching animals go about
their business."

"I've got dogs. I watch dogs."

"If you said wolves."

"Domesticated. That's my range."

"Wolves. You ever watch wolves? I can remember outside
Tha Binh."

"I admit to snakes. I watch snakes."

"Snakes are good," Mudger said. "You can do worse than
snakes."

"But only at the zoo."

The waiter brought coffee.

"There's news all right," Mudger said.

"Where from?"

"Van's in the hospital. All busted up. Shattered cheekbone.
Teeth and gums."

"Which one is Van?"

"He's the one whose sister I'm married to."

"Sorry," Lomax said.

"Christ, it's hilarious. Cao doesn't know where the hell
they are. All I have is Mercy Hospital."

"Not what city."

"Not what fucking state," Mudger said. "He'd like for
someone to tell him what fucking state he's in. He knows
about four words of English. Van, with easily double that
vocabulary, has a mouthful of wires and little silver wheels."

"I told you that about Selvy."

"They're out there somewhere. One of them's got a busted
face. The other one, it's all he can do to call Tran Le on the
phone. Don't you know she doesn't take his number down? All
she gives me is Mercy Hospital."

"I told you. Selvy. They took him light."

"He'll make the same mistake if he thinks whatever happened is any real indication. They took him light, okay. But
those boys can deal. I've seen them. They're not your typical
ARVN grunt. He's up to his ass in it. And it's climbing fast."

"I say he'll handle it."

"You say he'll handle it."

"The thing about Selvy. Selvy's more serious than any of us. He believes. You ought to see where he lives. Where he used to live. Buried in some rat-shit part of the city. Isolated from contact. He'd do it for nothing, Selvy. The son of a bitch believes."

"Believes what?"

"Believes in the life."

"The life," Mudger said.

"Eleven weeks at the Mines, incidentally."

"Was he at the Mines?"

"I told you. Selvy. Best I've ever run."

Lomax signaled for the check.

"How will they find him now?"

"I'm a bitch if I know," Mudger said.

"Unless he drops into Mercy Hospital for an appendectomy, how the hell will they find him?"

Lomax paid the check and went to the men's room. On the way out, Mudger stopped at the bar. The chimp was eating mixed fruit out of a plastic bowl.

"How much you want for the animal?"

"Not for sale," one of the men said.

"Name your price, go on."

The man turned on his stool.

"Not for sale. No sale."

"You shouldn't dress the animal up. It's degrading to the animal, having to wear clothes."

"What ar·· you?"

"You think it's cute, coming into a bar with an animal. It's a joke, dressing the animal up and coming into a bar."

"What are you, a Christian Scientist?"

"It's a joke," Mudger said.

"A Jehovah Witness. They don't give blood."

The other man turned toward Mudger.

"He's asking. What are you?"

"Tell him to piss up a rope," Mudger said.

"He's asking politely."

"Tell him to piss up a rope."

Mudger put his middle finger to his thumb as if to flick an insect off his sleeve. Instead he delivered a quick blow to the second man's ear. The man reacted as if shot. Then he turned back to the bar, head down, right hand covering his ear.

"Tell him to piss up a rope," Mudger said.

Lomax was standing alongside, watching. The man turned to his companion, speaking over the chimp's head.

"Piss up a rope, Stanley."

Sitting in the passenger seat as Lomax drove, Mudger looked out the side window. His gloom hadn't lifted. He thought of his own animals, the ones he'd managed to take out of Vietnam. He'd had to leave them behind on Guam, every one, under enforced isolation. In the end, practical considerations and endless technicalities forced him to abandon the animals to the whims of local authorities. There were things you couldn't do once the shooting stopped.

He thought of Saigon women in their silk blouses and sateen pants. Beds draped with mosquito nets. The relentless drenching heat.

He thought of people sharing hammocks in open-fronted huts outside Tha Binh. VC gongs sounding through the night. Parachute flares from a C-47 lighting up part of the sky. The roiling din of Medivac choppers landing nearby.

He thought of GIs heading down jungle trails with transistor radios, tossing gum wrappers into the bush. Occasional rounds from an M-60 machine gun. The sandbagged checkpoints. The fresh weapons being broken out of crates. The *punji* sticks smeared with human feces.

6

Richie Armbrister flashed a look at his laser-beam digital watch. The elevator gate opened with a crash and he followed Lightborne into the gallery. They went directly to the living quarters in the rear, where Lightborne began boiling water for tea.

"So, delay number two. What's going on, Lightborne? I paid money."

"And it's in a safe place. And the lady will get it as soon as she hands over the film can."

"With the film inside it."

"I remain confident, Richie."

"I have things. I have a number of projects."

"I understand," Lightborne said.

"Do you know how long I've been away?"

"Go back to Dallas, Richie."

"I've never been away this long."

"I'll handle it from this end."

The wrist watch, or chronometer, was the sole outward sign of Richie's wealth, excluding his DC-9. He wore heavy-weight khaki trousers, scuffed cordovans and a crew-neck sweater with a reindeer design, the wool unraveling at both cuffs.

He appeared younger than twenty-two, looking a little like a teenager with a nervous disability. High forehead, prominent cheekbones, large teeth. He seemed intense, over-committed to something, his voice keening out of a lean bony face—a face Lightborne could never look at without wondering whether he was dealing with a genius or a half-wit.

Not that Richie's accomplishments were to be questioned. He'd built an empire almost singlehandedly. He'd perfected the technology of smut, opening up channels of distribution and devising ingenious marketing schemes. At the same time he'd managed to remain legally immune, hidden in a maze of paper.

"I leave Odell behind."

"Who?" Lightborne said.

"I leave Odell here. Odell is my technical man for all film projects. You and Odell stay in constant touch, Lightborne. That way I know what's going on."

"I'm all in favor."

"Odell is my cousin."

"I understand, Richie."

"He's one of the few people around me that I would use the word knowledgeable."

"I know how much value you attach to that word."

"What with the people I'm usually surrounded with."

"Plus he's a relative."

"They're imbeciles. They dribble. They have to be told over and over."

"Believe me, Richie, I understand, I'm in sympathy, I empathize completely."

Lightborne poured steaming water over the tea bags. If Richie wanted to live in the barricaded warehouse where his materials were stored, that was fine with Lightborne. He himself, in Richie's position, might have chosen a quiet street in Highland Park.

If Richie elected to surround himself with people he'd known all his life—the bodyguards, the advisers, the relatives, the hangers-on, and the husbands, wives, girlfriends and boyfriends of all of these—Lightborne wasn't inclined to raise trivial objections, although in the same position he would have set up a board of administrators. Men and women skilled in diverse corporate fields. Perhaps an academic presence as well.

"I don't know about staying, Lightborne. Do I have time for a cup of tea?"

"It's your plane, Richie. The plane doesn't leave until you're ready."

"I'm ready. I'm anxious to scram."

"Drink your tea. I have a gift."

"There's an element in this business," Richie said. "They're taking more and more. They're very grabby. And something's been going on. My bodyguard thinks he's been seeing the same face, wherever we go, for the past three days. Not that his expertise is worth two dollars on the open market. But I'm better off home. Where I know where I am."

"You tell Odell I'm standing by."

"I'll be waiting for word. I'll be expecting. This is the big thing today. First-run movies. People want to tone up their fantasies. Feature-length is the right direction. I'll be waiting, Lightborne. I'll be looking forward."

"Finish your tea, Richie."

Earlier in the day, after searching in hardware stores, millinery shops, Fourteenth Street rummage dumps, Lightborne had finally found what he was looking for. He found it in a grocery store on Thompson Street, not far from his building. With Thanksgiving not too far off, the place was well stocked with specialty items. The Danish butter cookies, Lightborne noticed, came in circular metal containers, precisely the kind of thing he was looking for. He chose the super economy size.

"A little something I bought for your trip, to munch on the plane going back."

"What is it, candy?"

"Cookies," Lightborne said.

After displaying the shiny can, he wrapped it tightly in plain brown paper, very tightly, so that anyone watching Richie emerge from the building would have no trouble noting the circular shape. He used gummed tape, masking tape, glue and string to keep the wrapping intact.

"Cookies. Festive cookies. To make the trip go faster."

How much more pleasant it was to talk with Miss Robbins, who arrived about half an hour after Richie left. Not that he disliked Richie. Richie had human qualities. More than once he'd given Lightborne a token of his continuing friendship. String ties. A set of coasters depicting scenes of the Alamo. It was only fitting that Lightborne eventually reciprocate.

He asked Moll Robbins if she'd prefer another chair. She was sitting in the chair with the broken springs and had sunk considerably into it. She waved him off, eager to hear why he'd asked her to drop by.

"I'm still the chief skeptic in this enterprise."

"I remember your saying."

"Do you remember Glen Selvy? The man who was here the night I first mentioned the Berlin film."

"Yes."

"The man bidding on behalf of a certain someone."

"I remember," she said.

"That certain someone's been in direct contact with me."

"Lloyd Percival."

Lightborne sat back, stroking the side of his jaw.

"You've been active."

"On and off," she said.

"I was surprised when you said you hadn't finished the series."

"I got sidetracked."

"But you're back with it."

"It would seem."

"Then I'm glad I called," he said. "It's my feeling that a journalist on the scene tends to advance whatever is meet and just in a given situation."

"Hip hip."

"Of course my own role must be handled circumspectly. This isn't Lightborne the dealer in erotic junk, outgoing and colorful. This is a source close to the situation. This is a well-placed source. My name mustn't see print."

"I give the usual assurances."

"This footage is arousing mighty appetites. Let me tell you, I've been turning it in my mind. The utterly compelling

force of the man. He wasn't impotent, you know, despite earlier claims to that effect."

"Hitler, you mean."

"He had a remarkable impact on women. They sent him
love letters, sex poems, underwear. His motorcades, women
hurled their bodies at his car. Like a pop hero. Some modern
rock 'n' roller. Women threw themselves beneath the wheels."

"Surface affection," Moll said.

"Girls were constantly offering to yield their virginity to
him. We see his speeches, where women fell into states of
hysteria. We see collective frenzy. He had hypnotic powers
over women. I think this is clear."

"You're suggesting there's some basis."

"The rumors have never specified the old boy," he said.

"You're building a case."

"Think of the value such footage would have. And the
man with whom I originally discussed this matter, I recall
him clearly stating that I wouldn't be disappointed in the
identities of those who appear."

"Dead, I recall! your saying."

"This matter is fraught with every kind of pressure. I myself have put certain forces to work. I've also taken action to
deflect attention. I feel more secure now, people knowing
there's a journalist in the vicinity."

"How do people know?"

"I think they know."

"You feel they have ways of knowing."

"They know. I think they know."

He turned off one of the two lights in the room. Moll
decided her chair was in fact uncomfortable and pushed up
out of it, moving to a metal folding chair near the bookcase.

"He had youthful fantasies about a blond girl in Linz,"
Lightborne said. "There were other blonds later who were
more than fantasy. He may have had an eye for blonds. Also
an eye for actresses. His niece of course. An all-consuming
affair. When you get serious with nieces, this is suggestive of

a deep fire in the man." Pause. "He made drawings. He sketched her parts. At close range."

"That showed bad taste."

Lightborne made a worldly gesture.

"Before pop art, there was such a thing as bad taste. Now there's kitsch, schlock, camp and porn."

"But wasn't he in terrible shape at the end? Totally spaced on medication."

"My point exactly," Lightborne said. "I've made that point. He was enfeebled. I think it was his right arm, shaking wildly. They were using leeches for his blood pressure. He'd aged shockingly."

"You concede this is evidence against."

"I insist on it," he said. "I'm advancing theories largely for my own delectation. I admit. I'm making noises, merely."

"I never thought of him as a lover."

"Not your type."

"In addition to which I have to say I don't really understand why droves of people would pay money to see some gray old staticky footage of a funny-looking man running around naked, even if he was who he was."

"I've made that point. It's a vital question. *Who cares?* Yet I'm getting vibrations from all over. People with money and power. Forces are collecting around this thing, jumpy footage or not. You look a little bored, Miss Robbins."

"Not at all," she said. "It's just that I don't see what the appeal is. It's a little distasteful, frankly. Not that I'm above such things, Mr. Lightborne. But, really, all this activity for what?"

"Because it's him. Hitler. The name, the face. All the contradictions and inconsistencies. It would take an hour to list them."

"All great men. We know about great men and their public and private selves."

"Very furtive mind. Many doors locked. Hints, whispers of unnatural sexuality. Hush-hush even today. Women associ-

ated with Hitler tended to commit suicide or at least to attempt it. After his death, women all over Germany killed
themselves. Suicides unnumbered."

"Are you trying to depress me?"

"The bunker was an interesting mix. You had secretaries,
orderlies, SS guards, kitchen staff, so on. There were women
brought in off the streets by and for the SS men. You had
visitors from military units. There was a drunken revel, a sex
thing, in the SS rooms. How many people involved I don't
know."

"Maybe that's it. The footage."

"They thought he was dead. They were celebrating. But
he didn't do it till later. True, maybe that's it. But I'm holding
out hope for better."

"The old boy himself."

"We live in curious times," Lightborne said reflectively.

He thanked her for coming and promised to keep her
closely informed. They walked through the darkened gallery
toward the door. Moll bumped into a table and Lightborne
apologized, asking her to remain there while he turned on a
light. She noticed he didn't go for the wall switch but instead
walked to a corner of the room to turn on a small lamp, the
bulb perhaps twenty-five watts.

"It's getting so I don't like well-lighted rooms, or talking
on the telephone. I never had a suspicious nature. Old age, I
guess. First signs of deterioration."

"You've got a long way to go, Mr. Lightborne, I would
judge."

"First signs."

"We're all a little wary."

He nodded, standing in the dimness. She recalled the first
night she'd been here, the room getting progressively darker
as he went around turning off lights, giving her clues to Selvy's destination that night.

"Go into a bank, you're filmed," he said. "Go into a department store, you're filmed. Increasingly we see this. Try on a

dress in the changing room, someone's watching through a one-way glass. Not only customers, mind you. Employees are watched too, spied on with hidden cameras. Drive your car anywhere. Radar, computer traffic scans. They're looking into the uterus, taking pictures. Everywhere. What circles the earth constantly? Spy satellites, weather balloons, U-2 aircraft. What are they doing? Taking pictures. Putting the whole world on film."

"The camera's everywhere."

"It's true."

"Even in the bunker," she said.

"Very definitely."

"Everybody's on camera."

"I believe that, Miss Robbins."

"Even the people in the bunker under the Reich Chancellery in April 1945."

"Very definitely the people in the bunker."

"You believe that, Mr. Lightborne."

"I have the movie," he said.

He'd moved gradually to the end of the room, about twenty feet from the source of light, standing against a blank wall, suddenly disproportionate in shape, an illusion sustained by his own shadow on the wall behind him. His body seemed tiny. He was all head.

"Have you looked at it?"

He moved toward her a step or two, as though to whisper, a strange gesture considering the space between them.

"I haven't even opened the can."

He laughed.

"I'm waiting for technical help."

He laughed again.

"I'm afraid the whole thing will crumble if I open the can the wrong way. It's been in there over thirty years. There's probably a right way and a wrong way to open film cans when the film's been in there so long. There might be a preferred humidity. Safeguards. Recommended procedures."

"Who is your technical help?"

"Odell Armbrister."

This time Moll laughed.

"Richie's cousin," he whispered.

"Who is Richie?"

"Richie Armbrister's cousin. The Dallas smut king. The boy genius. That lives in a warehouse."

"Fascinating," she said.

Lightborne sank into a chair, wearied by these disclosures.

"Fascinating, yes. An interesting word. From the Latin *fascinus*. An amulet shaped like a phallus. A word progressing from the same root as the word 'fascism.' "

He was whispering again.

On a straightaway on U.S. 67, Glen Selvy, both hands on the wheel, decided to close his eyes and count to five. He didn't hurry the count. At five he even paused for half a second before opening his eyes again.

He was going eighty.

PAC/ORD had recruited openly. They needed administrators, clerical people, personnel investigators, career panelists, budget directors. As Selvy progressed through batteries of tests and interviews, he began to realize he was part of an increasingly selective group of candidates. Everybody else filed into Rooms 103, 104 or 105. Selvy's group convened behind an unmarked door.

There were weeks of further culling. Periodic technical interviews, or polygraphs. A progressively clearer picture. At intervals, candidates were asked to state their willingness or unwillingness to continue the program.

Selvy went on salary in a PAC/ORD division called Containment Services, Guidance and Support. For six weeks he checked personnel files and evaluated job candidates. This led to another series of tests, including thorough physicals. At

intervals, he was asked to state his willingness or unwillingness to continue the program.

He saw her waving: Nadine Rademacher.

She was standing outside a Howard Johnson's located near
a highway interchange. She got into the car smiling and
hefted her suitcase over the back of the seat as Selvy drove
off.

"Nice seeing Joanie. You could have done worse than
show up for a little home cooking. Where to next?"

"Where to next."

"All these ramps and levels. You be sure to pick a good one
now."

"I think we ought to just keep going in the same straight
line we've been going in ever since New York."

"Have we been going in a straight line?"

"Ever since New York."

"I'm glad to see you, Slim. Were you afraid I wouldn't
think you'd show up?"

"We'll have to go through that question point by point
some time."

"It's a tricky one."

"Where to next," he said. "Check the glove compartment."

"You're looking kind of tired and glum."

"There's a map."

"Tell you what I don't like. It's this little nip in the air. It's
too early and we're too far south."

Her hand came away from the glove compartment holding
the small dagger that Selvy had taken from the ranger about a
day and a half earlier. She waited for him to notice.

"What's that?" he said.

"Hey, bub."

"I use it for fingernails. A grooming aid."

"Is this what they call an Arkansas toothpick?"

"This is smaller."

"Being we're in Arkansas."

"You thought you'd ask."

"What's it for?" she said.

"I slash mattresses when I'm depressed."

They sent him to Marathon Mines. Here he attended classes in coding and electronic monitoring. There was extensive weapons training. He took part in small-scale military exercises. He studied foreign currencies, international banking procedures, essentials of tradecraft. For the first time he heard the term "funding mechanism."

His instructors conveyed the impression that he was part of the country's most elite intelligence unit. It was manageably small; it was virtually unknown; there was no drift, no waste, no direct accountability. He heard the words "Radial Matrix."

A great deal of time was spent studying and discussing the paramilitary structure of rebel groups elsewhere in the world.

They analyzed the setup the Vietcong had used. The part-time village guerrilla. The self-contained three-man cell. And *tieu to dac cong*, the special duty unit considered the most dangerous single element in the VC system. Suicide squads. Special acts of sabotage in ARVN-controlled areas. High-risk grenade assaults. Assassination teams.

They studied the Algerian *moussebelines*, or death commandos, groups undertaking extremely hazardous operations independent of local army control. They discussed the action of the FLN bomb network that operated out of the Casbah, maintaining a state of terror for nearly a year despite its limited numbers.

Selvy thought it curious that intelligence officers of a huge industrial power were ready to adopt the techniques of ill-equipped revolutionaries whose actions, directly or indirectly, were contrary to U.S. interests. The enemy. This curious fact was not discussed or studied. He heard the phrase "internal affairs enforcement."

Groups attached to various agencies, U.S. and foreign, trained at the Mines. From people belonging to some of these groups, Selvy kept hearing about the exploits of the original

chief training officer—the man, more than any other, responsible for the techniques and procedures currently employed.
Earl Mudger. Said to be in business these days somewhere in
the East.

"Remember chocolate cigarettes?" Nadine said.

Selvy drove along a two-lane road until they found a restaurant. It was a long room with a state trooper at one table
talking to a waitress in sneakers.

"Miss the lights?" Selvy said.

"Gotta be kidding."

"Times Square."

"Arm, leg, hip, breast."

"You think that woman might come over and take our
order sometime before sundown."

"She's visiting, Glen."

"What's he doing?"

"I think he's sniffing."

"That's what I think."

"I think he's getting ready to kick dirt."

"Call her over," he said.

"What's the rush?"

"Get back to our straight line."

When the food came they ate quietly. A small white worm
moved over a lettuce leaf in the center of Selvy's plate. He ate
around it.

"I used to work in Sample's Café in Langtry," Nadine said.
"I think it's uncanny the straight line goes past my sister, goes
past my dad."

"You want to see him, don't you?"

"I don't know," she said. "He was pretty close to being an
all-out bastard, no holds barred. It was only my mom made
things bearable. When she died, Joanie took off like a bat. It
took me a little longer. I was always slow to notice what was
going on. But I see it a little clearer now. The man just isn't
very nice."

"Lives alone?"

"You ought to see the house. It's a shack, just about. Half the things in our house my mom made out of old feed sacks. Dish towels, face towels, napkins, even a lot of our clothes. Pillow cases. Feed sack pillow cases. Feed sack dresses and skirts."

"Recycling."

"Poverty," she said.

About half a mile from the main highway they passed an abandoned farm. Selvy eased the car into some weeds. He reached into a carton in the back seat and removed the smaller of his two handguns, the .38. He walked through the front gate to a deep-water well not far from the main house. Holding the gun flat on his upturned palm, he tossed it about two feet into the air and watched it fall into the well. A blunt muffled sound came up to him.

Looking into the setting sun, Nadine squinted at him as he walked back to the car.

"What's this business about a straight line?" she said.

Back in Washington, he realized something was different. A man named Lomax came to his hotel. There was no mention of PAC/ORD or Containment Services. People he'd worked with didn't return his calls. He no longer seemed to be on salary.

Lomax took him for a ride in a black limousine. He said that Radial Matrix had severed all relationships with official agencies of the government. Systems planning would still be done out of headquarters in Fairfax County. All clandestine work would issue from this operation and its spin-offs. There was no other headquarters. There was no table of organization. There was no structure, no infrastructure. Only the haziest lines of command.

Lomax repeated what Selvy had learned at the Mines. Rebel movements drew their strength from the fact that their political and their military functions were one and the same.

Here, Lomax told him, business operations and clandestine activity are combined in very much the same way. One doesn't support the other. One *is* the other.

Selvy traveled in North America, then throughout Europe and parts of Asia. He gathered information on Radial Matrix competitors. He made undercover payments to representatives of prospective Radial Matrix clients. He paid secret commissions to agents of foreign governments. He arranged the disappearance of a trade commissioner on holiday in Greece. He financed the terrorist bombing of a machine-tool plant. Legitimate business expenditures.

Lomax called him back to the States. They needed a reader. Temporary assignment. Selvy's name had popped out of the computer.

Four days a week he went to a white frame house in Alexandria. A woman named Mrs. Steinmetz gave him private lectures, with slides, on art history. She accompanied him on visits to the National Gallery and the Hirshhorn. She showed him reproductions of sexually explicit art and discussed the esthetics involved.

Two days a week he went to a suite in an office building near Union Station. Here a Mr. Dempster explained House and Senate protocol and procedures. He gave Selvy reading matter on the subject. Eventually he provided a résumé— background, education, past employment, so forth. All of it was verifiable, none of it true.

The head of Percival's staff was impressed. He arranged an interview with the Senator. The Senator kept returning to the subject of Selvy's art background. He arranged a luncheon, during which Selvy was hired.

The black limousine turned up again. Lomax told him that until further notice he'd be paid by dead-letter drop. There was a pension scheme in the works.

For a month Selvy did staff work in Percival's office. The Senator arranged a small dinner at his Georgetown house. Selvy remained after the other guests left. They had a few.

They talked. They had another. The Senator showed him a room with a spinning wheel and an antique desk. Then he led him through the fireplace to the interior of the house next door.

"This is my true life," he said. "This is what I am."

They came out of the hills into ranch country, unbroken skyline and spare plains. They traveled slowly, stopping when possible along the main road for food and rest. Some days they went only twenty miles. Selvy didn't sleep much. The nights were cool.

On a small rise he spotted a curve in the road up ahead. He closed his eyes and counted to seven, easing the steering wheel left at four, when he'd estimated the car would reach the bend.

Richie Armbrister sat naked in the sauna. The man on the bench facing him was also naked. Through the steamy haze, Richie tried to get a good look at his face, without actually staring. The man was plumpish. Early forties, probably. Some gray at the temples. He seemed perfectly relaxed, which indicated he belonged here, or thought he did.

They exchanged a faint smile through the steam.

Richie got up and put his head out the door. In the passenger compartment a party was going on. People danced in the disco area while others sat around eating snacks and drinking. The co-pilot emerged from the flight deck through a beaded curtain and accepted a sandwich from Richie's bodyguard's girlfriend.

It was this bodyguard whose eye Richie was trying to catch. Daryl Shimmer. A rangy Negro skittering over the dance floor, all ripples and blind staggers. Richie wondered why this passionate concentration, so typical of his entourage, was forever being applied to ends other than his, Richie's, peace of mind.

Failing to attract Daryl's attention, he closed the door,

took a pitcher and poured more water on the heated rocks. Then he sat back down.

The man leaned toward him in the fog.

"We want to talk about a can of film."

"We being who?" Richie said.

"You and me."

"I don't want to do any talking about any can of film."

"It's on this plane. I think I speak for both of us."

"You think you speak for both of us when you say what?"

"That's it's on this plane."

"Nothing you mention is on any plane I know of."

"Richie, be a grownup."

"Do we know each other?"

"I'm called Lomax."

"Why are you here?"

"I could tell you I was supposed to meet another party. Aboard a different plane. There was a mixup. I found myself on the wrong plane. That's one version."

"Nobody checked? Nobody asked you?"

"Apparently I'm one of those people who blends well. I'm not noticeable. That's something I've had to learn to live with. Blending well. Failing to stand out."

"They know I'm here. Daryl and those. In case you're wondering."

"There's another version."

"I don't want to hear it."

"You're fully grown, Richie. You're not going to get any bigger. It's only right we treat each other as adults."

"Yeah, but for right now I have to start getting ready because we'll be landing soon."

"Certainly."

"Landing is bad enough with clothes on."

"I understand," Lomax said. "We'll continue later."

Richie got dressed and went out to the passenger compartment. He was stopped by a young woman named Pansy. She was Daryl Shimmer's girlfriend and for weeks she'd been trying to prevail upon Richie to get Daryl a dune buggy with chromed exhausts for his birthday. Richie was in no mood.

"Look around," he told her. "All these Vic Tanny imbeciles with their goggles, their male jewelry, their sculptured hair. It's like helmets they're wearing. It never moves, short of an earthquake. Get them out of here with their dipping shirtfronts, with their space boots. I want normal for a change. I want ordinary. People with real hair. I want less orgasmics around here. Everybody looks like they're climaxing. I walk into the warehouse, there's live bands, people writhing. I get on the plane, they're still shaking, it never stops. What happened to normal? Where is normal?"

About fifteen minutes later, as the plane approached D-FW, Lomax sat in a swivel chair, belted in, munching on roasted nuts. People were still dancing. He glanced over at Richie Armbrister. With the plane descending toward the runway, Richie had assumed a bracing position. His shoes were off. There was a pillow squeezed between the fastened seatbelt and his stomach. Another pillow lay across his knees. He'd bent his upper body well forward, head resting on this second pillow. His bony hands were clasped behind his knees.

Nadine crawled across the motel bed. Reaching over Selvy's body, she pointed one end of the cylindrical reading lamp right at his face.

"What are you?"

"Explain," he said.

"I'm analyzing your features."

"Racially, you mean. As to type and so forth."

"What are you?"

"An Indian."

"You don't look like an Indian."

"I've trained myself to look different. There's exercises you can do. Muscular contractions."

"Those aren't Indian features, Glen. You're not Indian stock."

"You can look different if you train. You start with a good mirror. It's like anything. Quality tells. You get yourself a quality mirror."

"If you're an Indian, that's not your name, what you've been telling people all these years. What's your real name, your Indian name?"

"Running Dog," he said.

III Marathon Mines

1

Van wasn't ready for solid foods. He was living on milk shakes and soup. He never complained, Cao noticed, but he was clearly more intense than usual. That was worse than complaints.

They listened to country music and kept on driving, through Lexington, Bowling Green, Memphis, Little Rock, Dallas, San Angelo, and on toward a pinpoint on the map called Ozona.

Road signs baffled Cao. The country grew rugged, empty and vast. He wanted to turn back. It was Van who kept them rolling. His cheek was still badly bruised. His upper lip was swollen and purplish. He referred to his road map constantly when he wasn't driving.

In Ozona, the lone town in a sprawling county, they saw a Toyota that appeared to match the one they were looking for. It was parked in a service station, off to one side, away from the pumps. A young woman sat on the fender drinking a Coke. Using binoculars, Cao checked the license. D.C. plates. Numbers matched.

The rangers were parked alongside the town square. Van showed his partner the map, gesturing excitedly at the line he'd drawn from New York, where they'd started, through a point tangent to the curve in the Ohio River near Huntington, where they'd been ambushed and humiliated, and down across four states and into Mexico. The line was straight and passed very near Ozona.

Cao was happy because Van was happy.

It was decided Van would telephone Earl Mudger. Van knew the place names and had an easier time pronouncing them.

Moll sat in the back of a checkered cab, thinking this was the best time of year, unarguably—the snap and clarity of autumn. The driver kept missing lights, mumbling to himself.

At one of these lights a car appeared on the right, a silver Chrysler. From the corner of her eye, Moll watched the driver's window come steadily down. Reflections gradually vanished, replaced by Earl Mudger's smiling face.

"I called."

"Once."

"I see," he said. "You have a point system."

"Did you leave a number?"

"There's a point system in effect. I lost points."

"I don't think you left a number."

"I called only once and I didn't leave a number. I'm dead. They're taking me away. A new low, pointwise."

The light changed. Her driver edged the cab forward. Mudger kept pace so that his front door was even with the taxi's rear door.

"My car or yours?" he said.

"I like it this way."

"Tell you what."

Horns were blowing. Her driver was mumbling again. They crawled up Central Park West. Mudger suddenly floored it. There was a split second of noisy tire-gripping and then the Chrysler sprang forward. Half a block away he braked into a U-turn and went slamming into a parking space nose first. The door opened and he came ambling out, crossing the center stripes just as the taxi approached. He kept on walking, forcing the cab to stop, and then came around the right side and opened the rear door. Moll slid over in the seat. Mudger got in and closed the door as the sound of horns grew thick behind them.

"We want the park," Mudger told the driver. "Flip an R first chance and make some circles in the park."

He looked at Moll.

"You like these old cabs."

"Character."

"I don't know how to talk to you. You know that? I think that's why I'm here. To learn how to talk to you."

"I thought our chat went fairly well."

"You had me on the defensive," he said.

"It was your territory."

"You don't know what to call me, do you? We have this little difficulty with names."

"It was your territory. You managed my arrival and departure."

"We have this little tension between us."

They were in Central Park, heading north toward the Eighty-sixth Street transverse.

"Here on business, I think you said."

"Lining up customers."

"What for?"

"The Mudger tip."

"Yes, your invention. I recall."

"Steel," he said.

Heading east they passed the volleyball courts where she'd played tennis with Selvy. These goddamn bastards. Who were they and what did they want?

"This is your territory," he said. "Which means I don't stand a Chinaman's chance."

"You're still managing the arrivals."

"Only my own."

"You're commandeering taxis. That little old man is terrified."

"After we ride around a while and get all this dialogue out of our systems, I think we ought to have some dinner."

"I've given it up," she said.

"What else have you given up?"

"You guessed it."

"Now why would you want to do a thing like that?"

"The humor's gone out of it. It's basically a humorous pastime, but lately the laughs have been few and far between."

"Two myths about women. Women see the humor in sex and appreciate men who do the same. Women care more for tenderness than for the act itself, the hardware involved—techniques, proportions, etcetera."

"Who's talking about sex? I'm talking about movies. Going to the movies."

"I said it, didn't I? Don't stand a chance. She left me gasping."

"What is it about our sparring and jabbing that gives you so much pleasure?"

"Does it show?" he said. "I didn't know it showed."

"I think that's called a shit-eating grin."

"It's my military smile. Can't seem to shake it."

"We've all read about the tough time you combat vets have had making the transition. One day you're standing around a provincial interrogation center, supervising the torture of some farmer."

"Better slow down," he told her.

"Next day you're back in the States, looking around, a little bewildered. It's no wonder you're still using the same smile. I know, the farmer was dangerous. The enemy was everywhere."

"You're way beyond your range."

"True," she said. "It's prim and smug for noncombatants to

criticize Those Who Were There. I understand that viewpoint and sympathize with it. Still, I've always felt the best view is the objective one, and sometimes this is made sharper and keener by distance. By thousands of intervening miles. The suffering we witness on either side can amount to a lie. But you're right, by and large. In my ridiculous urge to be fair, I definitely see your viewpoint. And I agree. I'm beyond my range. So let's stay closer to home. Things I've heard and seen."

The cab headed downtown along the western edge of the park.

"You and the Senator are chasing the same item. I know what it is, although I can't say I fully understand the various motivations. Doesn't matter. What's important is that a man was killed because of it."

"You think that's important."

"It merits consideration."

"I don't think it's so important."

He was crowding her a bit, edging her way, his left arm moving along the back of the seat.

"Are you learning how to talk to me?" she said.

"What?"

"You said you didn't know how to talk to me. That's why you're here, you said."

"I'm learning something. I'm not sure what it is. You think that's important. A man was killed. Did you think that was important ten years ago? In the days of your demolitions expert."

"You know about him. Of course."

"Of course I know. Late, great Gary Penner. And there you were, a slip of a girl, in your greatcoat with epaulets. How many people did Gary put into orbit, plying his trade? You ought to know. Living with the man. Having lived with the man. A few night watchmen. A few passersby. Arm here, leg there."

She looked out the window.

"You didn't take part directly. Enough fun just watching from the sidelines. But you've matured, haven't you? Terror isn't the erotic commodity it used to be. We know too much. We've seen. We've taken up organic gardening."

"You think I've matured, do you?"

"Somewhat," he said. "To a certain extent. Enough so that you've drawn a line."

The smile. The head tilting right.

"What you think is taking place, I'm flat-out telling you it's not that way. To the extent I straightened out the alliances for you once before, that's the way it still stands. There you go now. Putting me on the defensive again."

"In the flesh you have your convincing moments. I'm the first to admit."

"We have this tension. The air's a little crackly. Maybe I shouldn't let it bother me. Maybe it's auspicious. It might be I'm misreading the thing completely. Sometimes tension's to be encouraged. Sure, tension's a bitch of a stimulant some-times. See, down home everything's so smooth, so mellow, a man can be put off by the little mocking noises he hears in a place like New York. Sure, these little whipcracks, these hard edges. Personal relations work like machinery. The air is taut. People know what they want. There's a rasp, a little machine-like whine you hear in conversations in restaurants and shops. Women walk around with little numbers clicking behind their eyeballs. I wonder what they're seeing in there. My impres-sion, New York women, they're always keeping something in reserve, holding it back, saving the little extras. Who for, who for? Their analysts. That's why bald-headed Jews always look so happy. Nobody keeps a secret from a bald-headed Jew. They get all the leftovers, the most interesting parts, the greasiest and wettest and sweetest and best. Let me figure out how to decipher this suspense between us. I want to see if I can find out what it is people enjoy about these uneasy codes they keep sending into the air, all this nervous strain. Ten-sion's an edge, that must be it, a goading force, a heightener.

It betokens something good. Maybe there's a wild time in the works. What do you think? Who knows? Some all-out super-sonics."

He started edging toward her again. Twilight. The cab moving uptown now. Fifth Avenue's taupe stone buildings. That surfer's gleam rising to Mudger's face. His lustrous blue eyes seemed to have been attached to him independent of his other features. They were devices of a sensitivity and distinctness she didn't associate with Mudger, although she was willing to consider the possibility she was wrong. All she had to do was recall the number of varying moods he'd already composed and demolished in the relatively brief time they'd been in the taxi together.

She would have liked to suspend judgment, somehow to sabotage her own capacity to perceive the crux of things. When she was with Mudger earlier, in Virginia, sitting under the scarlet oaks, she'd felt they were communicating from either side of a semitransparent curtain or theatrical scrim. It was a weakness of hers. She liked drifting into strange terrains. It was what she'd had for a while with Selvy. That other son of a bitch. That son of a bitch in entirely different ways.

But things were clearer now. She was able to follow this man's line of attack, or that man's, or the other's, nearly to the end. The only real question remaining was a rhetorical one, a lament, uttered solely for effect. Who are these bastards and what do they want?

They passed a horse-drawn cab, four tourists huddled in the chill. Some kids chased each other across the road, causing the driver to start mumbling. Mudger sat with his head tilted back. She noticed the cuts and crosshatchings on his fingers, the eroded skin near his thumbnails.

"Who are you sleeping with these days?" he said.

"That's what my father used to ask me."

"Was he jealous?"

"Just sophisticated, that's all, and a little stupid."

"You should have slept with Percival. He knows interesting people. You could have had some sneaky fun. Junkets galore. You could have written a book. Lloyd's into everything. He'd love having someone like you to show off for. We talk, Lloyd and I. Not directly. There are channels. It never hurts to stay in touch."

He was getting ready to deliver another preemptive speech. Moll had noticed during their first meeting how he tried to establish prior rights to convictions and views he assumed she held. A tactic she found amusing.

"People are born conservative. They have to learn how to be liberal. In substance, at the bedrock, we're all of us conservative. People at the helm, I'm talking about. Lloyd's an instance of this. Slowly, surely reverting. Progress, mild reforms, old Lloyd's made a name. But those are the gleanings, the accidents, the random accretions. It all slides off eventually. It becomes sheer biology at a certain point." Here he smiled thinly, as though anticipating a joke on himself. "You return to your origins. What's old age but a kind of jaded infancy? You get physically smaller. You start to babble. You become sexually neuter."

"Poor Lloyd Percival."

"Now, myself, I'm getting out before any of those dire things can happen to me."

"Yes, you've said."

"The corollary to secrecy and power in this country is self-pity. I want to avoid that if I can."

The meter read twenty-one dollars.

"We're not getting anywhere, Earl."

"At least you call me by my name."

"It signifies an end to tension. To all these energies you tell me you detect in the air."

"I only sense what's there."

"Ride's over."

"That's regrettable."

"Your specialized bullshit versus my debased sensibility."

"She's warming up at last."

"If bullshit was music, you'd be a brass band."

"Don't stop now."

"It's over, really."

"What else do you have?"

"Nothing else," she said.

Mudger leaned toward the bulletproof partition.

"Flip an L," he told the driver.

"Flip an R. Flip an L."

"Old man doesn't like me, it appears."

"He belongs in the archives," the driver mumbled into his steering wheel.

"Picturesque old character."

"He's an oral history. Keep talking. I'll find a museum."

"Ought to be driving a hansom. You ought to be driving a hansom cab with a colorful personality like that."

Mudger sat back, smiling. It was an unsatisfactory way to end. Caricatures and gibes. Moll felt an injustice was being done to her own feelings, which were complex.

A downpour hit. The cab was stopped outside her building. Mudger sat in darkness, looking straight ahead. He didn't speak until Moll reached for the door, and then very quietly began. With rain beating down on the hood and roof, she had to concentrate intently to hear.

"I've seen you in motion, physically, only once. Walking toward my house that time. Getting out of the limousine and coming slowly toward the house. I remember it. It's engraved. It's the clearest picture I have of you. Physically in motion. Long legs. Long legs kill me. I'd die for long legs. I see you walking. You're tentative, not knowing really where you are. It's a lovely, a choice body. Forgive the crudeness. It's a choice body. Then you're standing still. Watching me in the doorway. I'd love to get my hands on that body. That's a little strong. That's crude. A little violent-sounding. But it's what I'd love to do. My hands, those legs. Feel those long legs wrapped around me. That's what I was thinking in that doorway. First time I saw you. Love to get my hands on that body. Has to happen, I thought. Must happen. I want that bitch. We'll fuck each other dizzy. We'll be walking in circles for two weeks. I'm trying not to be crude. Although I don't think you mind. You're way beyond minding a thing like that. Woman like you. Long legs like yours. You don't mind a little rough language, a touch of the unrefined. Legs like yours, and I'm only speculating, you can't possibly be put off by a little directness, a crude word now and again. This is number two. Second time I'm watching. Only this time you're walking away. Cunt. Aren't you? Only this time you're leaving, not arriving. Aren't you? Cunt. Bitch. Cunt."

He spoke softly all the way through, almost wistfully, even to the very end, so that his words were touched with a curious melancholy, a tone of longing. This was strange, of course, the voice he'd chosen, considering what he had to say. It was like a formal recital. Something learned for school. Yes, a recitation. A factual and rather pretty narrative. A calm and beautifully detached and rather touching enumeration of small truths.

She walked in the rain to the front door. Upstairs the first thing that caught her eye was the smoking pistol, the neon sculpture she'd bought to commemorate the final evening she'd spent at Frankie's Tropical Bar. With that other son of a bitch. That son of a bitch in entirely different ways. It was all so strange. She stayed depressed a long time.

The phone in Mudger's car was mounted on a panel behind the front seat, passenger side. When it buzzed he put his left foot on the accelerator, leaned far to his right and extended his arm over the seat to reach it, without taking his eyes off the road.

His driver had left a week earlier to take a job with the National Park Service in Arizona. Doctor's orders, he said.

Dry climate. Mudger knew he was going back to PAC/ORD.

It was Lomax in Dallas.

"Some progress, Earl."

"Tell me about it."

"I made contact. In fact I flew down on the kid's plane. What they call a carnival atmosphere prevailed."

"How'd you manage that?"

"Easy," Lomax said. "But I haven't located the item. Next step is the warehouse. Richie's jittery but I think I can get us inside."

"They have a moat, I understand, with crocodiles."

"They have dogs is what they have. It's a lot more secure than the DC-9."

"I heard from Van," Mudger said.

"Where is he?"

"Southwest Texas."

"How's his face? Still hurt?"

"They found the subject."

"Jesus, did they? That's fantastic. Okay, you said it. They'd get it done. Had me fooled, I admit. No more snide remarks about the rangers."

Mudger passed a Mercedes on the Jersey turnpike, heavy rain, the phone cradled between his head and shoulder.

"He wants to be found."

A pause while Lomax considered this.

"Explain, Earl."

"He wants to be found. That's the explanation. How the hell else could they have found him?"

"Why does he want to be found?"

"I don't know."

"Are they fixed or traveling?"

"They're still traveling."

"Where to, you think?"

The Mercedes came into view on the left. Mudger increased his speed.

"He's heading for the Mines."

"I guess, if he's led them down that far, could be."

"Sure, he's heading for the Mines."

"Does Van know he's being led?"

"Tell you the truth, Arthur, he was so goddamn happy I didn't have the heart to tell him."

Cao walked away from the roadside stand, eating a taco. He got into the microbus and Van drove off, obviously impatient. Propped on the dash was a Polaroid photo Cao had taken of his buddy standing in front of the statue of Davy Crockett in the town square in Ozona.

2

Talerico inspected the plants arrayed along the picture window in the living room. A police car turned into the street and went slowly past. Yellow cruisers. Cops with small neat mustaches, like army officers in World War I movies. He watched the car turn a corner and head toward the golf course. His wife had overwatered the Swedish ivy. He'd have to mention it.

His daughters kept asking about the Mounties. They'd seen pictures somewhere. Bright red tunics and wide-brimmed hats. The famous musical ride. Talerico didn't think of them as Mounties. They were the RCMP and if they wore bright red uniforms while bouncing around on their horsies, they weren't always easy to spot the rest of the time. He'd also been made aware of the provincial police. Not to mention the Toronto morality squad, whose officers liked to keep busy confiscating equipment and prints, and padlocking bookstores, peep shows and other outlets.

Talerico had come up from the Buffalo arm to develop

Toronto for hard-core, if and when it became legal. In the meantime he was dipping and dancing, teasing along the margins of what was legally distributable, checking out the under-the-counter trade and making contacts with local people the family might want to install as corporate officials.

His smallest daughter came into view, out on the lawn, playing with friends. After Buffalo, a city of sofa burnings and larger conflagrations, this place was easy to take. The kids, especially, loved it. His wife was right behind. He, Vincent, harbored secret yearnings for the familiar faces and voices. The mother, the sister, the cousins, the uncles, the nieces.

Still, it was only a couple of hours' drive to Buffalo and to all those smoldering ruins that were constantly being hosed down by overworked firemen. Here, once a week, to ease the longing for familiar things, he drove down to Pasquale Brothers on King Street and filled a couple of shopping bags with cheese, noodles, peppers, sausage, cold cuts, anchovies and olives.

He checked his watch. Two-hour time difference. Still a little early to call.

Talerico suffered from a facial nerve paralysis. About a year ago he got out of bed one morning to find that the right side of his face had more or less collapsed. It had slid down, like an acre of mud. He had trouble closing his mouth completely; the right corner didn't quite shut. His bushy mustache dipped far to the right and his voice occasionally sounded hollow.

The split was distinct. The left side of his face was normal. The right side was numb and set lower than the left. The right side was also expressionless. When he sneezed or blinked, only the left eye closed. The right eye hung there, frozen, staring blankly. It was slanted down, at an angle to the other eye. It was like an animal's eye, people said. A hawk, a snake, a shark. It was mysterious and fierce, staring out impassively, uninfluenced by what was happening on the other side of his face.

Vinny the Eye.

He went downstairs to the den. The phone down there was attached to a device called a blue box. It was roughly four by six inches, inlaid with digital keys. By dialing out-of-service numbers in nearby communities and then activating the blue box, he was able to switch the calls to points anywhere in the U.S. or Canada while being billed only for the short-range connections. It's the little things that give you the edge.

The long-distance target this time was Dallas. A man Talerico knew only as Kidder. He'd been told Kidder had a multiple answering service. On the ninth or tenth ring, a man picked up.

"B and G Realty."

"I want Kidder."

"Wait a second, I'll transfer."

Half a minute later a woman came on.

"Sherman Kendall Catering."

"Kidder."

"Who do I say?"

"Vincent Talerico."

He heard whispering. About five seconds of breathing. In the background a phone rang and the woman answered: "Tall Man Fashions."

Talerico heard the original male voice.

"Vinny Tal."

"Is this Kidder?"

"Talking."

"Do we know each other?"

"You know me as Sherman Kantrowitz. Or Sherman Kaye."

"Sure," Talerico said.

"You're the one with the eye? Or that's Paul?"

"That's me."

"I knew you before the eye. I knew you in Lockport with

Bobby and Monica that time. They knocked him down, I understand."

"He got put in a drum."

"Where?"

"I don't think it matters. Does it matter?"

"You don't want to reminisce, Tal. I understand. I assume this is long distance we're talking."

"I'm calling about a certain Richie Armbrister. Runs a lot of skin out of there."

"Preview Distributions. That's the parent. He's got about two hundred paper airplanes. Plus which he's got an accounting system that's totally bombproof."

"That's him."

"Why, you want to walk in?"

"Right now I'm interested in a particular piece of merchandise. I want to develop the kid. Bring him around to a different viewpoint."

"How personal?"

"I ought to visit," Talerico said. "Have a meal."

"Who from down here knows you're coming?"

"Nobody."

"Don't you want to tell somebody?"

"You're my field agent, Kidder. Keep an eye on this Richie kid. See if you can get inside his fortress. I'll be down soon. You'll show me the sights."

"Shouldn't you say something? That's the accepted way. You tell somebody you're coming down."

"I'm known for doing things unorthodox," Talerico said. "That's what makes me a legend."

His wife Annette was in the kitchen watching a Richard Conte movie in French on channel 25. Richard Conte was Talerico's favorite actor. The early Richard Conte.

He watched Annette leaning over the breakfast dishes, concentrating on the movie, trying to fathom it. No one concentrated the way she did. She got lost in things, profoundly involved. The next day, if you asked her, she wouldn't be able to tell you what she'd seen.

"Hey."

"You scared me," she said.

"Richard Conte gets shot in about two minutes."

"I didn't know you were there."

"He dies in the street."

"No, he doesn't."

"You put too much water in the Swedish ivy. I go away for a day and a half, you start watering in panic. How many times do I have to tell you? What do I have to do? Do I have to make a chart?"

"Let me watch this."

"He gets shot. He dies in the street."

"I'm too good to you," she said.

"You're not good to me. I'm good to you."

"I'm too good. That's always been my trouble."

"I'm good to you," he said. "You don't know how good."

"Ralphie used to tell me. 'You're too good to people. Don't be so good all the time.' He was right, as usual."

Talerico spread some jam on a slice of leftover toast.

"Who the hell is Ralphie?"

"Only my brother."

"That gets thrown out of college. That makes his parents ashamed. Which, that brother?"

"Stop hanging around. I don't like it when you hang around. Go out. Jog, like a Canadian."

He took a bite out of the stiff toast.

"When you water—listen to this, Annette. When you water, if you put too much water or do it too often, you cause little punctures in the leaf. You know which one's the Swedish ivy. It's hanging. It's the only one in the living room that hangs down. Now I'm going away again so I'm telling you so you'll be careful. Go easy. Don't be in such a hurry to empty the can. Too much water, the cells burst."

"You make me tired. You're why I'm tired all the time."

"I'm good to you," he said "You don't know what goes on out there."

Selvy held the magnum by the barrel. Dipping slightly, he moved his arm slowly back, then brought it forward, swiftly, tossing the gun, end over end, into the Rio Grande.

He walked back along the dirt road toward Sample's Café. There was a pickup next to his car at the side of the house. Nadine stood on the front steps, looking a little shiny.

"Changed your clothes finally," he said.

"I've decided to become a total blue-jeans person."

"Now that you're home."

"I might even sleep in them. That's an open threat. My dad's here."

"I know."

Some of the houses had been abandoned. Others were half ghosts, apparently still occupied, but with windows out completely, or with soft plastic sheeting replacing the glass, torn sheeting, sheeting rippling in the wind, and with sand everywhere, and tire tracks in the harder dirt, distinct reliefs, like tribal markings left behind to clarify local weather and geology.

Her father sat at the kitchen table, using a penknife to pick at the insides of a fluorescent light fixture. He was older than Selvy had expected, with a raw look about him, all brick and sand, and a tie-dyed blue bandanna around his neck. Functional, Selvy thought. Keep the sweat from moving freely.

"My dad, Jack Rademacher. Glen with one *n* Selvy."

They sat around a while talking about the weather. Nadine went out to buy an ice cream at one of the general stores up the road. There was a lull. Her father kept scratching at the fixture.

"I think she came in with beer."

"No thanks."

"I don't take a drink myself."

"Lately I've kept away."

"I never have. I never saw the point."

"I have," Selvy said. "But recently I decided to keep away. As recently as a day or two ago."

"What was she doing in New York?"

"Acting."

Jack shook his head, although not in disbelief. It was a comment, bitterly negative. He mumbled something about the ballast in the fixture. Needed new ballast.

"She saw her sister."

"In Little Rock," Selvy said.

"That one's damn crazy. We lost hope for that one early. What the hell's she doing out there?"

"Nadine went alone."

"She must be selling picture frames," Jack said.

He finished what he was doing and went upstairs. Through the window Selvy saw Nadine talking to a couple of small girls, dusty kids in dresses they'd outgrown. Jack came back down, carrying an old pair of boxing gloves, which he set before Selvy on the kitchen table. They were small and discolored, not very heavily padded, the leather peeling everywhere.

"I used to fight for money. Before her sister was born. The border towns. Their mother wanted me to give it up. I had over twenty fights."

"Weren't you past the age, even then?"

"I was fit," Jack said. "I never trained. I never ran the way they do. Didn't see the point. But her mother was carrying the first. What the hell, I stopped."

He carried the gloves back upstairs, returning a moment later. There was another lull. Nadine said something that made the two girls laugh. One of them jumped several times, laughing, the tips of three fingers in her mouth.

"You know about that training base," Selvy said. "You go

west to Marathon and then it's southeast of there, near where the silver mines used to be, off on some mud road."

"Mule deer, some dove and quail."

"Is it still there?"

"They pulled out in July."

"Where to?"

"Didn't say where to. Try Central America."

"Did they take everything with them?"

"They left some barracks standing," Jack said. "There were a dozen or so of those long barracks. Now there's two, maybe three."

"I'd heard they might move."

"I couldn't tell you why, exactly. They were never too free with information, were they? Always was a secretive kind of place. They had their reasons, I guess."

"Yes."

"If they didn't have their reasons, they wouldn't have plunked down in the middle of nowhere."

Selvy drove his car down to a lookout just above the river. He walked back up to the house.

That night he sat on a cot in an almost bare room off the kitchen. The temperature kept dropping. He heard the plastic sheeting on the windows of nearby houses whip and snap in the wind.

The girl came in.

"What's the plan?"

"No plan," he said.

"We're leaving soon, aren't we?"

"I thought you'd want to stay a while. He seems to like having you back. You want to stay, don't you?"

"Do I look like I've got long cow tits, wearing this sweater?"

"I don't know. Take it off."

"You want to go alone, don't you? Never mind. I didn't say that."

"Take it off. Then I can tell you."

She bent a leg back and kicked the door shut, lightly. She took off the sweater, and her shoes and jeans, and stood there in her briefs. Appliquéd beneath the elastic band were the words: *Not tonight—I've got a headache.* Selvy leaned back on the cot, knees bent up, to unlace his shoes.

"I'm beginning to think you maneuvered me here."

"What for?" he said.

"So you could leave me with someone. That way you wouldn't have to just slip out some morning with me in some motel room, sound asleep, leaving me there. You want to leave me with him."

He took off his shirt.

"If I had maneuvers in mind, I'd have left you at your sister's. I showed up, didn't I, after your sister's."

"That was different."

"How?"

"This is the end of the line," she said.

He smiled, stepping out of his pants. Nadine smiled too, moving toward him and delivering a mock blow to his arm. They tried to make love quietly. It was an old cot, and squeaked, and Jack was somewhere nearby, moving about. She kept on smiling, her eyes closed. When they were in bed together, everything about her suggested appealing healthiness. It bothered him. She seemed to think sex was wholesome and sweet.

Selvy would never understand her. All the more reason to think of her as the girl. But he was beginning to understand something else. Black limousine. Certain things were becoming clear.

After Nadine left to go to her room, he heard Jack come downstairs and knock at his door. He showed Selvy a photograph of three men he used to go fishing with. They stood in front of a pickup, wearing trail vests and wading boots.

"This one's Jack Brady. Same as me. Jack. This is Vernon Floyd. That one's Buck Floyd."

Selvy nodded.

"Now that pickup. I goddamn swerved to avoid a hole about so wide and my rear tires went for a walk on me. Truck swapped ends for sure. Now Vernon. He called me every name. Brother Buck couldn't talk for laughing."

He looked at Selvy, who nodded again. Then he took the picture back upstairs. Selvy listened to the sheeting as it snapped in the wind.

It was becoming clear. He was starting to understand what it meant. All that testing. The polygraphs. The rigorous physicals. The semisecrecy. All those weeks at the Mines. Electronics. Code-breaking. Currencies. Weapons. Survival.

All the paramilitary sessions. The small doses of geopolitics. The psychology of terrorism. The essentials of counterinsurgency.

What it meant. The full-fledged secrecy. The reading. The routine. The double life. His private disciplines. His handguns. His regard for precautions. How your mind works. The narrowing of choices. What you are. It was clear, finally. The whole point. Everything.

All this time he'd been preparing to die.

It was a course in dying. In how to die violently. In how to be killed by your own side, in secret, no hard feelings. They'd been grooming him. They'd spotted his potential, his capacity for favorable development. All this time. It was a ritual preparation.

We are teaching you how to die violently. This is the only death that matters, steel or lead or tungsten alloy, death by hard metal, taking place in secret. To ensure the success of the course, we ourselves will kill you.

He lay in the dark, smoking.

Sure. The rougher the testing, the more certain you can be they're preparing you to die. They want perfect specimens, physically and otherwise. It's less resonant if you're flawed.

So. He'd be able to sleep now. Good.

All conspiracies begin with individual self-repression.

They'd seen his potential. He'd checked off the right numbers in the elaborate profiles. They liked his style in the interviews. The computers approved.

Black limousine.

Of course. It was only fitting. All this time they'd been conveying him to the cemetery. In short hops. In stages. Now he knew. He'd sleep finally. Good.

He listened. The wind sound was haunting, a series of timed cries, level and clear. There was a change in direction and the wind's speed increased. The sound grew very different. The wind met creaking obstacles, banging through the hulks nearby, the ghost structures with windows blown out and doors leaning, weeds coming up through the floorboards.

The girl came to him in the dawn, moon-striped and pale, with dream-brown eyes, knocking over a chair as she crossed the room. She scrambled under the blanket. It was freezing and they couldn't stop trembling with cold-induced laughter as they pressed tight in the dark.

It hit seventy-five next day. They walked down the winding dirt road to the car, still parked near the river. Nadine sat on the fender. Selvy sat on the front end of the roof, his feet on the hood. The sky was glassy blue, marked by a single vapor trail formed in the wake of a passing plane.

"Are you as sluggish as I am?"

"No," he said.

"It's my biorhythms. They're way out of whack today."

"I'm great, I'm tuned."

"Biorhythmically I feel awful."

"You need a swim," he said.

The river wasn't wide here. On the Mexican side the rock wall was variously gray and copper, depending on the shadow line. Down here, with no buildings in view, no people around, it was all rocks and sky. A hawk sailed parallel to the cliff line where it ran straight for a fifty-yard stretch. He watched Nadine climb down to the lower bank, cautiously, skidding down the last dusty incline on her bottom, using her feet to brake.

Her voice was small, though remarkably clear.

"Got hit spang in the mouth with a pebble."

She stripped to her briefs and stepped into the water. The river twisted here. From his perch he could see material suspended in the areas of water that were touched by the sun. Mineral particles, brownish sediment. She slipped full-body into the river, dog-paddling in small circles.

"Not too cold. I thought it might be colder. Haven't done this in five years."

Her voice kept changing as she turned toward the opposite bank, then circled back this way. He saw her touch bottom at the near bank and stand erect, running her hands through her hair. When she spoke again he could tell by the pure tone of her voice that she was looking up at him.

"Hey, bo, come on down, get a little wet."

Selvy was looking across the river to the top of the rock wall. Two figures had appeared on the cliff line. First one, then the other ARVN ranger. He felt the briefest of regrets, thinking of his handguns. There was no mistaking the one he'd roughed up. Mustache. Wouldn't take his eyes off Selvy. The other one, the knife squatter, the one who'd waited motionless in the microbus, didn't mind tossing a look at Nadine.

She looked up that way, following Selvy's gaze. Then she turned toward the car again. Her voice was very small.

"I don't know more'n a monkey who they are."

Selvy remained on the car roof, watching them.

"They're not local people exactly," he said. "Why don't you stay right where you are for the time being? Put on your shirt if you want."

The two men remained for a long moment on the cliff line. Stetsons, sunglasses, tight denim pants. Nothing behind them but clear sky. Finally they moved back. Because of their higher elevation, from Selvy's vantage point, it took just two steps. They were out of sight.

The girl put on her jeans and climbed up to the lookout.
"This is turning into a Western," she said.

"What was it before?"

"I don't know what it was before. But it resembles a Western right now."

"Nothing like a swim," he told her. "You ought to be feeling better."

Selvy got in the car and started it up. Nadine kept looking over to the Mexican side. When the car started moving, she walked after it, opened the door and got in. He drove up to the post office. Less than a hundred yards away, tourists were emerging from a bus.

Selvy got out of the car and went over to talk to the bus driver. Above the curved windshield, in the slot where destinations are lettered, appeared the words: WILD WEST AND MEXICO. Nadine watched the imprint of her wet underwear gradually appear on her jeans.

He came back to the car and leaned against the door on her side. A few of the tourists drifted down this way, going into the general store, taking pictures of each other.

"I'm leaving the car with you."

"You want me to keep it for you."

"I want you to keep it."

"Keep it, period," she said.

"That's right."

The tourists slowly spread through town, mostly older people and eight or nine Japanese. Selvy walked over to the house. Through the front window she saw him speaking to her father. He came back out, carrying a can of beer and a soft drink, also in a can. He held them in one hand back against his hip.

Nadine remained in the car, sipping the beer. Selvy leaned against the door. A man asked if he'd move the car. He wanted to take a picture of his wife standing near the post office door. The car was in the way. Selvy said no.

In pairs and small groups, the tourists eventually reassembled outside the bus. The driver appeared, unwrapping a stick of gum. No one stepped aboard until he was behind the wheel.

Selvy tossed the empty soda can onto the back seat. The girl's jeans were wet, an explicit outline. Her shirt was wet in patches. She'd taken a map out of the glove compartment and was unfolding it elaborately, spreading it across the dash and up along the windshield. He walked over to the bus and stepped on. The door closed behind him with a splash of compressed air. In the brief moment before he slipped into his seat, Selvy noted something odd about the people, or the seating pattern, or something—he wasn't sure what.

It wasn't until they were well under way, heading west on U.S. 90, that he turned in his seat for a longer look. It was the Japanese. They were spread throughout the bus, singly or in pairs, nine of them, and they were all asleep. The other tourists talked, compared postcards, looked out the windows. It was as though the Japanese, secretly, by inborn means, had been able to communicate to each other the placid imperative: *sleep.*

He faced front again. They'd gone to sleep immediately and they continued sleeping despite the noise and motion. This apartness he'd always found interesting in Asians. This somehow challenging sense of calm. It only remained for him to discover whether they'd wake up simultaneously, raising their heads in unison.

3

All the windows were closed. The blinds were down. Lightborne double-locked the gallery door. Then he turned toward Odell and gestured, arms outstretched, palms up: what do we have?

Odell looked up from a book of etchings. He was older

than Richie, but not much, and fuller in the face, although with the same prominent teeth. The book was titled *Extra-terrestrial Sex Positions.*

Sixteen millimeter, he said. Considered an amateur film gauge at the time this footage was shot. No standard, or optical, sound track. Magnetic sound, if any, would have to be added. Problems there with certain projectors. Possible problems adapting 16mm to motion picture theaters. Schools and churches, yes. TV, yes.

"Wonderful," Lightborne said. "Schools and churches, that's wonderful."

He'd had to strain to hear what Odell was saying. Odell spoke rapidly and sometimes indistinctly, with much more of an accent than his cousin had—a run-on Georgia voice, a clip-clop, rather than Richie's slight but piercing twang.

Lightborne circled the small table that held the projector Odell had brought with him. They wouldn't be able to view the film until the following day. The projector had a defective part, Odell had discovered, and it was ten p.m.—too late to find a replacement.

Curiously, Lightborne wasn't disappointed. He found he was in no hurry to look at the footage. At some rudimentary level it was an experience he feared. He'd feared it all along, he realized. His involvement brimmed with fear.

Moll Robbins would be joining him for the screening. He wanted a disinterested intelligence on the scene. More than that. He wanted company. Human warmth. An interpreter of the meaning of his fear.

It was all so real. It had such weight. Objects were what they seemed to be. History was true.

Odell said he'd talked to Richie on the phone. Richie was barricaded in the warehouse. He was feeding the dogs infrequently, to give them a meaner edge. He'd had this feeling for months, Odell said. Someone was out to get him. Some dark force. There was a sniper somewhere, waiting for the right moment. He was sitting on a bed in some rooming house, cleaning his rifle scope. He had a bullet with Richie's name on it. Dallas, Richie would say. What am I doing in Dallas?

"All he talks about is John F. Kidney, Bobby Kidney, Martin Luther Kang, Jaws Wallace."

"What?" Lightborne said.

"I keep telling him what Rose Kidney told Tiddy Kidney." Long pause.

"What did she tell him?"

"That was Harry Truman."

"If you can't stand the heat," Lightborne said.

"That was Harry S Truman, wasn't it, said that."

Odell went on.

Richie was obsessed not only by his impending assassination but by the conflicting reports that would ensue. He'd been shot by one white male, or two white males, or one white male with a mulatto child. The rifle used had no prints, had several sets of prints, now being checked, or had several sets of prints but they'd been accidentally wiped off by the police.

Richie was especially obsessed by fingerprints being wiped off by the police, Odell said.

Lightborne went behind the partition into the living area. He turned on both taps in the wash basin, hoping this would lead Odell to think he was shaving. Then he sat at the foot of his cot and stared into the black window shade three feet away.

History is true.

Selvy got a ride from a man in a pickup, south from Marathon. The man was about seventy-five years old. There was a deer rifle on a rack at the back of the cab. Four hours till nightfall. The desert.

He saw it as a memory. Deep gullies at right angles to the road. Flash-flood warnings. Yucca stalk and ocotillo sticking out of the sand. Things don't usually resume existence precisely as you've recalled them. Spires, buttes, pinnacles, the eroded remnants, to left and right, in scaly rust and copper and sandy brown. Well ahead he saw the waveform, the scant silhouette, of the Chisos Mountains, palest slate, lying so completely in a plane it could not possibly be more than arbitrary light, a mood or fabrication.

Finally a car approached and passed. Then nothing again. A buzzard on a fencepost. Single windmill in the distance. Everything here was in the distance. Distance was the salient fact. Even after you reached something, you were immersed in distance. It didn't end until the mountains and he wasn't going that far.

They stopped for gas at the old frontier store, an adobe structure with a lone pump and the remains of a small covered wagon out front. Selvy went inside. There was a broad counter covered with rocks for sale. Along one wall was the owner's barbed wire collection. There were display cases full of sundries. In one case, Selvy spotted an item labeled Filipino guerrilla bolo.

The owner got it out for him. A long heavy single-edged knife with a broad blade. Flecks of rust. Small nicks in the cutting edge. Fifteen dollars.

"I always thought bolos were curved blades."

"Machete family," the owner said. "Vegetation, cane."

"From bolo punch, I guess I got the idea. An uppercut that comes way around. Got any honing oil?"

"I might find some."

"With all those rocks over there, think you can find one that's perfectly rectangular, about half an inch thick?"

"If you want a whetstone, I've got some Washita, if I know where to find it."

Selvy also bought a canteen and filled it with water. Then he paid the man and went outside. A teenage girl was cleaning the windshield. When she was finished, they moved back onto the road.

"Planning on making it before dark."

"There's time," Selvy said.

"I've my doubts."

"We're right about there. I'd say less than five minutes and we'll be there."

"You don't want to forget the walk."

"I'm tuned," Selvy said. "The walk is good as made."

A coyote loped across the road and disappeared in some brush alongside a gulley.

"What's that you got there?"

"Filipino guerrilla bolo."

"Where's your jungle?"

"I bought it for the name."

"You didn't get your money's worth unless a jungle came with it."

"I like the name," he told the old man. "It's romantic."

Along a slight elevation in the highway, he spotted the primitive road that led to the Mines. The man stopped the pickup and Selvy hopped out and started walking east. The trail was dusty except for isolated parts, hardened mud, where he saw signs of old tire tracks, mostly heavy tread.

The canteen was looped to his belt, left side. Bolo on the other side, at a forty-five-degree angle to his leg, cutting edge up.

He began to run. The canteen bounced against his thigh. He ran for twenty minutes. It felt good. It felt better with each passing minute. Prickly pear and mesquite. A memory unwinding. He walked for an hour, then ran for fifteen minutes. A dust devil swirled to his right. The weather was changing down there, far beyond the transient whirlwind. Something was building over the mountains.

Ninety minutes later he saw the barracks, two of them, surrounded by debris of various kinds, kitchen and plumbing equipment, a gutted jeep, a useless windmill, anonymous junk. This grouping of common objects he found briefly touching. Signs of occupancy and abandonment. Faceted in sad light. A human presence. In the rose and gold of sunset.

The wood-burning stove still sat in the long barracks. He found canned food in a locker. In the smaller building a dozen cots were ranged along a wall. He dragged one of them back into the long barracks and set it near the stove.

After eating he went outside, wrapped in a blanket. It was still clear in this area, broad scale of stars. No more than thirty degrees now, dropping. Dry cold. A pure state. An elating state of cold. Not weather. It wasn't weather so much as memory. A category of being.

The temperature kept dropping but this didn't signify change. It signified intensity. It signified a concentration of the faculty of recall. A steadiness of image. No stray light.

It was snowing in the mountains.

All behind him now. Cities, buildings, people, systems. All the relationships and links. The plan, the execution, the sequel. He could forget that now. He'd traveled the event. He'd come all the way down the straight white line.

He realized he didn't need the blanket he was wrapped in. The cold wasn't getting to him that way. In a way that called for insulation. It was perfect cold. The temperature at which things happen on an absolute scale.

All that incoherence. Selection, election, option, alternative. All behind him now. Codes and formats. Courses of action. Values, bias, predilection.

Choice is a subtle form of disease.

When he woke up it was still dark. Gray ash in the stove. He walked to the window, naked, and looked east into the vast arc of predawn sky. He crouched by the window. He crossed his arms over his knees and lowered his head. Motionless, he waited for light to burn down on the sand and rimrock and dead trees.

4

A set of tracks ran east and west along the front of the warehouse in downtown Dallas. It was a five-story building with corrugated metal doors and flaking paint. There was a loading platform out front. A small sign: PREVIEW DISTRIBU-TIONS. All the windows were boarded up.

Inside Richie Armbrister sat at a long table, tapping the keys of a pocket calculator. At his elbow a desk lamp burned. Nearby three dogs lay sleeping. In the gloom beyond was the figure of Daryl Shimmer, Richie's bodyguard, extended across an old sofa. Two more dogs near the sofa, sleeping. Beyond that, in total darkness, fork lifts and pallets and shipping cylinders, enormous ones, numbering in the hundreds.

Daryl was becoming increasingly morose and withdrawn. Physically distant. Richie noticed how he'd gradually been moving farther away. The sofa was a backward step, from Daryl's point of view. He'd spent the whole evening sitting in a fork-lift vehicle in the dark, about thirty yards away. He'd had to revert to the sofa if he wanted to sleep.

Everyone else was gone. They left singly, in pairs, in small groups, over a period of twenty-four hours, reverently, slipping out the north door. The warehouse was quiet for the first time since Richie had bought it.

There had been phone calls from a man who identified himself as Sherman Kramer. Daryl recognized the name. Kidder. A small-time operator. But with connections. Large connections.

A certain man was spending a lot of time in the parking lot across the street. Richie had watched him through a gap between two boards that were nailed across one of the windows. He spent most of his time near the Ross Avenue end of the lot, which was the far end in relation to the warehouse. He leaned against a car. Or walked back and forth. Richie thought it might be the man he'd found in his sauna aboard the DC-9. Hard to tell from this distance, looking through a dirt-smeared window.

Lightborne's phone was disconnected. No forwarding number. Richie had wanted to speak with Odell. He trusted Odell. Odell was family. Real family. The only number he had for Odell in New York was Lightborne's number. Disconnected.

He tried to concentrate on the figures before him. Avenues of commerce. That's all he cared about. The higher issues. Demography. Patterns of distribution. Legal maneuvers and technicalities. Bookkeeping finesse. He'd never even asked Lightborne what the footage was supposed to show.

He had visions of a mishandled investigation. They would fail to trace the rifle to its owner. They'd lose his autopsy report. Witnesses would move out of state, never to be heard from again. His funeral. A closed-coffin affair.

The phone rang. He watched Daryl start to rise. It rang again. Daryl came toward the table where Richie was sitting. He picked up the phone in a series of masterfully sullen movements, his face showing a blend of resentment and lingering obligation. Richie had doubled his salary on the way in from the airport and promised him a dune buggy with chromed exhausts for his birthday. This was in return for Daryl's sworn allegiance, no matter what.

"It's Kidder again."

"What's he want?" Richie said. "I don't want to talk to him."

"Same thing. A meeting."

"I don't have any can with any film. That's all I'm saying. That's the meeting. We just had it."

"He doesn't know anything about cans with films," Daryl said. "He just wants to arrange talks. Someone's coming."

"Not here. They're not coming here. Tell him the dogs."

"He says outside is okay. He has someone he's bringing.

Tomorrow, after eight sometime. Outside, inside, makes no difference."

"What should we do?"

"Ask him who he's bringing."

"Ask him," Richie said.

"He says no names available right now. A respected man in the field."

"Ask him what field."

"Too late," Daryl said. "He hung up."

Richie took a bite of one of the Danish butter cookies he'd carried back from New York. He pushed the container toward Daryl, who waved him off and headed slowly toward the sofa, his lean frame slumping. One of the dogs stirred, briefly, as Daryl dropped onto the sofa. The dogs were good dogs, Richie believed. Scout dogs. German shepherds. Trained in simulated combat conditions.

That was for break-ins. Close-quarter action. What about long range? There were bullets these days that went through concrete. On the other side of the parking lot and across Ross Avenue was the General Center Building. Excellent place for a sniper. Perfect place. He could stand on the roof and blast away, firing not only through Richie's boarded windows but through the brick walls as well. He'd leave the rifle on the roof and disappear, confident that the police would smear his fingerprints.

It was a hell of a party. Loud. The Senator liked noise at his parties. Young crowd mostly. He liked having young people around.

He moved sideways through the living room, from group to group, smiling, barking out greetings, clutching the upper arms of men, gripping women at the waist. Maneuvering around the cocktail table he came across a woman who reminded him of a Vestier nude he'd seen in a private collection in Paris—big-hipped, self-satisfied, status-oriented. An executive secretary.

Standing with her was a younger woman, much less monumental. Elbowing his way into the conversation, Percival wasn't surprised to see her suddenly *actuate*—the eyes, the smile, the tense and hopeful and solemn delight. Being recognized would never cease to be one of the spiritual rewards of public service.

"You are," he said.

Mouth moving.

"Museum. Fascinating, I would think."

Noise music laughter.

Of course he'd *expected* to be recognized. It was his house and his party. Still, it was always interesting, watching people release this second self of theirs. Women especially. Becoming shiny little space pods with high-energy receptors. Percival believed celebrity was a phenomenon related to religious mysticism. That ad for the Rosicrucians. WHAT SECRET POWER DOES THIS MAN POSSESS? Celebrity brings out the cosmic potential in people. And that couldn't be anything but good. What was the word? Salutary. That couldn't be anything but salutary.

As the older woman, the Vestier, looked on, Percival led this mellow child to the short staircase at the other end of the living room. There they sat, intimate chums, with their drinks, on the next to last step.

"Now then. P'raps we can talk."

"This is the really nicest house."

"You were saying. Museum. You mentioned."

"Where I work."

"You're associated with? Museums. I am passionate. Treasures, treasures."

"The Medical Museum of the Armed Forces Institute of Pathology."

"Jesus Christmas."

"Who did your décor?" she said.

"I did."

"It's so lovingly done."

She was half smashed, he realized. Roughly his own situation. A Pakistani put his left hand on the fourth step, as a brace, then leaned up toward Percival, diagonally, to shake hands. Percival thought it might be Peter Sellers.

"I really like your programs," the young woman said.

"I'm trying to think. Are you a Renoir? I see you as a little firmer. A Titian Venus. Not quite melted."

"I am just so charmed by this whole situation."

"Let me ask," he said. "An important question. But private. Calls for outright privacy. Repeat after me. This question."

"This question."

"Calls for."

"Who did the wallpaper?"

"Some Irishman with a crooked face *did* it. I selected the patterns."

"It really. It shows so much obvious love and care."

"Important, important question. Now wait. We need to ensconce ourselves. Because it's that kind of question."

"Ho ho."

"Exactly," he said. "Now follow me. How's your drink?"

"My dreenk she all right, señor."

He led her into the bedroom. She let her body sag to indicate awe. The canopy bed, the armoire, the miniature lowboy, the grain cutter's bench, the cloverleaf lamp table, the mighty oak rocker.

"Sit, sit, sit."

He found himself thinking of Lightborne. It may have been the sight of the phone. He'd been trying to call Lightborne, who had promised him a screening. They'd talked twice on the phone and Percival had disguised his voice, in a different way, each time. He was trying to figure out how to handle the screening. Lightborne had assured him it would be private. Still, there'd have to be a projectionist in the immediate vicinity, and Lightborne would probably want to be present as well. How to view the footage without being recognized. Preceding that, however, was the problem of contacting Lightborne. Percival had been calling for two days. A disconnect recording every time. No forwarding number.

He sat at the end of the bed, watching her rock.

"You had a question, Senator."

"Call me Lloyd."

"I am so charmed by this."

"You have an extraordinarily expressive mouth."

"I know."

"English-expressive."

"I would like to ask, confidentially. Are you thinking of the presidency? Of running? Because I have heard talk. Young people find your programs extremely appealing."

"No, no, no. That's a dead end, the presidency."

"I think you'd find young people very supportive."

He watched her drink.

"I'm having trouble with the Titian concept," he said. "Your mouth is so English. Do you know Sussex at all?"

"Tallish man? Wears striped shirts with white collars?"

"Call me Lloyd," he said.

He got up and closed the door. He stood behind her chair, gripping the uprights, and rocked her slowly back and forth.

"Except the Sunbelt would be a problem," she said. "You wouldn't find a power base down there."

The phone rang. He moved quickly to the side of the bed, realizing belatedly that it couldn't be Lightborne, that Lightborne didn't know who he was, much less how to reach him. It was his wife, back home. A picture came immediately to mind. She is sitting up in bed. Her face gleams with some kind of restorative ointment. All over the room are volumes of the Warren Report along with her notebooks full of "correlative data." She is wearing a pale-blue bed jacket of puffy quilted material.

"What do you want?" he said.

"Wondering how you are."

"Go away. Will you go away?"

"I am away."

"I'm having a noisy, noisy party and I love it."

"I don't hear a thing," she said.

"I'm in the bedroom and the door is closed."

"Who's with you?"

"Oswald was the lone assassin. When will you get it through your thick skull?"

"There's someone with you and I don't give two shits, if you want to know the truth."

"She's a girl with lambent hair," he said.

"What else? Jesus, I mean what else would she be?"

"I'll put her on."

He carried the phone over to the rocking chair and asked the young woman to tell his wife where she worked.

"The Medical Museum of the Armed Forces Institute of Pathology."

Percival took the phone from her and walked back across the room. This time, addressing his wife, he whispered fiercely.

"See what you've done to me?"

"I've done? I've done?"

"I have no patience with this kind of thing."

"That doesn't make sense, Lloyd."

"It's all been drained out of me."

"What kind of thing?"

"I'm bone dry," he said.

He went downstairs, circulated briefly and came back up with two fresh drinks. He stood behind her chair, rocking.

"Senator, you had a question."

"It all started with a question."

"I'm sure waiting."

"Yes, yes, yes, yes."

He swiveled the rocker a few degrees to the right so that she could see him, and vice versa, in the mirror over the lowboy. He felt completely sober. He felt clear-headed to a remarkable degree.

"How would I look in a beard?" he said.

Ignoring the mirror, she glanced back over her shoulder, as though only.the real thing, the three-dimensional Senator Percival, could serve as a basis from which to develop a mature reply. He was gratified to see she was treating the question with the attentive care he felt it deserved.

"Would you recognize me as Lloyd Percival if you saw me in a beard? Dark glasses, say, and a beard. If you saw me in an unlikely place. A more or less run-down area. Far from the splendor of Capitol Hill."

Talerico walked through the arrivals lounge. He was wearing a vested suede suit and carrying a Burberry trenchcoat over one arm.

He saw Kidder waiting in the baggage area. Definitely a type. They ran to types, these people with nine phone numbers and a different name for each day of the week. A man who looks pressed for time or money. A man who operates in a state of permanent exhaustion. He was probably no more than thirty years old. A shame. Fatigue was his medium by now. He needed it to live.

"Vinny Tal, how are you?"

"Head winds."

"Twenty minutes late. But no problem. We drive down there. You talk to this Richie. Nice and smooth."

"It's arranged."

"It's more or less arranged," Kidder said.

They went outside and got into Kidder's bent Camaro. He started up, turned on the lights, and they moved off.

"Vinny, I want to ask. Frankly. What's wrong with your face? What happened to cause that?"

"This woman I knew, about a year ago, threw lye in my face."

"That's awful. That's awful."

"Lye."

"What for? Why?"

"I was so fucking handsome she couldn't stand it."

Kidder hit the steering wheel with the heel of his right hand.

"Shit, you had me thinking."

"It was driving her crazy, just looking at me. She had the permanent hots. She had to do something. It was wrecking her life."

"You had me going. Vin."

"It always gets a reaction. The lye. It has that effect on people. Lye."

The door on Talerico's side squeaked. Something rattled around in the trunk. He was sorry he hadn't arranged to rent a car. He owned an Olds Cutlass Supreme. He was accustomed to a measure of comfort. This thing here was a coffee pot.

"Let me ask. Vin. Ever been down here? Everybody has two first names down here."

"I watch TV."

"That's in case they forget one of them. Which they aren't too bright, some of them."

"First time down."

"I have to say I frankly like it. It's humane. People walk around. They're living."

"We're almost there, or what."

"We're still in the airport," Kidder said. "This is the airport."

The car made Talerico think of his youth. Six or seven guys piling into an old Chevy. Chipping in a quarter each for gas. It was depressing to think this Kidder rode around in the same kind of car. This Kidder here.

"What kind of harassment up there? They harass people in Canada?"

"You have the FBI. I have the RCMP."

"Which means what?"

"Which means they can kick in my door any time of day or night."

"That's Russia."

"My ass, Russia. There's a thing called a writ of assistance. With a writ of assistance they come pouring in. It doesn't have to have my name on it, or my address, or whatever it is they're searching for. It's wide open. First they come pouring through your doors and windows. Then they fill in the blanks."

"It must feel good to be back in the U.S.," Kidder said.

"I'm thrilled."

"We're out of the airport. We just left the airport."

"Keep up the good work."

"That was the airport line right there. We're definitely out."

"You talk to this Richie?"

"I talked to the dipshit who answers his phone."

"You didn't get in the warehouse, in other words."

"Tal, it's a warehouse. What's so special? You say you want to develop the kid. Does it make a difference where? You talk. You make your point."

"Tell you what I found out, asking around independently. His dogs don't bark. They're trained to be silent. They come at you without warning."

"See?" Kidder said. "Good thing I didn't try to get inside. You should have told me earlier. What if I'd tried to get inside?"

"They come out of the dark, leaping," Talerico said. "Trained to go for the throat. But silent. They don't even growl."

"What's this thing you're after?"

"Dirty movie, what else? Too hot for this Richie to handle. I'm doing the kid a favor."

"How'd you hear about it?"

"I got a call from New York."

"The relatives. Always the relatives."

"Paulie gave me a call. What? Ten days ago."

"I never met the man," Kidder said. "I know the man's reputation."

"He called me. That's how I heard."

"How did he hear?"

"Somebody named Lightborne called him. Out of nowhere. Said he was lining up bidders. Wanted to know if Paul was interested in bidding."

"Interested in bidding," Kidder said.

"Can you imagine that?"

"Interested in bidding."

They would try to talk girls into getting in the car. Seven guys in the car, not too many girls were interested. You didn't ordinarily find girls that curious. They kept a zip gun under the driver's seat. They never went anywhere without the gun. This guy Kidder here. That was about his level. His sex life is probably restricted to the back seat of the car. He keeps a Navy flare in the glove compartment.

"Tell you what I could go for," Talerico said. "I could go for some zookie."

"What's zookie?"

"Jewish nookie."

"I had to ask, right?"

"It always gets a reaction. Zookie. It has that little sound people like."

"See those lights?" Kidder said.

Twenty minutes later the car eased into the dark parking lot located across the tracks from the warehouse. A single freight car sat on the tracks. *Ship It On the Frisco!* Kidder turned off the headlights and they sat facing the warehouse. It was cold. Talerico got out of the car to put on his trenchcoat, then slid back into the seat. This wasn't what he'd had in mind.

Half an hour later they saw a figure emerge from beneath

the freight car, coming up from a position on all fours. Slender young man. Black. Wearing a heavy sweater. Carrying a flashlight.

"His name's Daryl Shimmer. He looks after the kid."

"Who looks after him?"

Daryl came toward the car, looking around him every few steps. Ten feet away he put his left hand under the sweater and lifted a small gun out of his belt. He approached the driver's side.

"Shit," Talerico said wearily.

Daryl had the gun in Kidder's face. A .25 caliber automatic. Talerico could read the imprint *Hartford Ct. U.S.A.* above Daryl's long dusty thumb extended along the barrel.

"I know you people looking for some motion picture. We don't know where it's at. Now Richie there, it's all he can do to piss inside the bowl, the way you people keep pressuring. We're saying get back. We don't know the whereabouts. We don't want to know. We're walking away. It's all over, we're saying. You locate the motion picture, more power to you. Don't even tell us about it."

"Listen, hard-on," Kidder said.

Daryl bit his lower lip.

"Get that thing out of my face. That's in bad taste, a pointed gun. That's ugly."

"Who you talking?"

"Scumbag."

"I fucking shoot."

"Anything I hate, man, it's being pointed at."

Overlapping dialogue. Volume increasing all the time.

"You ought to put some meat on your bones," Talerico said quietly. "You're awful thin. I hate to see that."

"Shut up all around."

"You ought to eat more of that soul food."

"Get that gun," Kidder said. "If you don't get that gun. Point it out of here."

"Who you talking?"

"Dipshit. You hard-on."

Daryl had the gun right in Kidder's cheek and he was biting his lower lip again. Kidder was screaming at him, coming up with names Talerico hadn't heard in years.

"You ought to spend more time with people," Talerico said softly. "You're alone too much. I don't like to see that. It's unhealthy. Look at you. You don't know how to behave around people. You ought to get out more. And you ought to eat more. You ought to put some meat on those bones."

Another figure appeared. This one at the side of the freight car. He came walking toward the Camaro. Daryl, keeping the gun in Kidder's face, directed the flashlight into the car.

"They're ready to listen, Richie."

"I heard that yelling. We don't need that here. Yelling."

"This trouble's yours," Kidder said. "This is yours."

"I came out to show we don't have anything to hide. I came out in good faith. I don't know anything about the item you want. You keep putting pressure. It's aggravating."

"The pressure's in your head," Talerico said.

"I didn't even bring the dogs, to show good faith. To make an appearance. I thought this would lessen the mystery. You wouldn't want to get in there so much if you saw me, if you saw there's nothing special and that I don't have the item."

"He wants his Bugs Bunny teeth kicked in," Talerico explained to Kidder.

"This is yours," Kidder kept shouting. "I'm looking at you right here."

Richie was wearing an oversized peacoat. His hands were stuffed into the deep pockets. He nodded in Talerico's direction. A gesture meant for Daryl—shine the light on the other one.

Talerico turned the right side of his face toward the light. The dead side. The side with the chilled meat. His fierce eye stared blankly.

"I'm not even here," Kidder was shouting. "The whole thing's over."

"He wants to eat this gun," Daryl said.

"You stupid bastards. You cuntlaps. You don't know where you're standing."

Talerico had heard this kind of dislocated shouting before. It reminded him of his cousin Paul. When Paul faced trouble, he got meaner, he got deadly. And sometimes he shouted things that connected to the situation only in the loosest of ways, if at all. Talerico had seen his cousin terrorize people—cops more than once, men with guns—simply by displaying rage that bordered on the irrational. He was obviously possessed. Too real to deal with. Once they see you don't mind dying, they're in serious trouble and know it.

All in all, Talerico was impressed by this aspect of Kidder. Kidder was tough. He didn't take shit. He screamed and ranted. The closer he got to dying, the more he seemed to control the situation. The more he intimidated the opposition.

It wasn't bluff, either. That was clear. It was genuine outrage and meanness and fury. Kidder was definitely impressing him. He didn't think a man that exhausted could summon such insanity.

"I want to make like a statement here," Talerico said.

"I feel we welcome that," Richie said. "Whatever we can exchange in the way of views, that means it's looking up."

"You died five minutes ago. You've been dead five full minutes. You're so dead I can smell you. That's my statement."

"I don't want to know who he is," Richie told his body-guard.

"Look at the eye," Talerico said.

"If you know who he is," Richie said, "don't tell me."

He turned and headed toward the warehouse, slipping around the freight car and out of sight.

"Eat and run," Kidder screamed.

"You're going, aren't you?" Daryl said.

"I'm looking right at them."

"You're going. You want to go."

"They don't know the words. They're someplace else completely."

Daryl bit his lower lip. He squeezed the trigger and Talerico jumped into the door and bounced back and then found the handle and had the door open. He walked quickly, head down, his ears belling electrically. He went past the warehouse and then made a left. There were banks, shops, hotels. Very little traffic. No cabs in sight. He'd have to call for a cab.

He made a right and saw the Southland Hotel. It was roughly ten p.m. Very dead here in the urban core. He'd get a cab to take him to the airport. First plane out. New York, Chicago, Toronto. His overnight bag was in the back seat of Kidder's car. He went over the contents mentally. Nothing there that might be traced to him. Not even a monogrammed shirt.

A cab pulled up at the hotel as Talerico approached.

Sooner or later, in this line of work, in acquisitions, you were bound to find yourself in a stress situation, especially if your business took you to a part of the U.S. where everybody owns a gun of one kind or another, for one purpose or another.

Cowboys.

Earl Mudger stood outside Lien's, a Vietnamese restaurant located above the Riverwalk in San Antonio. He'd stopped off here, instead of flying directly to Dallas, in order to have dinner with an old war buddy, George Barber, who was now attached to the Air Force Security Service, stationed at Kelly.

He was glad he'd thought of it. They'd enjoyed themselves in all the time-honored ways. Affection, sentiment, vague regret. He was waiting for George to get his car from a nearby lot and take him to the airport for the short flight to Dallas.

George had filled Mudger in on the latest hardware. It was a complex sensation, hearing that specialized language again, studded as it was with fresh terms. It reminded Mudger of Vietnam, of course. The brand names. The comfort men found in the argot of weaponry.

It also reminded him of the surreal conversation he'd had, long distance with Van, just before he'd left home to come down here. With Tran Le on the extension, translating when necessary, Mudger had listened to Van explain that he wanted to approach the subject by air. They'd traced the subject to an old encampment somewhere between U.S. 385 and the Rio Grande where it loops north above Stillman. It wasn't enough for Van to say he wanted a helicopter. He tried to specify type, size, trade name, model number and technical characteristics.

All this nomenclature, which wasn't even English to begin with, eventually defeated Van, who said he'd settle for whatever Mudger could come up with. Thanks largely to George Barber's efforts, Mudger came up with a two-man patrol helicopter, a Hughes 200, one of the types used by U.S. customs agents to keep up with border smuggling. As an afterthought, Mudger asked George if a stretcher pannier could be fitted externally to this type of aircraft. It could.

Tran Le wanted to know what a "subject" was.

George drove up and Mudger got in the car. Vietnam, in more ways than one, was a war based on hybrid gibberish. But Mudger could understand the importance of this on the most basic of levels, the grunt level, where the fighting man stood and where technical idiom was often the only element of precision, the only true beauty, he could take with him into realms of ambiguity.

Caliber readings, bullet grains, the names of special accessories. Correspondents filled their dispatches with these, using names as facets of narrative, trying to convey the impact of violent action by reporting concatenations of letters and numbers. Mudger loved it, both ironically and in the plainest of ways. Spoken aloud by sweaty men in camouflage grease, these number-words and coinages had the inviolate grace of a strict meter of chant.

Weapons were named, surnamed, slang-named, christened, titled and dubbed. Protective devices. Bearings of perfect performance. Reciting these names was the soldier's poetry, his counterjargon to death.

"I guess I ought to hit it," George said, "or you'll miss your plane."

Mudger didn't really care. This operation was slop. Maybe it was true, what people seemed to suspect. Without PAC/ORD behind him, things were slipping badly. No doubt PAC/ORD itself was helping manage the process of deterioration. This whole thing should have been handled by now, without his presence becoming necessary. The other thing, Van and Cao and the adjustment, was an even greater mess, at least potentially, having the foreordained character of some classical epic, modernized to include a helicopter. But he was the one who'd let it go on. That was stupid. He wanted to be in his basement shop, right now, pounding a heated steel blank with a double-faced hammer.

Early man roaming the tundra. You have to name your weapon before you can use it to kill.

Lomax was motionless in the cashier's shack.

It occurred to him that one day soon areas such as this would be regarded as precious embodiments of a forgotten way of life. Commerce and barter. The old city. The marketplace. Downtown.

What are we doing to our forests, our lakes, our warehouse districts? That's how it would go. What are we doing to our warehouse districts, our freight yards, our parking lots?

He was tired, hungry and cold. The man who handed out

tickets and collected money had left some Ritz crackers stacked on a piece of wax paper. Lomax edged them away with his elbow. Other people's food. Other people's refrigerators. He'd always been vaguely disgusted by things he'd happened to see in other people's refrigerators.

He heard a man shout. The sound had the tone of an insult. Briefly someone's head became visible over the top of a car parked about fifty yards away. The voice again, screaming insults. A second figure appeared, moving toward the car.

Lomax sucked in his breath and removed the automatic from his waistband holster. He put his left hand on the door handle, ready to push it open if necessary. It was possible his silhouette could be detected in the very dim light cast by a streetlamp not far away. He remained motionless for several minutes. Some more screaming. No one else around. The old city. The abandoned core.

The second figure moved off, toward the warehouse. Lomax opened the door of the shack. There was a gunshot. He moved quickly to the nearest car, crouching down behind it. Someone passed within twenty yards of him, moving quickly, a man, head down, as if he were walking into a stiff wind. Lomax looked over the trunk of the car. Someone was walking in the opposite direction, slowly. Also male. He disappeared behind the freight car.

Lomax stayed where he was for three full minutes, listening. Then he headed toward the car where the shooting had taken place. He held his gun against his thigh. That arm he kept stiff, not swinging naturally as the other arm was. He saw himself leaving the scene. A jump in time. He saw himself getting off a plane at National in Washington. He saw himself selling condominiums on the Gulf Coast.

Both doors were open. On the ground on the driver's side was a man, breathing deeply. Lomax crouched five feet away, his gun directed at the man's head.

"Who are you?"

The same worried breathing. The deadweight respiration of a deep sleeper.

"Who are you?" Lomax said.

"Fuck off. I'm hit."

"I know you're hit."

"The slug's in my throat. I feel something."

Lomax leaned to his right for a better look. The man had been shot on the left side of the face, below the cheekbone. With the doors open, the car's interior light had come on and Lomax could see powder burns rimming the hole in the man's cheek. There was blood all over his mouth.

"What's your name? Who are you?"

"Mind your own business. Let me breathe."

"I can get you an ambulance. Would you like that?"

"If I start choking, put your finger down my throat. I'd appreciate your doing that. I hate that feeling of choking. I fucking dread it."

"No promises," Lomax said, "unless you tell me who you are."

"I'm Sherman Kantrowitz."

"Who are you, Sherman? Who were those other people?"

"I'm the son of Sophie and Nat."

"Who were those people?"

The same uneven deep breathing. The search for a rhythm.

"Who do you work for, Sherman?"

"I want to swallow but I'm afraid."

Lomax saw himself playing eighteen holes a day. The sun is shining. There's a sweet breeze from the Gulf.

Tran Le.

The fields were tawny and sparse. Three-quarters of the wheel and more. Winter's pure alcohol in the air.

Tran Le standing by the window.

Her eyes were large and dark and had a special dimension

inward, an element of contriteness, as of a child always on the verge of being punished. Without this softening depth, her face might have had too much contour. The lines of her cheekbones and jaw were strong and exact, and she had a full mouth, wide and silver-pink and sensual, and a little greedy in a certain light, a little coarse. Again a counterpoise. It mocked the childlike eyes.

She moved from window to window now. Small lamps swung on the patio. A cane chair stood beneath a tree. The end of a red canoe jutted from one of the stables. She crossed to the other side of the room. Leaves turned slowly in the pond. The scarlet runner hung over the edge of a small shed. It was quiet, minutes till sundown, a tinted light in the fields. She watched the ponies graze.

5

It took the cabdriver about sixty seconds to write out a receipt. Moll watched a pair of dog-walkers stop near the curb to give their pets a chance to sniff each other. Cute. She took the receipt and went up the stairs to the front door of the brownstone.

In the vestibule she rang the bell and waited for Grace Delaney to buzz her in. Nothing happened. She rang again. It was after eleven but this was Monday and Grace always stayed until midnight, or later, on Mondays.

Moll had a set of keys. Before opening the door, she peered through the glass panel, her view obscured by the crosshatched metal grating on the other side of the pane of glass.

She entered the building and started climbing to the third floor. She walked with her head twisted to the left and angled upward so that she might see ahead to the landing and the next bend in the staircase.

Both doors on the third floor were locked. She climbed the

final flight. Two keys to the door of the outer office. On the second try she fitted each to its respective lock. Only one lock had been fastened.

All the lights were on. She entered hesitantly, calling Grace's name. She walked through the outer area into Grace's office. The usual clutter. Proofs, correspondence, photographs. A bottle of hand lotion on the coffee table. A paper cup nearly filled with vegetable soup.

She stood in the middle of the room, feeling a dim presentiment. Something about to happen. Someone about to appear. She picked up the phone and dialed Grace's home number, if only to break the mood. A recording came on, overamplified and dense: *"This is Grace Delaney. I'm not here right now. No one is here. At the beeping sound, leave your name and number—"*

Of course. Nobody is where they should be. Moll realized how wrong she'd been to feel apprehensive. The action was elsewhere, and included everyone but her. By refusing sexual alliance with Earl Mudger, she'd sealed herself off from the others. That was the effect, intended or not. There was no danger here. No one watched or listened any longer. Security. Why did it feel so disappointing?

She fastened both locks and walked slowly down the stairs and out of the building.

Grace Delaney sat near the immense Victorian birdcage in the lobby of the Barclay, off Park Avenue. She checked her watch several times and eventually walked over to one of the house phones. A man answered.

"I'm checking the vent in the bathroom."

"First you get me here," Grace said. "Then you make me wait."

"I'm in the middle of checking the vent."

"I'm coming up."

"We want to be sure the room's lily white. Don't we want that?"

"We want that."

"Of course we do," he said.

Fifteen minutes later she got off the elevator at 12. The room was located along the main corridor. Lomax let her in. The curtains were drawn. Only one light was on—a small table lamp—and he'd placed it on the floor, apparently to make the lighting as indirect as possible. He helped her off with her coat and hung it in the closet.

"That dress is a winner."

"Second-string," she said. "A relic."

"You know how to wear clothes. Clothes hang well on you. You have a sense of what looks good."

He sat on the edge of the bed and took off his shoes.

"You're a New York woman," he said. "A classic type."

"Shut up, Arthur, will you?"

"No, really, in the best sense."

She took off her dress and put it over a chair.

"I never thought I'd end up in bed with a man who wears Clark's Wallabees."

"I don't wear them in bed."

"At least they're not Hush Puppies," she said. "Good Christ, think of it."

Lomax stood up to get out of his pants.

"What's wrong with Clark's Wallabees? They're a damn good shoe."

A pair of chambermaids talked and laughed as they walked past the door.

"What about some room service, Gracie? Scotch, bourbon? This is Scotch weather. This is the season."

"I've got my flask."

She sat before the mirror in her bra, panties, stockings and garter belt. A bobby pin was in her mouth as she rearranged her hair. Lomax stood nude, briefly; then he slipped under the covers, watching her.

"Did you have to cancel something?"

"Just Moll," she said.

"My schedule's a super bitch."

"Only I didn't cancel, I just split. Meaning to ask, Arthur. Who was this friend of hers? What friend was she talking about?"

"You mean the collection."

"I told you she had someone who could get her access to Percival's collection."

"Him we forget about."

"Were they lovers?"

"Yes indeedy."

"Where is he now?"

"Doesn't matter," Lomax said. "Far away."

"You seemed rather interested, Arthur, at the time."

"Fact-gathering, that's all."

"And what are the facts?"

"Maybe he gave her access, maybe not. I haven't thought about it lately. Onward and upward."

Grace walked over to his side of the bed. He put his hands on her breasts, over the bra, for a long moment. It seemed part of a set program. Then she went into the bathroom, leaving the door open.

"What happened in Dallas, Arthur?"

He didn't answer. She came out holding her handbag. She took the silver flask out of it and walked over to the far side of the bed. She sat there, removing her stockings.

"What's this lamp doing on the floor?"

"A little mood thing," he said.

"Sure it's not bugged?"

"I ought to know how to sweep a room by now."

"Sen-si-tive."

"Bastards, I wouldn't put it past them."

She faced him, reclining on top of the covers, the flask between them.

"Which bastards?"

"PAC/ORD."

"Aren't they your bastards, ultimately? Don't you still have a channel?"

"Did I tell you that?"

"As long as it's not the tax man," she said. "As long as you're keeping the tax man away from my door."

Lomax leaned over to lick her navel. Someone pushed a room-service tray along the corridor.

"It's ongoing," he said. "I have to keep fending off. Tax fraud is no joke."

"Pricks."

"Willful omission."

"Isn't there a statute of limitations?"

"Not for fraud," he said.

"This was years ago."

"You were a political. They love politicals and they love big-time mob figures. And they love to make their cases around February or March. Instills fear in the tax-paying public. That's when you see pictures of your favorite mob figure coming down the courthouse steps. Late February, early March."

"Why aren't they content to just seize my bank account or car or whatever?"

"They favor prosecutions in cases like yours. Of course it depends on how much money's involved. You were tied into some very radical adventures, Gracie. You were playing around with some large sums of money. Willful omission. Multiple filing schemes. Terribly naughty girl."

"The movement was a living thing," she said dryly.

"I'll show you a living thing."

"It was one's duty to beat the system."

"You want a living thing?"

"What have they got, exactly?"

"I've seen your paper. They keep the paper. There's all kinds of computerized data. But they keep the paper. There are clear indications of fraud. As I say, I've been fending off. Fortunately for you, there's a chain of mutual interests."

Grace ran the tip of her index finger over his lips. She drank from the flask and passed it to Lomax. Street sounds barely audible. He took a brief surprised swallow.

"This isn't Scotch."

"It's vodka."

"This is Scotch weather."

"Wod-ka."

"Should I call room service?" he said to himself. "Then I'd have to get dressed."

"Tell me about Dallas, Arthur."

"Cold and dark."

"You've dropped wee hints."

"You make me do these things. It's not to be believed, what you make me do."

"What we make each other do."

"It's because I've lost the faith."

"You don't give a rat's ass. I understand, sweet."

"Take off your top, why don't you?"

"Due time, love."

"I don't believe. I used to believe but now I don't."

"I understand, pet."

She turned toward him, moving closer—the flask, in her left hand, resting on his chest.

"It was frankly nasty," he said.

"You tell such charming stories."

"Ain't it the truth."

"Let me get all curled up and toasty and snug."

"What happened, various sets of people were maneuvering for position. That's standard. I stationed myself according to plan, waiting for Earl. This can be a full-time occupation. It happens with him. Fierce enthusiasms. The earth is scorched for miles around. Other times, where is he? He says thus and so but he's not where he's supposed to be, he's in

Saudi on some leasing deal. In the meantime I find myself face to face with a guy who has a bullet in his throat. It's very dark. What's going on? After a lot of prodding, I find out he's free-lancing for Talerico, Vincent, a middle-level mobster. Everybody's after the same thing. We knew about the Senator's interest. We knew about Richie's interest, the kid, Armbrister. Now we have the families in all their Renaissance glory. What happens then, a car comes barreling around the corner and I go diving out of sight. I'm underneath a pickup truck, peering out, feeling this is the onset of a midlife crisis."

"The dark night of the soul," Grace said.

"For what, or whom?"

"When the priests stop believing, what does it mean?"

"Of course it was Mudger. He was sitting in the back of an ordinary cab. I crawled out and walked over. Told him what I knew. He suggested I get in, which I did, and we drove off."

"Leaving the man with the bullet in his throat."

"That happens, Gracie."

"Don't call me Gracie."

"Do you want me to call you what Earl calls you?"

"What's that?"

"Never mind," he said.

"What does Earl call me?"

"Take off your top."

"Tough darts, bubie."

She drank from the flask and resettled herself.

"Do I go on?"

"You're in the cab," she said.

"Earl, anyway, tells me he's disillusioned. The whole thing's a mess. Let the families have the goddamn footage. He no longer wants it."

"What does he want?"

"He wants to start a zoo. He wants to buy a huge tract somewhere and build some kind of safariland. Animals running around, people with cameras, I don't know. Part zoo, part natural habitat. He wasn't clear on details. He'd only thought of it on the flight up from San Antonio. It's part of Earl's nostalgia for Vietnam. He had a zoo there."

"I wonder if I'd like him," Grace said. "Moll did and didn't."

"You don't like anyone. Who do you like?"

"She wrote an interesting piece. Uneven and loose as hell. But her best work really. I was genuinely upset."

"Earl calls you FCB."

"What does that mean?"

"It's a joke name. Doesn't mean anything. Earl made it up. Actually we both made it up."

"I don't think I'd like him."

"You wouldn't like the Senator either. You don't like anyone."

"I'm old and tired," she said.

"The Senator is also out of the running. On to something else. A touch more traditional."

"Who cares? Do I look as though I care?"

"You're still young," Lomax said. "I'm the one who's old. I feel old."

"You're younger than I am, Arthur, and I don't even care."

"I feel old. I'm the old one. Forget chronology. If I were a dog I'd be only six years old, chronologically, but I feel ready for the meat machine."

Grace removed her brassiere and lay facing the ceiling. Lomax put the flask on the small table by the bed. His radio pager started beeping. This was a small device he'd lately taken to carrying everywhere. It was in the closet right now, in his coat pocket. Unlike the pagers generally in use, this one operated within a radius of one thousand miles from the originating signal. Activated by computer, the device enabled Earl Mudger to contact Lomax wherever he was, whatever he was doing, within that radius. When the beeping started, Lomax was to call a certain number and receive whatever instructions had been prepared for him.

The noise stopped after fifteen long seconds. Grace looked over at him, waiting for some reaction.

"I'll tell you who I give credit to," Lomax said.

He clasped his hands behind his head.

"Who are the only ones who believe in what they're doing? The only ones who aren't constantly adjusting, constantly wavering—this way, that way. Being pressed. Being forced to adopt new stances."

"The families," she said.

"They're serious. They're totally committed. The only ones. They see clearly, *bullseye*, straight ahead. They know what they belong to. They don't question the premise."

"Are they still in the running then?"

"They *are* the running," Lomax said. "There's just that old lunk, the art dealer, who's probably sitting on the film can himself, thinking all he has to do is arrange an auction."

"What does FCB mean?"

Lomax glanced over at her, a hint of small bitter amusement in his face.

"You're sure," he said.

"Tell me, yes, I'm curious."

He pulled his right hand out from behind his head and used the middle finger to groom first one sideburn, then the other.

"Flat-Chested Bitch," he said.

Her mouth went tight. Supine, she rolled rightward, swinging her left arm up and over to deliver a roundhouse blow to the area just above his right eye. He folded up, oddly, as though he'd been hit in the groin. Both hands covering his right eye, he turned away from her, his body compact, close to the edge of the bed.

"It's a joke name," he said.

The second blow, a hammerlike left, caught him behind the ear. The radio pager began beeping again.

"It doesn't mean anything," he said. "It's just the way we communicate, in abbreviations, in codes sometimes. We give everybody a different kind of name. Some are a lot worse than yours."

Grace lay back on the bed, listening to the paging device emit its programmed series of noises. Her mouth was still rigid but she was breathing normally, as though spasms of violence were common in her life.

Moll sat in the tub, trying to turn the pages of the early edition of the *Times* without getting them wet.

Interesting item back near the obits.

Learned today that Senator Lloyd Percival was married last Thursday in Bethesda, Maryland, hours after his divorce became final.

Bride is Dayton (DeDe) Baker, 20, a specimen trainee at the Medical Museum of the Armed Forces Institute of Pathology, Washington, D.C.

Funny but puzzling.

Ceremony performed in the meditation suite of the Stone Hollow Country Club by the Rev. Penny W. Parker, founder of the Humanist Missions.

Jesus.

The story, amid some typographical chaos, went on to quote the Senator, 61, as saying today that he felt "reborn, revitalized—ready to attempt bold new ventures." He was interviewed with his wife before the couple left for the airport, en route to an undisclosed destination.

The next day at the office, on an impulse, Moll looked for the story in the late city edition. She found that a paragraph had been left out of the earlier version. She filled in the rest by walking down the hall and checking the magazine's files.

The bride's father was the late Freeman Reed Baker, a well-known authority on Persian art and culture. He was also the central figure in a scandal involving the disappearance, fifteen years earlier, of rare examples of ancient erotica—

carpet-weavings, textiles, metalwork—from a legendary private collection in Isfahan.

I am beginning to understand.

At the time of the apparent theft, Dr. Baker had been special curator of the so-called Forbidden Rooms, a restricted area of the collection.

Very sexy stuff.

He died of natural causes three years ago in eastern Turkey, still under a cloud of suspicion. The treasures have not been recovered.

Back in her cubicle, Moll wondered if Lightborne had seen the story. If so, he'd be saying a mental farewell to Lloyd Precival. The Senator has clearly abandoned fortress Berlin, *Nazis in motion*, preferring the reassurances of desert stillness. The art of mystics and nomads. Old-fashioned contentments.

6

Selvy found a Sam Browne belt in someone's foot locker in the long barracks. He put it on. A decent enough fit. He liked the feel of the shoulder strap that extended diagonally across his chest. He thought he might figure out a way to attach the bolo somehow, knowing that the original belt had been designed, by a one-armed British general, to support a sword.

He stood outside the barracks. A clear day. Occasional small whirlwinds in the area. Memory. A playback. He watched a raven soar toward the mountains, wind-assisted, rising at first gradually, a continuous and familiar fact, and then in spasmodic surges, peculiar stages of rapid ascent, wholly without effort and seemingly beyond the limits of what is possible in the physical world—imperceptible transitions that left the watcher trying to account for missing segments of space or time.

Large soaring birds were the only things here that lived without reference to a sense of distance. Or so he imagined, Selvy did. He'd once exchanged stares, at fifteen feet, with a red-tailed hawk that had lighted on a tree stump at the edge of a deserted ranch, perhaps twenty miles from this spot, during exercises with live ammunition. That was how he'd come to believe in the transcendent beauty of predators.

That day was like this one. A morning of startling brightness. Clarity without distracting glare. The sky was saturated with light. Everything was color.

He was twenty yards from the barracks when he realized two cats were at his feet. He stopped and turned. Three more cats moved this way. He knew what it meant. Still more cats came out from under the barracks. They followed him, moving around his feet, mewing. Cats approached from another direction now, the windmill. An image unwinding. After ten paces he crouched down and they were all over and around him, scratching, crying out, at least fifteen cats and kittens, allowing themselves to be petted and rubbed, or just stretching in the sun, purring, or sniffing at his clothes, all of them looking healthy and well fed.

Levi Blackwater was here.

At the Mines, back then, he'd been an unwelcome presence in most gatherings of men. An ordinary boy from Ohio, named out of Genesis, he'd served as technical adviser to ARVN forces in the relatively early days of U.S. involvement. Out on a reconnaissance patrol, he'd been captured by the Vietcong, and tortured, and had come to love his captors. Eight months inside a prison building in a VC base camp in a mangrove thicket. Fish heads and rice. They strung him up by the feet. They held his head under water. They cut off two of his fingers.

The more they tortured him, the more he loved them. They were helping him. He considered it help.

At the Mines he cooked and worked in the laundry and did odd jobs. The men knew his history and stayed away from him. Selvy was an exception. He went to Levi for lessons in meditation.

Moll was suspicious of quests. At the bottom of most long and obsessive searches, in her view, was some vital deficiency on the part of the individual in pursuit, a meagerness of spirit.

She sat in the dark, listening to Odell fiddle with the projector.

Even more depressing than the nature of a given quest was the likely result. Whether people searched for an object of some kind, or inner occasion, or answer, or state of being, it was almost always disappointing. People came up against themselves in the end. Nothing but themselves. Of course there were those who believed the search itself was all that mattered. The search itself is the reward.

Lightborne wouldn't agree. Lightborne wanted a marketable product, she was sure. He wasn't in it for the existential lift.

Odell turned on a lamp and approached the screen in order to make sure it would be parallel to the strip of film itself when it moved through the projector gate. While he was doing this, Moll glanced over at Lightborne.

"What was it doing when you arrived?" he said. "Was that rain or sleet? I need new boots. I'd like to find something with some lining this year. This is a bad year, they're saying, looking long range."

He'd been making the same nervous small talk ever since Moll walked in. Twice now Odell had turned on the light to make a last-minute adjustment somewhere. Both times Lightborne had immediately started talking. In the dark he was silent. He chewed his knuckles in the dark.

Once more Odell turned off the lamp. Moll began to feel that special kind of anticipation she'd enjoyed since childhood —a life in the movies. It was an expectation of pleasure like no other. Simple mysteries are the deepest. What did it mean, this wholly secure escape, this credence in her heart? And how was it possible that bad, awful, god-awful movies never seemed to betray the elation and trust she felt in the seconds before the screen went bright? The anticipation was apart from what followed. It was permanently renewable, a sense of freedom from all the duties and conditions of the nonmovie world.

She felt it even here, sitting in a hard straight chair in a shabby gallery before a small screen. She felt it despite her knowledge of the various dealings, procedures and techniques that surrounded the acquisition of the film.

A two-dimensional city would materialize out of the darkness, afloat in various kinds of time, all different from the system in which real events occur. Yet we understand it so readily and well. They connect to us, all the city's spatial and temporal codes, as though from a place we knew before.

"I had the phone turned off," Lightborne said. "A temporary measure. To mute out the sound of certain voices."

He started to say something else but his voice drifted off and the only sound that remained was the running noise of motion picture film winding through the transport mechanism of the black projector.

A bare room/black and white.

Plaster is cracked in places. On other parts of the wall it is missing completely. The lights in the room flicker.

Three children appear. A girl, perhaps eleven, carries a chair. Two younger children, a boy and a very small girl, drag in a second chair between them.

The children set the chairs on the floor and walk out of camera range.

There is a disturbance. The picture jumps as though the camera has been jarred by some brief violent action.

A blank interval.

Again the room. The camera setup is the same.

A fourth child appears, a girl. She walks across the room

and climbs onto one of the chairs, sitting primly, trying to suppress a bashful smile.

The boy and oldest girl carry in two more chairs. A woman appears, very drawn, moving toward the seated child. The lights flicker. Another girl appears; she notices the camera and walks quickly out of range.

The boy and oldest girl carry in two more chairs.

The camera is immobile. It does not select. People pass in and out of its viewing field.

The woman sits next to the small girl, absently stroking the child's hand. The woman is blond and attractive, clearly not well. She appears weak. It is even possible to say she is emotionally distressed. The oldest girl stands next to her, speaking. The woman slowly nods.

The boy carries in another chair. Three more adults appear, a man and two women. They stand about awkwardly, the man trying to work out a seating arrangement. The boy and oldest girl carry in two more chairs.

The once bare room is crowded with chairs and people.

The lights flicker overhead.

"What do you think?" Lightborne said.

"I don't know what to think."

"You know who it could be? Magda Goebbels."

"The first woman?" Moll said.

"Those could be her children. I'm saying 'could be.' I'm trying to supply identities. Make a little sense out of this."

"Do you think it's the bunker?"

"It could be the doctor's former room. Hitler's quack doctor was allowed to leave. Goebbels took over his room."

"The three others," Moll said.

"I don't know. They could be secretaries, the women. The man, almost anything. A chauffeur, a stenographer, a valet, a bodyguard."

"Magda Goebbels, you think."

"I'm saying 'could be.' This isn't what I expected. I wasn't looking for this at all."

Nothing much had happened thus far but Moll found something compelling about the footage she was watching. It wasn't like a feature film or documentary; it wasn't like TV newsfilm. It was primitive and blunt, yet hypnotic, not without an element of mystery.

Faces and clothing were immediately recognizable as belonging to another era. This effect was heightened by the quality of the film itself, shot with natural lighting. Bleached grays and occasional blurring. Lack of a sound track. Light leaks in the camera, causing flashes across the screen. The footage suggested warier times—dark eyes and fussy mouths, heavy suits, dresses in overlapping fabric, an abruptness and formality of movement.

Four adults and five children, all seated, fill the screen. They face the camera head-on.

Time passes.

"What's that jump?"

"It could be the shelling," Lightborne said.

"That's the second time."

"The Russians are a quarter of a mile away. Nuisance fire. In an all-out bombardment, they wouldn't be able to film. Aside from the steady concussion, the place would be full of smoke and dust."

The blond woman slowly rises and walks off camera.

"She knows what happens."

"What do you mean?" Moll said.

"The children."

"What happens?"

"Goebbels has them poisoned."

Another room.

This one, although small and narrow and with an incomplete look about it, contains a writing desk, sofa and chairs. The walls are paneled. There's a picture in a circular frame over the writing desk.

A woman sits in one of the chairs, facing an open door that leads to another room. She turns the pages of a magazine. There's a trace of self-consciousness in the way she does this. Finally she decides to look directly at the camera, smiling pleasantly. This puts her at ease.

From her next reaction, it is clear that someone in the adjoining room is speaking to her.

She sits with her legs crossed, paying no attention to the magazine pages she continues to turn. A light-haired woman in her early thirties, she wears a dark tailored suit, a bracelet, and what appear to be expensive shoes. She has a small worried mouth (even in her present good humor) and a somewhat shapeless nose. Two distinct shadow lines make her cheeks look puffy.

She gestures toward the open door.

"Where are we?" Moll said.

"Still in the bunker. It's not inconsistent, the two rooms. See that picture over the desk? If we could see it from a better angle, being in a circular frame, that could be his portrait of Frederick the Great, which would make this room his living room."

"Whose living room?"

"It's a possibility. It could be. And through that open door, that's his bedroom. Whoever's shooting this film, it could be he's shooting one room, he's stopping, he's walking over to the next room."

"Editing in the camera," Moll said.

"We're getting everything. What do you think? We're getting the one and only take of each scene."

"It's certainly unprofessional. But I can't say I mind."

"Those kids and those others are sitting in the first room waiting for the camera to come back. Maybe that's why the thing seems so real. It's true. It's happening. I didn't look for this at all."

Another woman enters the room. The blond woman from the first sequence. Magda Goebbels—if Lightborne's speculation is correct.
She hands the younger woman a flower. Expression of delighted surprise. It's a white boutonniere. The woman takes it into the next room.
Visual static. Flash frames.

"What are we looking at?"
"I don't know," Lightborne said.
"If that's Frau Goebbels standing there, who's the woman who just disappeared?"
"That shouldn't be hard to answer."
"I want to hear you say it."
"You know as well as I."
"Who is she?"
"It's real," Lightborne said. "I believe it. It's *them*."

The routine persisted.

In the late morning sun, Selvy placed the bolo knife on a bench in the littered compound. Seating himself on an overturned crate, he began working with oil and whetstone on the base of the blade. A snowy tom rolled in the dirt nearby. Directly ahead the spare land extended to the bottom of an enormous butte, its sloping sides covered with rockfall.

He saw it as memory, as playback. The border of appearances. Within is perfect color, the sense of topography as an ethical schematic. Landscape is truth.

When he looked up, ten minutes into his sharpening, he saw Levi Blackwater approaching from the southeast. Had to be him. There had always been something physically off-center about Levi. Nothing so distinct as a limp or even an ungainliness of stride. The right shoulder sagged a bit. Maybe that was it. And the head tilted. And the right arm hung slightly lower. All apparent as he drew nearer.

He was a tall man, balding, and wore the same old field cap with ventilating eyelets. He was pale, he was sickly white, as always. Soft baby skin. A little like skin that's been transplanted from another part of the body. He stood smiling now. That knowing smile. Dust devils spinning fifty, sixty yards away.

"I came in to feed the cats."

Only Levi could speak of traveling to this remote site as "coming in."

"Where are you when you're out?"

Levi kept smiling and stood in profile, turning his head left toward the barest stretch of desert. He came forward to shake hands. It was the right hand that lacked two fingers, severed by his captors. Selvy had forgotten the directness of Levi's manner of looking at people.

"I always knew if anyone came back, Glen, it would be you."

"Not much left, is there?"

"Everything you'll need."

"I won't be staying, Levi."

People use names as information and Selvy believed the use of that particular name, Glen, indicated that Levi was deeply pleased to see him and wanted to suggest a new level of seriousness. In the past he'd often called Selvy by his rarely used first name, which was Howard. A teasing intimacy. It had amused Levi to do this. His eyes would search Selvy's face. Those fixed looks, curious and frank at the same time, were irritating to Selvy, even more than hearing the name Howard. But he'd never complained, thinking this would put a distance between them.

Levi had been tortured, had spent extended periods of

time in a dark room not much larger than a closet, and conse-
quently had things to pass on, knowledge to impart, both
practical and otherwise. He'd found tolerances, ways of
dealing with what, in the end, was the sound of his own voice.
He'd come out stronger, or so he believed, having lived
through pain and confinement, the machine of self.

"This is a stop then? On a longer trip?"

"You might say."

"A way station," Levi said.

The phrase seemed to please him. His liquid eyes peered
out of the shadow cast by the visor of his hat. He wore a
soiled fatigue jacket, torn in places.

"I see you've brought along some metal."

"An antique," Selvy said.

"We were just getting started when you left."

"I know."

"We were beginning to see results, I think. I'm happy
you've come back, even for a while. It's gratifying. You're
looking well, Glen."

"Off the booze a while."

"You ought to stay, you know. There are things you can
learn here."

"True. I believe that."

"The less there is, Glen, the more you're tested to find the
things that do exist. Within and without. It works. If you limit
yourself to the narrowest subject, you force yourself to concentrate to such an extent that you're able to learn a great
deal about it. You already *know* a great deal about it. You find
you already *know* much more than you'd imagined."

"I believe that."

"With no limits, you wander back and forth. You're defeated at the outset."

"That's why you're here, Levi."

"Both of us."

"Tighter and tighter limits."

"To learn. To find out what we know. When you left, we

were just starting out. Damn shame if you didn't stay for a time. I've learned so much. So very much of everything."

He was squatting on the other side of the bench where the knife lay on several old newspapers, the only things Selvy could find to soak up the honing oil. Levi let a fistful of sand gradually spill to the ground. The sky was changing radically. Dust rising in the wind. Darkness edging across the south-westerly wheel of land.

"I'm born all the time," Levi said. "I remember other lives."

Staring.

"Creature of the landscape."

Smiling.

"Gringo mystic."

The wind lifted dust in huge whispering masses. Toward Mexico the mountains were obscured in seconds. The butte in the middle distance still showed through in swatches of occasional color, in hillside shrubs and the mineral glint of fallen rock.

"I feel myself being born. I've grown out here. I know so much. It's ready to be shared, Glen."

"I'm on a different course right now."

"You were making real progress."

"I'm primed, Levi."

"Yes, I can see."

"I'm tuned, I'm ready."

"I don't accept that."

"You know how it ends."

"I don't understand."

"You know what to do, Levi."

"Have we talked about something like this?"

Sand came whipping across the compound. Above and around them it massed in churning clouds. Wind force increased, a whistling gritty sound. Levi took off his field cap and jammed it in his pocket. His jacket had a hood attachment, tight fitting, with a drawstring around the face and a zippered closure that extended over the mouth. Levi fastened this lower part only as far as the point of his chin.

Selvy recognized a sound apart from the wind. He got to his feet and took off the Sam Browne belt. He threw it in the dirt. Damn silly idea. He had to admit to a dim satisfaction, noting the confusion in the other man's eyes.

"There's no way out, Glen. No clear light for you in this direction. You can't find release from experience so simply."

"Dying is an art in the East."

"Yes, heroic, a spiritual victory."

"You set me on to that, Levi."

"Tibet. Is that the East? It's beyond the East, isn't it?"

"A man chooses a place."

"But this is part, only part, of a longer, longer process. We were just beginning to understand. There's so much more. You think you're about to arrive at some final truth. Truth is a disappointment. You'll only be disappointed."

Selvy went into the long barracks and started ripping apart a bed sheet, planning to fashion some kind of mask, basic protection against the blowing sand.

Levi followed him in. Selvy watched him detach the hood from his jacket. He moved forward and put it over Selvy's head, slowly fastening the drawstring. His eyes, always a shade burdened with understanding, began to fill with a deep, sad and complex knowledge. He raised the zipper on the lower part of the hood. Selvy, feeling foolish, turned toward the door.

Outside he went to the bench and picked up the bolo knife. He heard the sound again. There it was, *color*, black and bright red, a small helicopter, bearing this way, seeming to push against the wind.

Little bastards must be serious, out flying in this weather.

He walked about a hundred yards beyond the compound. The sand stung his eyes. He heard the motor but kept losing sight of the aircraft. Then he saw it again, off to the left, shouting distance, touching down near a gulley, trim, vivid in the murky gusts, its spiral blades coming slowly to a halt.

Inside the projector the film run continued noisily.

The first room.

There are now six children and five adults, all seated, facing the camera. Among the adults are the two women from the flower sequence in the furnished room.

The smaller children are restless. Several adults wear rigid smiles; they look like victims of prolonged formalities. Two children trade seats. A woman turns to whisper.

For the first time the camera is active.

In a long slow panning movement, it focuses eventually on a figure just beyond the doorway. A man in costume. After an interval of distortion, the camera, starting at the man's feet, moves slowly up his body.

Oversized shoes, turned up slightly at the points.

Baggy pants.

Vest and tight-fitting cutaway.

A dark narrow tie.

A wing collar, askew.

A battered derby.

A white boutonniere in the lapel of the cutaway.

A cane hooked over his wrist.

This footage has the mysterious aura of an event that cuts across time. This is because the man, standing beyond the doorway, is not yet visible to the audience of adults and children in the immediate vicinity. The other audience, watching in a dark room in New York in the 1970s, is aware of this, and they feel a curious sense of preview. They are seeing the man "first."

"Is it?" Moll said.

"It could be."

"Jesus, it's almost charming."

"But do I want it?"

"He looks so very old."

"Do I need it?" Lightborne said.

The camera is trained on the man's face. Again it moves, coming in for a medium close-up.

Eyes blank.

Little or no hair alongside his ears.

Face pale and lined.

Flaccid mouth.

Smoothly curved jaw.

The famous mustache.

Head shaking, he acknowledges the presence of the camera. It pulls back. The man moves forward, walking in a screwy mechanical way. Here the camera pans the audience. As the man enters the room, the adults show outsized delight, clearly meant to prompt the children, who may or may not be familiar with Charlie Chaplin.

Back on the performer, the camera pulls back to a corner of the room, providing a view from the wings, as it were.

He's a relatively small man with narrow shoulders and wide hips. It's now evident that his pantomime, intended as Chaplinesque, of course, is being enlarged and distorted by involuntary movements—trembling arm, nodding head, a stagger in his gait.

"Do you want me to tell you what this is?"

"He's not bad, you know," Moll said. "Despite the tottering and such. He's doing fairly well."

"This is one of her home movies."

"Whose?"

"We saw her before."

"Eva Braun, you mean."

"This is her idea. She was a home-movie nut. She had movies made of herself swimming, walking in the woods, standing around with *him*. He's in some of them."

"He's in this one."

"But he didn't like Chaplin, if I recall correctly. I think he's on record as not being a Chaplin fan."

"I believe it was mutual."

"On the other hand he was a gifted mimic. He did imitations."

"Who did imitations? Say it."

"There were resemblances other than physical. He and Charlie."

The figure shuffles toward the camera, his cane swinging. Behind him, in a corner of the screen, one of the small girls earnestly looks on.

Briefly the man is flooded in light—the bleached and toneless effect of overexposure. With the return of minimal detail and contrast, he is very close to the camera, and his lifeless eyes acquire a trace of flame, the smallest luster. A professional effect. It's as though the glint originated in a nearby catch light.

He produces an expression, finally—a sweet, epicene, guilty little smile. Charlie's smile. An accurate reproduction.

"They were born the same week of the same month of the same year."

"Is that a point?"

"Within days of each other."

"But is that a point?"

"It's a fact. A truth. It's history."

"You're overwrought, Mr. Lightborne."

"Not that I'm convinced it's him. It's not him. He didn't empathize with the tramp character at all. Why is he doing this?"

"For the children, presumably."
"Who do I sell this to?"

Three-quarter view. At first he seems to be speaking to the smallest of the children, a girl about three years old. It is then evident he is only moving his lips—an allusion to silent movies. One of the women can be seen smiling.

"Hitler humanized."
"It's disgusting," Lightborne said. "What do I do with a thing like this? Who needs it?"
"I would think it has considerable value."
"Historical. Historical value."
"It's almost touching."
"Has to be one of her home movies. That bitch. What is she, stupid? Artillery shells are raining down and she's making movies. That whole bunch, they were movie-mad."
"You're certain about the children."
"Cyanide."
"So here we are."
"I expected something hard-edged. Something dark and potent. The madness at the end. The perversions, the sex. Look, he's twirling the cane. A disaster."

Flash frames.

"I set things in motion."

New camera setup.
This is the sole attempt at "art." The camera faces the audience head-on. The members of the audience are attempting to pretend that the Chaplinesque figure is still performing at a point directly behind the camera.
Two adults remain, an unidentified man and woman. Both gaze dutifully past the camera, forcing tight smiles. Of the six children, only three seem interested in the illusion. One of the

others kneels on the chair, her back to the "action." One looks directly at the camera. The smallest climbs down from her chair.

There is a general shifting of eyes. The members of the audience are clearly being prompted by someone off-camera.

"I put powerful forces to work."

Silently they applaud the masquerade.

The hoods of their ski parkas kept getting blown off their heads. He saw the bright orange lining.

He gave a neighborly shout. *Hey.* Louder. One more time. He saw the ranger on the left reach out and touch the other's arm. Both had him in view now. They turned into the wind, which was at his back.

They came toward him like skiers cross-country, absorbed in economy and method, leaning into the force of the storm, each step a deliberate and nearly ritual movement, diagonal stride with poles.

He forced the lower part of the hood up over his nose so that only his eyes were visible. He saw the bright nylon lining intermittently. He had his feet firmly planted in the dirt, to maintain balance. They emerged from a swirl of dust, vanishing in a single stride.

He held the long knife across his stomach. Handle in his right hand. Blunt edge resting lightly in his left. He was rocked by the wind. The sound gathered density.

Moving slowly, not appearing to struggle, they emerged again, still empty-handed, he noticed, one of them unzipping his parka, vanishing, the other vanishing, the first transformed now, an apparition, ballooning bright nylon, the second emerging, undoing his jacket, which likewise filled with wind, and they came more quickly, released from their trekking pace, orange lining wind-billowed, metal at their belts. These bursts of unexpected color. The beauty of predators.

Strong sense of something being played out. Memory, a film. Rush of adolescent daydreams. He'd been through it in his mind a hundred times, although never to the end.

They moved in, showing spear-point bowies. One of them edged off to the side. He seemed to think if he moved slowly enough, Selvy would forget about him. The other one, in clear sight, stopped his maneuvering, as an afterthought, to remove the parka he wore. Selvy wanted to ask him what the fuck he thought he was doing.

When they closed in, Selvy used a backhand slash. Motion only. Drawing reaction. He turned to meet the man coming full-tilt, coming too fast, giving up alternatives. He went to one knee, throwing the man off-stride. The ranger's face registered mistake. Selvy used his free hand to push off from the ground, giving him added spring. Stunned breath. He found the midsection, realizing he'd used too much force going in.

He was attached, in effect, to the man he'd stabbed. He shoved his left forearm up against the ranger's chest, pressuring forward, trying to withdraw the knife at the same time. The man sagged to the ground, all mash, Selvy slipping down with him part of the way. When he turned, rising with the knife, too late, the other ranger was on him, white-eyed, wincing with every thrust.

He could see sand in the man's lashes. They held each other briefly. The tension left Selvy's face, replaced by deep concentration.

What he needed right now was a drink.

Van lessened his grip in stages, letting the body ease to the ground. He walked over to Cao, whose mouth was wide open. Sand came skimming along the ground in broad flat masses.

The blowing dust, which had been part of things, inseparable from events, was now a space away, the landscape, the weather, small rough particles striking Van's face and arms. He reached for his parka and put it back on.

He put the bowie knife back in its sheath. He rolled up his jeans and took a second, smaller knife that was clipped to the outside of his boot. Working carefully with this utility model he cut the drawstring on Selvy's hood. Then he sliced the fabric down along the zipper. He put the knife away. With both hands he opened up the hood and lifted it off Selvy's head.

He knelt there, still breathing heavily. The wind force decreased. He realized he was looking directly toward the helicopter; the fuselage was briefly visible. On all fours he searched for the guerrilla bolo. It was five feet away, nearly buried. He lifted it out of the sand and used it to cut off the subject's head.

It was something he'd done before and seen others do. Heads on poles in the high noon slush of rice fields. A discomfort reserved for the spirits of particular enemies.

He dragged Cao's body to the aircraft. The weather kept easing and he saw the butte he'd nearly flown into before setting down. He went back for the other man's head, first emptying out a duffel bag to carry it in.

He thought Earl would want to have it. Evidence that the adjustment had been made.

"There's another reel," Odell said. "Where's everybody going?"

Moll was heading toward the door. Lightborne went around turning on lamps. Briefly he stood near a three-foot-high fertility figure—wood and horsehair.

"I knew it would be no good. A document, with gestures. I was always the chief skeptic. I told everybody. Did they listen? Or did they keep calling me up? Long distance, local, from airplanes. I'm a dealer in knickknacks. I shouldn't have to turn off my phone to avoid hearing things."

He moved toward a wall switch, running his hand through a streak of yellowish hair over his right ear. After flicking on the light, he slipped behind the partition into his living quarters. Here he turned on more lights. Then he sat on his cot and stared into the black window shade.

Odell left his seat by the projector to unlock the door for Moll Robbins. He wore white cotton gloves, important when handling master film. As she stepped out, he gestured toward the screen.

"Who are those people?" he said.

Lightborne could hear Odell close the gallery door and walk over to the projector. Apparently he was getting ready to screen the second reel. A few moments later the lights in the gallery went out, one by one. Lightborne remained on his cot. There was a noise outside, just a yard or two away, it seemed. He lifted the window shade. It was one-thirty in the afternoon and a man with tinted glasses was sitting on his fire escape.

It was Augie the Mouse. He sat facing the window, his back against the vertical bars, knees up, hands jammed into the pockets of his long strange charcoal coat, big-buttoned, rabbinical. He had a small pointed face. His hair was dark and wild. He kept sniffling, and every time he sniffled he moved his head to the left, as though to clean his nose on the worn lapel of the coat; he couldn't get his nose that far down, however, and kept rubbing his chin instead—a detail he didn't appear to notice.

"What do you want?"

Augie cocked his head. The window was shut and he couldn't hear what had been said. Lightborne thought of running out of the room. He thought of shouting for Odell. But the man was just sitting there. His casual attitude finally prompted Lightborne to open the window.

"What do you want?"

"I still don't hear you."

"What do you want?"

"You're seeing things. There's nobody here."

"Broad daylight," Lightborne said, not knowing quite what he meant.

Augie seemed to take the remark as a compliment.

"People can see us from those windows."

"They can see you. I'm not here. They see some old man moving his lips."

"Is this a new hangout for derelicts? The streets are no longer adequate. Is that what I'm meant to conclude?"

"You see these glasses I'm wearing?"

"I can call my colleague, who's right in the next room there."

"These are called shooting glasses," Augie said.

Down on Houston Street, Moll watched a flock of pigeons fly over a two-story building into the back alleys. Seconds later Lightborne saw the same pigeons turn a bend and hurry toward a nearby roof.

"Do I have something for you?"

"I'm beginning to hear," Augie said.

"Did somebody send you to pick up something from me? Is that it? An item?"

"I'm taking form."

"Is it something that fits into a round can?"

"You're beginning to see me," Augie said. "I just arrived from my country place."

Lightborne heard something behind him. It was Odell, standing on this side of the partition. Augie didn't seem upset at the sight of another person. He sat sniffling, hands still in his pockets.

"What happens now?" Lightborne said. "Do I tell my colleague to go get it and bring it out to you while I remain here as insurance? He knows the handling procedures. Is that what happens?"

"No."

"What happens?"

"You invite me in."

"We can do that," Lightborne said. "We can do it inside. Fine, sure. But all this is assuming you tell me who sent you."

"Hey. I'm not here to audition."

"I don't necessarily mind parting with the item. But I'd like the option of knowing the recipient."

Augie let his head slump to one side, closing his eyes at the same time. Weary disappointment. I come here to do a simple job, he seemed to be thinking, and they start in with their complications, with their ballbreaking little remarks. Opening his eyes, he waited a long moment before moving his head to an upright position.

"Maybe you notice how far into these pockets my hands go. Practically half an arm is in there. That's made possible by the pockets being conveniently ripped out. What my hands are in there holding, if you want a clue to size, it takes both hands to hold, and I'm not talking about dick. You know dick?"

"I know," Lightborne said with a sigh.

"It's not dick I'm holding."

He invited Augie in. Odell, surprisingly, seemed to grasp the nature of the situation, and said nothing. All three went into the gallery. The second reel was running. One of the women from the earlier footage—unidentified—was teaching the oldest of the girls how to waltz, leading her stiffly around the floor. Briefly visible were two smaller girls, running from the camera.

Lightborne turned on the two nearest lamps and asked Odell to halt the screening and get everything repacked. Augie the Mouse strolled around the gallery, browsing, both hands still in his pockets, holding the sawed-off whatever-it-was.

Lightborne wondered if they'd blame him for what was on the film. All he could do was suggest possible outlets. They could sell it to one of the networks for a news special. They

could sell it to the Whitney Museum or the Canadian Film
Board. He'd come up with a list of suggestions. What else
could he do? Could he tell them people like to dress up?
Could he tell them history is true?

Moll felt like walking. After early rain, the day had turned
warmer and very bright. Movies in the afternoon. The rude
surprise of sunlight when you emerge. What is this place?
Why are these people so short and ugly? Look at the hard
surfaces, the blatant flesh of things.

When she reached Tenth Street, a limousine seemed to
approach her, moving slowly down Fifth Avenue, veering
toward the curb. She felt herself reacting.

Days later, trying to hail a cab outside her building, she
watched another long black car move toward her. She was
certain this one would stop. She waited to see the back door
slowly open. It was raining lightly and the wipers cut a pair
of arcs across the windshield.

But the car kept on moving, droplets of rain gleaming on
its surface. She watched it head onto the transverse road on
the other side of Central Park West, where it disappeared in
the trees.

Levi Blackwater surveyed the remains from a small rise
about sixty yards away. He was motionless, positioned in a
crouch, leaning slightly forward on his toes. His left hand, as
though acting independently of his field of concentration,
gathered a quantity of loose dirt.

The land was a raked paint surface. The power of storms
to burnish and renew, he thought, had never been more
clearly evident. The sky was flawless. Things *existed*. The day
was scaled to the pure tones of being and sense.

The last sweeps of weather had caused the body to become partly buried. Levi knew who it was from the color of
the trousers and the single russet boot still visible. He also
knew what to do with the body. He remembered.

You approach death with a clear mind. You choose the right place. They'd discussed this often. Glen used to talk about pure landscape. He loved the desert. When you leave the earth-plane, there's a right place and a right way.

Levi knew everything there was to know about Glen. His childhood and adolescence on army bases. His father's steady ascent through the ranks—nicer houses, bigger backyards. His mother's piteous drift into lassitude, amnesia, silence. Glen spoke of these things with intense detachment, already a student of the process of separation. They camped, the two men, in the desert, talking into the starry dawn.

Glen wanted to be left in a sitting posture. What was known as an "air burial" would be provided. No receptacle for the body. No actual burial. He would be placed on a wooden framework or rudimentary platform of Levi's devising. Left for the air, for the large soaring birds. They'd discussed it often.

Levi had always wanted to giggle when Glen mentioned this. It was such an oversimplification. It left so much out.

Still, he would do as his friend had asked. In his own excessive way, Glen believed. He believed easily and indiscriminately, taking to things with a quick and secret fervor. It was a tendency which Levi had hoped to moderate, given the opportunity.

He let the dirt pass through his hand. He got to his feet, cap low over his eyes, and walked in his crooked way toward the body, slowly. Glen would get his air burial, yes. But first Levi would sit and chant, directing the escape, the separation of the deceased from his body, as taught by the masters of the snowy range.

This was a *lama* function, and therefore an enormous presumption on Levi's part, but he knew the chant, after all, and he had love in his heart for the world.

It was a day of primal light, perfect arrangements of color. No voice could speak this. A raven swayed in the wind.

After chanting, he would try to determine whether the

spirit had indeed departed. Levi wasn't sure he knew how to do this. But he believed he would *feel* something; something would *tell* him whether he was on the right path. He knew for certain how you started. You started by plucking a few strands of hair from the top of the dead man's head.

A NOTE ON THE TYPE

This book was set in Caledonia, a Linotype face designed by W. A. Dwiggins. It belongs to the family of printing types called "modern face" by printers—a term used to mark the change in style of type letters that occurred about 1800. Caledonia borders on the general design of Scotch Modern, but is more freely drawn than that letter.

Composed by Maryland Linotype Composition Company, Inc., Baltimore, Maryland. Printed and bound by The Haddon Craftsmen, Inc., Scranton, Pennsylvania.

Typography and binding design by Virginia Tan.